THE
BETWEEN

DAVID HOFMEYR

PENGUIN BOOKS

PENGUIN BOOKS

UK | USA | Canada | Ireland | Australia
India | New Zealand | South Africa

Penguin Books is part of the Penguin Random House group of companies
whose addresses can be found at global.penguinrandomhouse.com.

www.penguin.co.uk
www.puffin.co.uk
www.ladybird.co.uk

First published in the United Kingdom by Penguin Books 2020
Simultaneously published in the United States of America by Delacorte Press,
an imprint of Random House Children's Books, a division of
Penguin Random House LLC, in 2020

001

Set in 10.5/15.5pt Sabon LT Std
Typeset by Jouve (UK), Milton Keynes
Printed and bound in Great Britain by Clays Ltd, Elcograf S.p.A.

A CIP catalogue record for this book is available from the British Library

ISBN: 978-0-141-35448-4

PENGUIN BOOKS

THE
BETWEEN

Also by David Hofmeyr:

STONE RIDER

For Adam and Brune,
who live between London and Paris

How can I accept a limited definable self when I feel, in me, all possibilities?

        – Anaïs Nin, *The Diary of Anaïs Nin, Vol.* 1

First you lift. Then you float. Then you Fall.

That's how it happens – the **FALLING**. It's frightening and it hurts. It feels as if your bones are being crushed. Your insides ripped out. Your body is being force-fed through a meat mincer. It disorientates, disturbs and it dazzles the mind. Flips normal upside down, inside out and back to front.

Yes. These things are all true. But it's not the Falling that matters. It's what happens after.

SOL

1

Between school and home lies a path through the woods. It's Friday afternoon and the sun falls from a cloudless blue sky. It's baking hot. No hint of wind. We're alone on the narrow path. But in my gut, I get that nervy feeling. A darkening. Something, hidden in the trees, is following me.

'I had that dream again last night,' I tell Bea to distract myself.

'No kidding? The same one?'

'Yeah. Kinda. I woke and found myself in an empty house. I stepped out on to the street and the whole place was deserted. Everyone had vanished . . .'

I don't have the courage to tell her the rest – a new part of the dream. The tall, spider-like creature I saw moving among the bombed-out buildings of a desolate city.

We hit a thorny stretch of the path, crossing a park in the heart of London, cut off from the clamour. I feel dizzy in the heat. Bea leaps up, fluid and light, snaps off a dead tree branch, lands and dances forward, swinging the stick like a sword.

'I can interpret the dream, if you like,' she says.

'No you can't.'

'Easy.'

'Fine. Go for it.'

'It's panic,' Bea says.

'*What?*'

'Blind panic you'll never find *The One*. Always be alone. Always searching.' She laughs and stabs the air. 'Got Anaïs Moon written all over it.'

Anaïs Isabel Moon. Me. But, to everyone other than Bea (for reasons of her maverick lawlessness), I'm just Ana. Three letters. Two syllables. A palindrome. I was born abroad, in Paris. The Old Man and Frankie were studying at the Sorbonne. Frankie, Business. The Old Man, Arts. They were both in a phase – experimenting.

We pass under the eaves of a hunkered oak, its branches like arms, wide and bent, and here the path is walled in by nettles and thorns. Something moves, at the edge of my vision, in the shadowy green. A figure? The sprawl of wings?

I spin round. See nothing.

It's back again – that raw, uncomfortable feeling, a sense of being watched. It quickens my step, plays a drumbeat of dread in my heart.

'Hey, what's the rush?' Bea says, matching my pace.

I shake off the weirdness and look at her, at all the nuances that make her *Bea*. The tiny dot on her nose where the ring gets replaced. Dyed-black hair, just so, in a deep V over her left eye. A pity, if you ask me, because her eyes are startling.

'God, this heatwave,' she says, tugging a button loose. 'It's *September*.'

'Bea . . . do you think we'll always be friends?'

She stops, looks at me. 'Are you literally crazy? What brought *that* on?'

'Nothing. It's just –'

'Put it this way, Moon. You'll be the one walking me down the aisle for weddings number one, two *and* three.'

'Only three?'

She walks on. 'The fourth, fifth and sixth will be in Vegas, baby. And, if I'm in the mood, the seventh might even be you.'

'Right. Good to know.'

'Point is, of course we'll always be friends, you idiot. In what world could you desert someone as charismatic and amazing as me?' She looks at the path ahead. 'But you want the truth?'

'Always.'

She turns to me. Smiles. 'Truth is I'd go to the ends of the earth for you, Moon. Wanna know why?'

'Why?'

'Because you'd do it for me too. If I was mad and lost, you'd pull me back from the brink you would. That's who you are.'

'You make it sound easy.'

'Make *what* sound easy?'

'Knowing who you are. I never know who I'm supposed to be.'

'All that back and forth between Frankie and your Old Man getting to you?'

She's got one of those minds, Bea – quick-fire, straight to the point.

'Sometimes I feel like I'm lost in the middle, you know?'

'Yeah. I know.'

'And Zig makes the whole thing harder. I mean, I thought it'd get easier. That, at some point, it would just . . . make sense. I'd forget everything before.'

'But you don't,' Bea says. 'You never forget. It changes you.'

'I'm one person with her,' I say. 'Someone else with him.'

Bea looks away. Shadows filigree her skin. Eventually, she nods, and I can't tell if she's agreeing with me or just acknowledging my point of view, until she says, 'Hey, at least you get the option.' And the air punches out of me.

'I'm sorry, Bea . . . I didn't –'

'Forget it, Moon. Bygones.'

My family moved from Paris back to Bristol when I was two, but I have no memory of this. The idea was to give me English schooling, which Frankie considered a vital academic stepping stone to an autonomous life. The Old Man thought it was a load of crap. Then, when Bristol's work opportunities dried up, we moved to London. The marriage dissolved a year later. But it was rotten and badly formed from the start (obviously). The Old Man living in the closet, *that* didn't help. Plus Frankie's affairs. I was ten. My world had been perfect: the River Severn, the smallness of Bristol, trips to Wales and Cornwall. When I was thrown into the Big Smoke, I sank. Until Bea arrived.

She moved down to London from Northumberland and was full of edges and stubbornness and we looked at each other on her first day in class and we clicked.

Then her father died. As quick as a sentence, he was gone. Afterwards came the disbelief. Then the struggle to make sense of it. And, while Bea and Mrs G. argue about most things, they agreed when it came to the sudden loss of Avi Gold. He had deserted them. Their way of making sense of it – blaming him. I didn't judge.

Bea and I bonded over hurt and books and film, anything to sweep away reality. We conspired against all things messed up, corrupt and wrong in the world.

We were outsiders, on the outside of every side.

We were best friends.

'Look,' Bea says now. 'Maybe you're not *meant* to be anyone. Maybe you're just, you know, meant to *be*. Live in the now and all that.'

'Maybe,' I say. 'But *sometimes* I wish I could just flick a switch and make everything go back to the way it was before. Back to normal.'

Bea pulls a face and drags her hair across her forehead, then she bends the stick between her thumbs until it snaps.

'I read the craziest shit online the other day,' she says, flinging the remnants into the scrub. 'Imagine this. You're standing in a room with a baby.' She glances at me from under that dark shank of hair. 'Same age as your brother.'

'*Half*-brother.'

'And this baby, you know for a fact, is Adolf Hitler.'

'What?'

'At least, he'll grow into Adolf Hitler. Now, what if I told you there was no comeback if you killed the baby? No repercussions. You wouldn't be tried and you wouldn't go to jail. So, the question is this: would you do it? Would you kill Hitler?'

'Are you taking the piss? Would I kill *Hitler*?'

'Yeah.'

'That's hypothetical. It can't happen. It's a paradox.'

'*Clearly*, it's hypothetical. But humour me. The baby, we can take as a given, *is* Hitler. He *will* go on to murder millions of people. *My* people.'

'It doesn't make any sense.'

'Would you do it, Moon? That's the issue. We're not debating plausibility.'

I imagine myself in the room. I see the baby in his cot laughing, kicking his pudgy legs. I think about Zig. And I can't. I *can't*. But then I give the baby a perfect little Hitler moustache and my resolve hardens. Darkness stirs in me.

'Yeah. I would. I'd kill him.'

Bea smiles and nods. She says nothing.

'Is that the right answer?'

'There are no right or wrong answers,' she says, kicking at the nettles.

We walk in silence, considering this. Then we stop dead. The sky is clear. The heat thick on my skin. Someone is on the path ahead. And, in my bones, I know . . .

This. Will. Hurt.

2

Erika Jürgen. A year above us, two years older. Flame-red hair and a wicked temper. She blocks the path in front of three shoulder-to-shoulder girls who look skittish. Louella Caden, Zoe Pierce, Evin O'Keefe. Two have their phones out already, filming. Meaning it's no accident they're here. They planned this. A bird, I don't know what kind, cries and a shadow flits over the path. I feel Bea bristle next to me and the urge to turn and run is fierce – it's primal. But we don't.

'Well, well, well,' Erika says, grinning, sauntering towards us. 'Look what the universe has gone and coughed up.'

It's been building, this fight. Last week, they cornered Bea in the changing room. Someone spat a derogatory comment at her, which wasn't smart. Bea doesn't back down. It escalated quickly, ended only with a teacher intervening.

'Hurrying home to Mummy and Daddy?' Erika says in a sing-song voice.

The other girls snicker in solidarity. We say nothing.

'Oh, that's right. I forgot.' She's warming up, enjoying this. 'Gold doesn't *have* a daddy, does she? My bad.' Hysterical laughter. Slaps on the back.

'Shut up, Erika!' I can't stop myself – the words blaze out.

I sound panicky.

'Oh, don't get me started on *you*, freakshow.' She pouts and runs a hand suggestively over Zoe Pierce's cheek. 'Daddy still a fruit?'

Her minions double over, like it's the funniest joke ever.

Bea lets go a sigh. 'Jürgen,' she says, her voice quiet. 'D'you have any idea what they'll say about you when – *if* – you leave school?'

The laughter dies. Erika's face blooms red. 'You better watch it, Gold. Whatever you're gonna say, be very, very careful.'

Bea smiles. 'You understand the question, though, right?'

Erika says nothing. Her eyes slide from me to Bea, momentarily off balance, a boxer recouping from an unanticipated, lightning-fast jab.

'It's binary,' Bea says. 'Yes or no. Either you understand or you don't.' She looks unafraid and I can't tell if she's acting relaxed or if it's real.

Erika takes a step towards us. I feel a spurt of anxiety. The trees seem to crowd the path.

'They'll say,' Bea continues, blithely unaware of my fear, 'absolutely nothing. You'll disappear, like a fart into the ether. You'll be forgotten.'

*

Dr Alice Augur leans back into her leather chair, which is ergonomic and stylish. She's slim, in her late thirties. She's wearing designer glasses and a sharp black knife of a dress. Ruby garnets at her throat, like drops of blood. 'Why not turn back?' she says in a calm, smooth voice.

I shake my head. 'Delaying the inevitable. They'd have been on to us the next day. There are rules. Someone calls you out, you face them.'

'I see. And this feeling of someone following you, I assume it was them?'

'Erika and the others? No. It wasn't them.'

Dr Augur steeples her fingers. 'Someone else?'

'I can't say.'

'Can't or won't?'

'Take your pick.'

'I'm on your side, Ana. I'm here to help.'

'Are you?'

Dr Augur lifts a pen and wobbles it between her fingers. 'Ana, you can trust me. Tell me what you saw. In the trees, following . . . if it wasn't the other girls . . . then, in your opinion, what was it?'

'In my *opinion*?'

'Yes.'

A rhombus of sunlight falls across Dr Augur's desk. I shift in my seat and stare at a pair of framed photographs. A man – intellectual-looking, darkly handsome. Two laughing kids at Euro Disney. The perfect family.

Dr Augur rolls her pen. 'This is a safe place, Ana. Nothing can hurt you here.'

'Not true. You're trying to get inside my head. *That* hurts.'

Dr Augur gazes at me, the epitome of cool. Uncrackable.

'All right,' I tell her. 'But, remember, you asked for this.'

She opens her palms to me, an invitation to proceed.

'There are things,' I tell her. 'I don't know what they are. I don't know where they're from. But they're coming for me. I feel it. And they're getting closer.'

'Things?' She glances round the room.

'That's right.'

'That . . . aren't from here?'

'No.'

'OK. Go on.'

'They're watching me. I see them all the time.'

Dr Augur frowns. 'You believe people are following you?'

'Not people. I told you, *things*. They were there, before the fight. In the trees.'

'I see,' she says, as much to herself as to me. I imagine the cogs in her brain twitching and turning. 'And . . . are they menacing?'

'Some are. I feel the danger pouring off them. Others seem more . . . I don't know, benevolent. As if they want to warn me.'

'Warn you about what?'

I shrug and squint out of the window at a bright blue, sun-baked London – city of a thousand cranes – a half-made place, eternally under construction.

'I saw one on the way here,' I tell her.

'Oh?'

'It was on the other side of the road. I couldn't make out its face – it was blurred and sort of indistinct. Its body was more a shadow than physical.' I'm aware, as I say this, how ridiculous it must sound to her. But I know what I saw. 'It was just standing there, facing me. Even though I couldn't see its eyes, I knew it was looking at me. Then a bus shot past and it was gone. It vanished.'

Dr Augur adjusts her glasses. 'I see.'

'You always say that. But you *don't* see. You don't believe me.'

She looks at me squarely. 'I believe you're very clever, Ana. Few of my young patients would use a word as particular as "benevolent". I also believe in the mind's extraordinary power. That, if you want something to be real, then –'

'Look, why do we even have to do this?'

'We don't,' she says, raising her shaped eyebrows, scribbling something down on the notepad on her desk. 'You're welcome to leave now and we'll tell your parents to fetch you and inform the school you're not inclined to return.'

'That's a joke . . . What are you writing?'

'My notes, Ana.'

'You're telling them I'm not normal, right?'

Dr Augur looks up from the tight scrawl on her notepad (spidery handwriting that's impossible to read upside down). 'Define normal,' she says.

'You only say that because you're a shrink.'

'Psychologist.'

'Same difference.'

An uncomfortable quietness settles on the room. Dr Augur spins her pen on the desk, between thumb and forefinger. It bobbles like the dial of a compass.

'I'm lost,' I say finally. 'That's what you're writing down.'

'Is that what you think?'

I clench my hands between my knees. Say nothing.

'All right,' she says, putting the pen aside. 'Let's come back to the figures later. First, I want you to tell me what happened with Erika and Bea. And don't leave anything out. Be specific. It's important we acknowledge everything. OK?'

I sigh and slouch back in my chair, a kind of scooped Scandinavian minimalist thing – comfortable enough to relax in, but not enough to let you fall asleep.

I stare at the wall clock over the door, willing the hands to accelerate.

Dr Augur watches me. 'Ana,' she says. 'What exactly happened?'

Erika surges forward. But Bea, light on her feet and laughing, dances out of the way, causing Erika to stumble, swinging her fists, red-faced with rage. Bea, cool as you like, taunts Erika, beckoning her to come after her again. Which I figure is tempting fate, because Erika looks set to murder someone. It then becomes apparent that *someone* means *me*. Instead of going after Bea, she turns and she looks in *my* direction.

And, like a bulldozer, she comes.

Next thing I know she's got me pinned up against a tree. It happens fast. Before I can react, her hand is at my throat and I can't breathe and I'm seeing dots and Erika is staring at me, stony-faced and contemptuous.

I'm powerless. Trapped.

Then Erika's eyes go as wide as plates and she jerks backwards.

It's Bea – she's pulling Erika off me and then she's hitting her and hitting her and hitting her and I'm falling and, at the edges of my vision, everything bends. The light changes colour. It turns silvery and then blue, and then it vibrates.

No.

It shimmers.

3

A dream. A stupid dream. I'll wake up and everything will go back to the way it was. But the world doesn't work that way. Sometimes things just happen and, like *that*, nothing is the same. I lie on my bed and chart a pattern of sepia water stains on my ceiling, like clusters of faraway planets.

It was agreed – by the headmistress, Mrs Tsukishima, and the board – that, to protect the school's reputation, only suspension would suffice. A month. Served to both Bea *and* me. Readmission hinging on one proviso: Psychological Evaluation.

One week down so far, one to go.

My phone buzzes.

Moon! You OK?
Barely.
F**kin parental won't let me see you.
Mine either. You're banned.

Lol. Been to the shrink yet?
Once. You?
Same. It sucked.

'ANA!' Frankie, downstairs, yelling up at me to get moving.

'All right! All right!' I yell back. My thumbs fly over the screen.

Bea, I gotta talk to you.
Me too.
I think I'm losing it.
You're not losing it.
She's still in hospital.
Only been a week.
**I'm switching today. Off to the Old Man's. I can
    sneak out. You?**
Of course. The Usual?
Done.

Downstairs, Frankie's back is turned. She's brewing her morning coffee with her keep-your-damn-hands-off-my-state-of-the-art-Italian-espresso-machine. It's Sunday. She's in her suit, despite the heat. Ziggy is at the kitchen table in his high chair, flicking mashed banana with a spoon. In the corner of the kitchen, the telly blares out a depressing news story.

POLICE GIVE UP HUNT FOR MISSING TEEN.

I slump into a seat opposite Zig.

Frankie swivels round, espresso cup in hand.

OK, I'll admit it: she looks good for forty-five. I've seen men stop in the street to leer at her toned legs (courtesy of Seb, her Pilates trainer) and it never fails to creep me out. Francis, aka Frankie Solana – her readopted maiden name. Early in her banking career, she was identified as a bona fide investment wunderkind. The move to London was a career thing – a haul up the corporate ladder.

'How'd you sleep?' she says.

'Fine.'

'No nightmares?'

'As a matter of fact, I dreamed I was living with a family in Australia. In the outback. We were hunted by dingoes and crocodiles and killer snakes.'

'Sounds terrifying.'

'I loved it.'

She takes a sip. 'So you're seeing Dr Auger again tomorrow?'

Cuts to the chase does Frankie.

'Do I have a choice?'

Frankie moves to the stove. The ingredients are prepped and waiting in glass bowls: chives, eggs and grated cheese. She's making omelettes and I know what they'll be like – runny in the centre, burned brown at the edges.

'I don't get it,' she says, cracking an egg.

'What's to get?'

'Your school isn't free, Ana. And who's paying for that girl's private medical bill? *You?* Your *father*? But you don't think about that, do you? The universe only exists for you.'

'So . . . you're saying I'm a solipsist?'

'A *what*?'

'A person who believes only the self exists or can be proved to exist. So the world, and everything in it, is just an invention of their subconscious mind. Technically, that makes you a figment of my imagination. I made you up, Frankie.'

She shakes her head, works the spatula. 'If only you applied that brain. You're a straight-A student, Ana. And now you're getting into *fights*?'

'We didn't start it.'

'*We*. That Beatrice Gold.'

'She saved my arse, Frankie. If it wasn't for her –'

'A girl's in *hospital*, Ana. Shattered collarbone, broken nose, you name it. I mean, really! Sometimes I don't know who you are any more.'

Frankie sighs. The pan sizzles.

'I take it you're not offering me a lift,' I say.

'I don't have time,' Frankie says. 'This one's important.'

'Right.' I watch Zig's attempt to squeeze out of his high chair. Fifteen gargantuan years lie between us. That and a different surname. Ziggy *Thorn*.

'I've been working on it for months,' Frankie says. 'You know that.'

'Yeah, yeah. I get it.'

Ziggy worms out of the chair's harness and now he's a few short moves from cracking his skull open on the hard marble floor. I stand and mooch round the table, shove Zig upright in the chair, clip him in properly and return to my seat.

Flip. Scrape. Flip. Frankie sees nothing of this.

'You act like you got the worst deal in the universe,' she says.

'Where's the proof I didn't? It's logically and mathematically possible I *did* get the worst deal. Someone must have. Why not me?'

'I give up. I really do.'

'Well, now you know where I get it from.'

'This is your father's fault.'

'Can't argue with that. It *could* be the Old Man's fault.'

The Old Man. Michael Moon. Aka Dad – which, if Moon legend is anything to go by, I've declined to call him from birth.

Frankie swivels and drops a plate down in front of me (more emphatically than necessary, if you ask me) and here's the omelette (runny in the centre, brown at the edges). Frankie picks up her espresso cup and takes a neat, controlled sip. 'You're welcome,' she says. She looks slick in her suit, but also a little baffled and sad. She glances at her watch and downs the espresso, goes to Zig and kisses him on the cheek and ruffles his hair. For a second, I feel like an intruder watching a stolen moment between mother and child. There's an easy tenderness in the way she looks at Zig that stings. She unclips him and lifts him into the air and Zig laughs. Frankie carries him outside the room and I hear a brief exchange in the corridor. The nanny.

Frankie returns – alone. And I swear she almost looks guilty.

She sweeps up to me and her hand finds my shoulder. 'Ana . . .'

'I'm fine. Just go.'

'I love you, Ana. You know that, right?'

'I know.'

'You could tell me the same thing.'

'I could.'

She sighs. 'Whatever this is, I don't pretend to understand it, but I'm here. OK? I'm your mother, regardless of this Frankie charade. Your *mother*.'

I say nothing, let myself become petrified, as hard as wood.

'We'll get through this,' she says. 'Together. We're a family. Maybe not a normal one. But then . . . well, maybe there's no such thing.'

As always, she smells of expensive leather, strong coffee and, weirdly, chocolate, despite never touching the stuff (bad for the perfectly toned abs). She stands next to me, hand still resting on my shoulder – just sitting there.

'I'll see you next week,' she says. 'OK?'

'Fine.'

'Are you going to wish me good luck?'

'Who has a meeting on a Sunday?'

'It's an informal meeting.'

'Right. Well . . . good luck.'

'Can you say it like you mean it?'

'Break a leg, Frankie. Knock 'em dead, Frankie. Do whatever it is you do so well. You'll get the deal. You always do. You're Frankie Solana. Super-achiever.'

'Ana . . .'

'*What?*'

'Nothing. Just . . . be safe. OK?'

I don't look at her. I stare ahead. And, when I turn round, she's gone. But her smell lingers – the chocolate, the coffee. Suddenly I feel like crying. And the world outside the door seems like a black precipice. I leave the omelette untouched.

4

I stand in front of the burgundy-red door of 7 Underwood Lane, Earls Court. Heat burns off the walls. The sky is a mindless blue, almost black. Before I get the chance to knock, our front door flies open and I'm hit with this: hair – shaved on the top and sides and, at the back, drawn up into a ponytail of beaded dreadlocks. Ears – pierced and run through with twisted ash-black bones. A scarlet kimono – silk, with black and white herons, gaping open, revealing a hairy chest, rib bones, a potbelly and . . .

'Christ, Gad!'

Gad bunches the kimono at his navel with a fist. '*Pardon, chérie. Ça va?*'

Unbelievable. Zero embarrassment. *Nada.* Zip. *Rien.*

Committed eco-warrior, Moroccan Frenchman and (to my profound and unceasing embarrassment) practising nudist, Gad Moudnib. Aka the Hippie.

Welcome to stage two of my Brilliant Imploding Life.

A week with Frankie. A week with the Old Man. On and on. Ad nauseam.

'How bad was it?' the Hippie says, stepping aside (pronouncing 'was it' *waz eet*). By 'it' he means the past few days with Frankie.

'Beautiful.'

'*Ah bon?* That horrible, huh?'

'Worse.'

'*C'est la vie.* Now you are here.'

I turn and look at him, throwing my satchel down on a couch. 'You heard what happened, right?'

He flicks his hand and spits a plosive 'whatever' sound, as if to suggest the whole school-suspension thing is a storm in a teacup, entirely unworthy of his attention. He understands solidarity, I'll say that for the Hippie.

He follows me into the kitchen.

'Where's the Old Man?' I ask, flinging open the fridge door, enjoying the blast of cool air. I haul out the orange juice. Down it straight from the carton.

'On the terrace,' the Hippie says. '*Comme d'habitude.*'

I find him in Downward Dog, arse in the air, face beetroot-red. I drop into one of two LA-style, retro plastic-strip garden chairs and sigh, long and deep.

'Darling,' the Old Man grunts. 'Manageable week?' He glances up at me and switches from Downward Dog into Leg Raised.

Gad follows me out, commandeers the second chair and takes a sip from a glass of slug-green juice. He flips through the *Sunday Times* magazine on the table, crossing a leg over his knee. The kimono sluices open.

'Jesus, Gad. Clothes aren't optional, you know.'

'Ana,' the Old Man wheezes. 'Don't be such a prude. A nude body is a glorious and natural thing.'

'Peeing is a natural thing, but you don't see me squatting on the front lawn.'

Gad, to his credit, laughs.

We watch the Old Man power up through Warrior into Reverse Warrior, until finally he salutes us with Mountain Pose. We clap. Me ironically. Gad with gusto.

'How's your mother?' the Old Man says, towelling his arms.

'No change.'

'Still a complete nightmare then?'

'This is my cue to leave,' Gad says, standing up and giving a mock bow. 'I bid you lovely people adieu. My citizenship test waits.'

The Old Man blows him a kiss and Gad departs, humming.

'She hasn't signed the divorce papers yet,' the Old Man says. 'Can you believe it?'

I shrug.

'The master manipulator at work,' he says. 'Incredible. Same way she's managed to get her sixteen-year-old daughter to see a psychologist.'

'Seventeen.'

'What?'

'I'm seventeen. Not sixteen.'

The Old Man throws the towel over Gad's empty chair. 'Now let me look at this beautiful face.' He cups my cheeks in both hands. His palms, despite the yoga, are dry from countless hours handling clay in his ceramics studio. 'I see you, sweetheart,' he says. Like the bloody Na'vi in *Avatar*. The Old Man's way of saying 'I love you'.

'Are you eating properly?' he says now, frowning.

I pull away.

'You know what you need?' he says, narrowing his eyes.

'Enlighten me.'

'A dog.'

'A *what*?'

'One of those beautiful chocolate Labradors. Dogs can centre a person.'

'You're *allergic*.'

'Your next appointment,' he says, changing tack. 'It's tomorrow?'

'Yeah.'

'How many more sessions do you have?'

'Six.'

'It makes me mad. You don't need this. We should go to Brighton. There's this Wellbeing Festival there. Love and wholesomeness, that's what you need. And trees.'

'Right. And a dog.'

'It's normal,' the Old Man says. 'This'll pass. It's a phase. Life is full of phases, one after the other, you'll see.'

Yeah, right. A phase. Like marriage.

'You're on a journey, Ana. All you have to do is find the real you.' He taps my chest bone. 'The Ana Moon in here.'

Vintage Old Man. Michael Moon believes in the healing power of trees and forest walks and staring into night fires. He believes in crystals and reiki, that the heart is the most important organ in the body, and that kindness trumps intellect any day of the week. What he *doesn't* believe in is psychotherapy. But Frankie does.

'I forgot to get something from the High Street,' I tell the Old Man, plunging my fingers between the plastic straps of the chair, widening them, then pinching them back in place. 'It won't take long. An hour tops.'

'Get what?'

'A book. It's on our English Lit. reading list for next term.'

'What book?'

'*Equus*,' I reply. 'It's a play by Peter Shaffer.' Which is true – both the title and the author *and* that it's on our reading list. The only thing I leave out is my real intention: to meet up with the one person everyone thinks is leading me astray. Bea.

'It's all about horses,' I tell the Old Man when I see him frown.

'Hardly,' he says. 'It's about far more than that.'

'Can I go?'

The Old Man levers himself down into a chair and reaches for the paper. 'You're not under house arrest, Ana. But suspension's a big deal.' He snaps the paper open in his hands. Then his eyes find mine. 'Tell me you'll be right back.'

'I'll be right back,' I tell him. 'I promise.'

5

'MIND THE GAP!' a voice commands in a disaffected monotone, as if the gap might be a black and bottomless pit, but anyone falling through would raise no more than an eyebrow. This is The Usual – *our* place. The Tube. Circle Line to be exact. Bea claims there's no better place on the planet to talk. Safe, surrounded by the indifference of strangers. Going round and round in a giant, endless loop.

We step into the carriage and plant ourselves on seats near the door, sipping frozen lattes. Here sit the usual suspects: an old woman opposite us with shopping bags at her feet, a load of tourists, a man in shorts and a T-shirt wet with perspiration. Countless others staring gloomily at their smartphones.

'So?' Bea says.

She's wearing a fitted lime-green jumpsuit. On anyone else it would look ridiculous. On her it's perfect. She seems delicate, otherworldly almost. I catch my reflection in the dark glass of the carriage window. Curly auburn hair. Cheeks pale and shiny. I'm taller than Bea; my bony shoulders curve inwards. But my go-to mustard-yellow hoodie looks OK, despite the heat. And my black skinny jeans too, torn at the knees and worn to silver, and my Stan Smith trainers, a month old.

'*Moon*. Tell me what happened, with your shrink.'

'Nothing.'

'*Nothing?*'

'Not a single thing worth repeating.'

'So you're saying your shrink *doesn't* hold the key to universal understanding and consciousness? No shit, Sherlock. Mine neither.'

'She says it's a process.'

'Bloody hell, Moon! I don't see how the school gets away with this.'

'I know. Tell me about it.'

Bea slides her bum down in the seat and kicks her legs out across the aisle, drawing a hostile sigh from the woman opposite. 'Know why shrinks are *called* shrinks?' Bea says, staring down the woman.

'Nope. But I get the feeling you're about to tell me.'

'It's from headshrinker,' Bea says, turning to me. 'I looked it up.'

'*Head*shrinker.'

She grabs my arm at the elbow. 'Which was taken from cannibal tribes in the Amazon that literally shrank the heads of their victims.'

'Right. So . . . what does it mean in *this* context?'

Bea lets go of me. Shrugs. 'I dunno. Maybe it's all about shrinking our inflated egos. See, here's the thing, Moon. I reckon they're scared of us.'

'They're not scared of us.'

'Yes they are.'

'Why?'

'Because we *feel* more than them. Their lives are small, so they try to make *us* small, label us, put us in boxes. It's diabolical when you think about it. They're trying to make us *less*. I mean, so what if we're messed up and full of craziness? So what?'

I don't answer, because right then I get a prickling feeling on my scalp. That sense again – I'm being watched.

My heart thuds. I look round the carriage. And I see *him*.

He stands diagonally across from us. He's wearing faded black jeans with a fat belt, high-top boots, a white T-shirt (tight) and a leather bomber jacket with a faux-fur collar. He looks muscular and tough, like he could bash through a brick wall. His hair is short, dark and wavy. I guess of Middle Eastern or African descent. His eyes are coal-dark and calm – gunfighter eyes – and his lips are full and . . . oh, let's just go ahead and say it, he's beautiful. And he's staring . . . Right. At. *Me*. Yours truly.

'Hello? Earth to Moon?'

I look away. I look back. Bloody hell. His eyes. They don't waver from me.

'Moon! You're doing that thing you always do. You're disappearing, Moon. You're off in your head again. Hello? Anyone home?'

Maybe in my don't-even-think-about-it mustard-yellow hoodie and skinny jeans I've still got it, but this is weird.

Fine. Two can play this game. A stare-off. But this guy must be a professional poker player – he's inscrutable. And there's something in the steeliness of his look, like he's probing, asking questions.

'Aaaah! Now I get it. Moon, you're forgiven! God, he's a dish.'

I glance briefly at Bea. I look back and he's edged closer.

My heart slams. My palms are clammy. I feel like bolting. I take a sip of my coffee and pretend to fuss with the lid. When I look up, he's right in front of us.

'Hi,' Bea says.

He looks at us, from Bea to me. *It's you*, he seems to say. And my heart quails, because I swear his lips don't move. The words just form in my head. They appear there. Like that! But then my brain kicks in and dismisses the idea.

'Let's start with a name,' Bea says. 'And we'll go from there.'

He looks focused, like he's trying to work something out. 'I'm Malik,' he says. This time aloud. Dead sexy voice. Husky.

A change comes over his face, as if he's affirming something.

'I'm Bea,' Bea says (God, I'm envious of her ease). 'Beatrice Gold. And this here is my best friend in the world, the gorgeous and prodigiously clever –'

'Ana,' he says. 'One "n".'

I try to speak but my voice is mutinous. The train lurches. My heart kicks like a caged animal.

He gives a low, throaty laugh and points at the black scrawl on my Starbucks cup. 'Don't worry. I'm not a stalker. The barista wrote it on your cup.' His lips curl into a grin. His teeth are white and the right kind of crooked. 'So . . . does *Ana* speak?'

I open my mouth and then shut it again. Like a damn fish.

'I get it,' he says. 'Low-profile. Smart.'

Uh . . . *what*?

'It's just you two?' he says, glancing round the carriage.

'What, two's not good enough for you?' Bea deadpans.

'Where are the others?' he asks.

The *others*? OK, that does it. He's a psycho.

'I suppose you could ask me the same question,' he adds, his face darkening. 'Truth is, I needed space. Last mission . . . it didn't go well. All over Sol news.'

'*What* news?' Bea says.

'They didn't make it,' he says. 'None of the last three have.'

OK. All right. Stay calm. Don't lose it. Just because he's Tobias-Eaton-aka-Four-in-*Divergent* hot doesn't mean he's not an axe murderer.

'What did you say your name was again?' Bea says.

'Malik.'

'Right, well. Look, Malik, I don't know what the Buck Rogers you're talking about and I don't really care. To each his own. But listen –'

35

The train wheezes and the brakes whine and swallow her words. We pull into a station. The doors crash open and the carriage crowd disgorges on to the platform.

'This is me,' he says, glancing up. 'See you at the Haven?'

The *what*?

He moves past me and my fingers graze his and that sends a shock up my arm. I watch him shoulder through the crowd, glancing back once, and still I don't speak. A thrill of adrenaline pumps in my blood. *Wait*, my body screams. *Don't go. Stay.*

I sit, transfixed, breathing hard, turned to the window as the doors slide shut. He's a stranger . . . and yet I feel like meeting him was meant to be. Inescapable. *But why?*

In the middle of the crowded platform, he turns again and his eyes find mine. And I feel two things at once. Affinity with him, a closeness. But also a nameless dread. The train screeches and speeds up and hurtles us into darkness.

He was staring at me – at *me* – as if no one else existed in the world.

Here. With me. Gone.

'Well, that was weird,' Bea says. 'And, by the way, you're a pickup artist of the first order, Moon. Should have your own vlog, teach others.'

'Get lost,' I say.

'In your defence,' she adds, 'he *was* fit, that boy. I'd like to take him home and . . . well, finders keepers. I know. I'm just sayin'. Dreamboat.'

I put my hand against the glass, feel the train shake. I stare at my reflection in the window and the black beyond.

'Don't worry,' Bea says. 'You'll see him again.'

'Think so?'

She smiles. 'Of course. Only seven point seven *billion* people in the world. Why not? Odds are totally in your favour.'

'You're not helping. You know that, right?'

'Moon, listen. You've gotta snap out of this not-talking-to-boys malarkey. No chat equals no kissing. And no kissing equals no shagging. You're seventeen, not twelve.'

'Whatever. I dated Ennis for, like, a month.'

'Dated? It was more like a week. And anyway he wasn't right for you.'

'No. Turns out he *was* right for Katie, though.'

'True. And Sarah-Jane. And don't forget about Jaleesa. Not bad for one month's work. All while supposedly dating you.'

I shake my head. 'It felt like I *knew* him, Bea.'

'*Ennis?*'

'Malik. Dark-eyes. Like meeting him was somehow . . . inevitable. You know? I mean – look, this is gonna sound dumb, but weird things have been happening to me lately. Things I can't explain. Things you won't believe.'

'Oh yeah? Try me.'

I turn and look at her, knees touching, her jumpsuit rucked up, the train bucking us back and forth. 'Do you remember everything, Bea? From the woods? The fight. What you did. Pulling Erika off me, hitting her like that.'

'Moon, it wasn't like –'

'Because I don't. Not really. It gets blurred for me. Confused and mixed up. I see shadows. Everything warps. The air shimmers and –'

'*Shimmers?*' Now she's laughing at me.

I bite my lip and feel a burning heat up my neck. 'See? Never mind. I knew you wouldn't believe me. No one ever does.'

'No. Moon, listen –'

'Forget it. Forget I ever said anything. Just leave it.'

Bea gives me an exaggerated frown, as if she's offended by my tone. 'Jeez. What crawled up your arse?'

A clamp tightens round my throat, making it difficult to breathe. I'm getting irritable. My pulse is thumping and Bea is looking at me with an expression that feels judgemental, even though I know it isn't. 'Nothing,' I say. 'It's nothing.'

I pull my hood down to my mouth and feel my heart turn to a lump of coal.

'Ana?' Bea says. Her voice is softer.

I don't answer. I lose myself in the sideways lurches and rhythmic thumps. I can feel her looking at me, and then her hand, over mine. I remain still. The darkness is powdery-black under my hood.

Suddenly the train brakes. HARD. A screech, followed by a loud crash, rips me wide-awake. Then I'm flying over seats and the world is tilted and my head slams into a metal pole with a sick *smack!* A flash of blue. The lights buzz. I sit upright, dazed, rubbing my temple. I can feel a lump already – a stickiness.

Then I see her. Bea. Lying on the floor. Not moving.

Panic catapults me from the seat and I lurch across the aisle. I skid next to her, drop to my knees and haul her up into my arms. Her body is limp, beads of sweat on her forehead and her hair, damp in my hands. I feel her wrist, a faint pulse.

She opens her eyes and looks at me.

'Bea? Oh God. Bea!'

She blinks at me. Turns her head from side to side, a look of bewilderment on her face. 'What happened?'

'You're OK,' I tell her. 'We're all right.'

But then I look around.

The other passengers – the old woman, the tourists, the sweaty man in shorts, all of them – they're not moving. Not moving *at all*.

They're frozen. It's as if they're in limbo.

'Stay here,' I tell Bea, resting her head gently on the floor. 'I'll be right back.'

She nods, bleary-eyed, and mumbles something.

I leave her and I walk down the carriage accompanied by the loud squeaking of my Stan Smiths. My head throbs. I stand in front of the old woman. She doesn't move. I wave my hand in her face. No reaction. It's like she's been turned into a Madame Tussauds wax model. I try the tourists. Same thing. The man in the shorts. No response. Not even an eye twitch.

OK, it's official, I'm freaking out. 'Bea!' I yell. 'The hell's going on?'

She doesn't answer.

The lights flicker, then go out entirely.

The carriage is plunged into darkness.

I see nothing. Then silhouettes. Pale faces.

The lights snap back on. I look at Bea in panic. She raises her head, stares at me strangely.

'You OK?' I shout.

She waves her hand at me. *OK*, she mouths back.

I walk on to the sliding doors of the carriage. In the glass lies my reflection and a wall of foreboding darkness. We've stopped between stations. I try the door button. Nothing happens.

'HELLO!' I shout.

No answer. I look at Bea again. She's sitting upright now, rubbing her head.

'HELLO!' I pound the door with my fist. 'Is there anybody out there?'

Silence.

Which makes sense. We're in the middle of a tunnel.

The loudspeaker crackles and hisses. I wait for the driver's voice and nothing comes.

I'm on the verge of yelling out again when the carriage lurches and I'm thrown backwards. We're on the move. I plant my feet as we gather speed. I look back at Bea.

'Hey, Bea!' I yell. 'Just hold on, OK? I'm coming.'

But we're moving at pace now – *fast* – and I'm struggling to stay upright, let alone get back to her. I shouldn't have left her.

My heart jackhammers. 'It's OK!' I shout. 'I'm coming. It's fine.'

I'm wrong. It isn't fine.

We pull into a station and the train slams to a stop. But I can't move.

At the edges of my vision, everything bends. The light changes colour. It turns silvery and then blue, and then it vibrates. Now the temperature in the carriage plummets and my breath turns to fog and the windows frost over. The next thing I'm aware of is a complete shutdown of noise. It's as if an invisible dome has clamped down over the carriage, blocking out every sound. Then I feel my body become weightless. And I lift into the air.

I'm floating.

What the hell? I'm *floating*.

My hair sails up around my face and I see Bea and all the other passengers, stone still in their seats beneath me. It's as if the Tube has transformed into an interstellar rocket and I'm the only one blasting through space in zero gravity. Which is 100 per cent not possible. But as I try to get my head round this, I hear it.

A sound like nothing I've heard before. A frightening, pain-wrought and drawn-out noise. Not human. Not animal. Something else. Something primeval.

SKRAAAAAAAAAAAAAAAAAAAAAAAAAAAAAAAAA-AAAAAK!

Bird-like and quick, a shadow flashes past the frosted windows. I spin round. Loud screeches fill the air. A stench like a gutted beast.

And I see it now. And every part of me is afraid.

It crawls through the space from the next carriage along. A humanoid thing. Naked and hairless. Head, torso, arms and a pair of long, sinewy legs leading to clawed feet. A network of dark capillaries fan like roots beneath pink wrinkled skin. On its back, buckled and bony wings bend to the carriage walls. Eyes, black holes staring from a gaunt, misshapen face. Its mouth, stretched and huge, revealing rows of teeth. It drags itself forward using long hooks on its wings to haul itself along the carriage floor ... towards Bea. I try to move – to get to her – but it's impossible. Bea is between me and the beast and, like me, she's floating.

This isn't real. This can't be happening.

The creature lurches towards Bea.

'NO!' I shout. My voice is hollow, like an echo.

It's close now. So, so close.

Oh God.

No.

Nononono.

NO!

It's *on* her. It leans into her, slavering. Digs its barb-like hooks into her.

'Don't you touch her!' I scream, throat closing.

The creature looks at me with ferocity. It cradles Bea's limp body in its talons. I get a sense of its hunger, its impatience. I'm feeling light-headed. Dizzy.

'You leave her alone,' I plead, my voice desperate and small. 'Please, just . . . leave her. Take me. Take *me* instead.'

The world begins to spin. Everything blurs.

Thump!

I slam down on to the floor, flat on my stomach. The coffee splatters. The lights glare on and, when I raise my head, the creature is gone.

And so are the other passengers, every single one.

And so is Bea.

Vanished. Disappeared.

Gone.

LŪNA is the temptress; she flatters to deceive. Paired with Sol. Similar; not the same.

LŪNA

6

I feel sick. My head pounds. Every nerve in my body feels shredded. Bea's gone. *Taken*. I stumble through the train in a state of numb fear, and find nothing. Every carriage is empty, as in not-a-single-soul-on-board empty. One carriage after the other, I find no trace of her or anyone else.

But how? People don't just disappear. They *don't*.

I try to replay what happened, but my memory is fuzzy. I get the feeling the whole episode lasted, I don't know, a minute or two? A minute or two of madness.

I remember feeling weird, blacking out maybe. Then the crash.

I remember the scream and that hideous thing – black eyes, pink skin, wings bent to the walls of the carriage – the creature. I remember it reaching Bea.

And then? What then? Nothing. I fell. I hit the ground hard, and when I looked up the train was empty and Bea was gone.

I double back to the carriage where I started and I stare at the crushed Starbucks coffee cup on the floor – *hers* – her name still scrawled on the side.

Bea

I stare at the bare space where she'd been lying. I pull back my hoodie, and look up and down the deserted carriage. Nothing. I swallow hard and a bitter taste lingers in my mouth. My teeth ache. A persistent noise crackles in the back of my head, as if there's a swarm of locusts in there.

I lean against the train wall to stop from hyperventilating. *Shit.*

Shit. Shit. SHIT!

I blunder through the carriage in a daze. I find a door broken open. I shoulder through it and race up and down a deserted platform, shouting for help.

My voice echoes in the empty space.

I feel sick. My head pounds. I put my hands on my knees and breathe hard.

I need to get help.

I give the train a last glance, and then I turn and race to the WAY OUT sign and I hurl myself up the nearest escalator, which, like the platform, is abandoned. Two, three, five stairs at a time. At the top of the escalator, I trip and sprawl on the floor.

'Anybody,' I wheeze. '*Some*body. Please.'

No one hears me. The station is deserted, which can't be right. I try to recall if any stops on the Circle Line had been closed for repairs, but I'm positive there weren't. *Which station is this?* I forgot to look on the platform.

From the floor, I cast about for a sign, but see nothing and nobody – not a single Tube official or even a tourist. I'm alone. Alone, without Bea.

I stand up and run. I reach the unmanned turnstiles, vault over them and race up a set of stairs to the exit – and slam into a barrier. A metal mesh gate pulled down.

There's a gap, though. I shove myself into the tiny space between wall and gate and squeeze through, sobbing.

I'm out. I pound up another short flight of stairs and I'm on the pavement.

I drop to my knees and I cough and I take a deep, shuddering breath and I pummel the pavement until the skin of my knuckles is raw. I look up and read the station's name: SLOANE SQUARE. Which means I'm three stops from home, but nothing will ever drag me back down into the Underground. Only Bea.

And she's gone. *Gone.*

There are people on the street. A mother and her young daughter see me and the mother draws her daughter in close and they quickstep round me.

'Wait!' I yell after them. 'Wait, I need help. Please. Please help me.'

My voice sounds like a crow. They rush away and don't look back.

I feel for my phone in my pocket and pull it out. Dead. Blank. No battery. The ground spins. I take another long breath and look up at the sky.

And this makes me panic even more. Because here it is . . .

Anomaly number 1: The sky is grey.

7

Grey. In the space of three Tube stops, about seven minutes, the sky has turned from a stark blue to an iron-grey. There is no sun, just a vague halo of light beyond the clouds. An earthy basement smell lingers in the air. The cement pavement is dark and sodden, and the cold cuts like a knife. It's a bitter, bright cold.

Keep it together, Ana – get to the Old Man's and raise the alarm.

That's what I need to do. That's the priority now. *Get to the Old Man's. Get to the Old Man's. Get to the Old Man's.* I repeat the phrase in my head, over and over, the only coherent thought I can marshal.

Lightning flashes across the sky. Thunder. I run home in a downpour. I don't stop for breath, not once, not even when I see things that are impossible – like cars floating low over the ground. I'm losing it. I'm nuts. I keep my head down and ignore the world around me. I run.

By the time I arrive at the Old Man's front door, I'm a mess. Wet through. My lungs are bursting, my nerves jangling and my ears buzzing.

And that's when I see it . . .

Anomaly number 2: The door is black.

8

Black. As in not red. Black. As in this-door-has-never-been-black-it's-always-been-burgundy-red-but-now-is-for-no-good-reason-black. I run my hand over the surface, expecting to find fresh paint. But it's blistered and peeled – *old*. I take a step back and look at the number: 7. Above the letterbox, tilted to the left. OK, so at least *that's* normal. *That* hasn't changed. The Hippie's been promising to fix it for months. Once he went so far as bringing out his ancient toolbox. He set it on the step, gazed at the number and came back indoors. He said he preferred it offset.

I look at the road sign, shivering, dripping in the rain. Underwood. I'm in the right place. *Why wouldn't I be? I know where I live, don't I?*

So what the hell's going on?

A helicopter, or something like a helicopter, roars overhead. The sound of its blades chopping the air reverberates in my chest. *Bea*, it says inside me.

Bea. Bea. Bea. Bea. Bea. Bea.
BEA!
I'm hallucinating. It'll pass. This is all a dream.
It doesn't pass. It isn't a dream.
The door swings open and here's the Hippie.
Except . . .
Anomaly number 3: The Hippie's wearing a suit.

9

A suit. A three-piece, buttoned-up dove-grey suit. I say nothing, because I can't speak. It's not just what he's wearing that's wrong, there's something else. Something *off*. His dreads. His dreads and his goatee and his earrings – they're all gone. It's so incongruous I feel like slapping him on the back and roaring with laughter. It's actually getting funny. The Hippie's in a suit! It's a joke. Any second now Bea will leap out from behind the door and yell '*Surprise!*'.

But she doesn't.

'You don't like the grey?' the Hippie says, looking crestfallen, which makes no sense. He's indefatigably upbeat. 'You prefer the blue? *Merde. Oui.* The blue suit.'

The *blue* suit? He ushers me inside and I watch him shut the door behind us. I want to scream at him. I want to shout for help. I want to blurt out what's happened. But I can't. For no reason I can fathom – other than a deep, atavistic sense of something being terribly *wrong* – I say nothing.

What can I tell him? A creature came into the Tube and snatched Bea away right in front of me?

'*Ça va?*' the Hippie says. 'You look a little . . . different.'

I shake my head. 'I'm just . . . I got caught in the rain.' My heart's pounding. I'm freezing. I feel like I'm about to be sick.

'*Oui*,' he says. 'Of course. Where is your coat, your umbrella, *chérie*? You will catch your death. This cold rain every day . . . it is getting – how you say? Tiresome.'

Tiresome? It's been blue skies and hot-as-hell all week.

'How was it?' the Hippie asks, although it's weird thinking about him as the Hippie when he's nothing like the version I remember.

'How was what?'

'The week?'

'The *week*?'

'That bad, huh? Cannot say I envy you, bouncing from one place to another like this. *Très difficile, non?* Anyway, you are here now.'

He follows me into the lounge, smoothing his suit. His *suit*. I take a deep breath and try to settle my nerves, but that's like telling a cornered tiger to take it easy.

'Are you sure you're OK?' he says. 'You are not yourself, *chérie*.'

'I'm OK,' I mumble.

'You have cut your hair,' he says. 'Not so?'

'No. It's just wet.'

'*Qu'est-ce qu'il s'est passé?*' he says.

'Wh-what do you mean?' I stammer.

'You have a bump. On your head.'

'It's nothing.' My hand touches it instinctively, feeling the hotness, the slipperiness of rainwater on my skin.

Then it hits me. If Bea was snatched away on the Tube by some monster, and the Hippie isn't the Hippie any more, and the door isn't the door and the sky isn't the sky . . . then what else is wrong in the world?

I turn and look at Gad. 'Where's the Old Man?' I know his answer before he opens his mouth. The terrace. But I'm wrong.

'In the conservatory,' Gad says. '*Comme d'habitude*.'

And it hits me . . .

Anomaly number 4: We don't have a conservatory.

10

A conservatory. *When did that happen? How?* The Old Man sits with his back to me. He's barefoot, wearing his check shirt and scruffy jeans. On the table in front of him, under his fingers, lies an open book. The table is the same battered cedarwood thing we've always had, and here are the two garden chairs crying out that the world is normal. But the rain drums on a glass roof . . . and I stand in the doorway in shock.

And that's when I notice the smell. Most days, the house reeks of incense, which Gad and the Old Man light by the shedload. Today, it smells . . . *animal*.

No. That's not true. I'm imagining things.

The Old Man turns his head, as if sensing me. 'That you, darling?'

What do I say? I want to tell him about the door, the Hippie, the sky. *Everything.* Most of all, I want to tell him about Bea.

But I don't. I can't.

'Come,' he says, waving his hand. 'Join me.'

His voice is the same – the tone, the manner – no different. But something doesn't fit. Then I see. Despite the rain, he's wearing his sunglasses, a pair of aviators he bought in Cornwall on a Family Moon holiday (back when Family Moon was still an actual thing). He reclines in his seat and gazes up at me in a way that seems unfocused. 'Let me look at your face,' he says. I take a dazed step towards him and he reaches out his hand and his fingers find my chin. 'Holding up OK?'

The buzzing in my ears begins again.

We've been here already.

My teeth ache. My head hurts.

The Old Man strokes my cheek. His fingers travel onwards, finding and feeling out the contours of my mouth, my nose, my eyebrows, my cheekbones, as if he's familiarizing himself with the topography of my face – a face he's always known.

'Something's different,' he says, frowning. 'What's wrong?'

Wrong? What *isn't* wrong?

I get a sick feeling in my stomach and pull back. When did it begin, the day's weirdness? With dark-eyes. Malik, he said his name was. *He* was the start of it all.

'Ana?'

'I'm fine,' I say.

'How's your mother?' the Old Man says. 'Still a complete nightmare?'

Stop it. *Stop this*. We've had this conversation.

I take a deep breath, let it out. I feel exhausted.

The Old Man grabs my hand in his. 'What's up with you, darling?'

'On the Tube,' I say, voice trembling. 'I . . . something happened.'

'On the *Tube*?' he says. He squeezes my hand and I realize his skin feels different, clammier than normal. Softer.

'Bea,' I say. 'We . . . I was with her and she . . . she's . . .'

'Ana, what are you talking about? Who's Bea?'

That hits hard. I snatch back my hand, a maelstrom of thoughts whirling in my head.

Who's Bea?

I get the sudden feeling Bea was never with me, that we never met on the Tube. That I imagined it all. The boy. The floating. The creature. It never happened. None of it.

'Ana?'

'N-nothing,' I stammer. 'I just . . . nothing. Forget it.'

'You sure you're OK, Ana?'

'I'm . . . it's just . . . I'm not feeling great.'

'Oh, sweetheart. You should get some rest.'

'What did you do to the door?' I whisper, unable to say anything else.

'The door?'

'The front door. Why's it a different colour?' My voice sounds edgy. I'm struggling to breathe, gripping the arm of the garden chair, white-knuckled.

The Old Man turns his head towards the interior of the house and frowns. 'Ana,' he says. 'What are you talking about? What's got into you?'

That's when I recognize the animal smell.

Wet *dog*.

The Old Man reaches out to my face and I step backwards and his hand wafts in the air, trying and failing to reach me. I look at his dark glasses, searching for the eyes beyond, but all I find is my own back-to-front reflection. I watch his hand, flailing in the air, and my gut squirms. I look at the book lying open on the table. And I see them. Strings of neat dots raised on the page.

Braille.

And here it is . . .

Anomaly number 5: The Old Man's blind.

11

I'll accept the rain and the clouds. I will. Weather's a weird thing. It can be clear and then rain in the space of an hour. It *can*. It happens. The black door? OK, the door is odd, but maybe Gad (I can't call him the Hippie, not any more) replaced it. I don't know. It doesn't make *much* sense, but the door can be explained away too. Same as the suit and the lopped-off dreads and the damn conservatory. People get tired of things, change it all up. It's normal, part of everyday life. But this thing with the Old Man? This is *not* normal. The Old Man could see a few hours ago, and now he can't.

And nobody but *me* seems to find that strange.

I'm lying ramrod-straight in my bed in my room, staring at the ceiling, covers pulled to my chest, fully clothed except for my trainers, door locked.

My bed? *My* room?

The door, the window, my bookcase, desk and chair – everything is exactly where it should be. The disturbing part is that only some things are different. But they're *big* things: Gad, the Old Man, the dog.

I look at my shaking hands and splay them in the air like stars.

How long have I been like this, lying here, freaking out? Minutes? Hours? I ran from the conservatory. I had to find space to think, to process everything that's happened. But no amount of thinking can erase the tapping of the Old Man's stick on the tiled floor outside. His long white stick.

There's a light knock at the door. A pause. 'You OK in there, darling?'

'I'm OK,' I lie. 'I'm fine.'

But things are about as far away from fine as Mars from Earth. Bea's been taken. *Taken.* She's disappeared from existence and then *this* happens, *this* place. This is not my home. This is not my life. And this man in the corridor, being all nice and dadsy, is *not* the Old Man.

And maybe I'm different too.

Maybe he knows that.

A whimper comes from outside my door. A skittering of claws.

When I ran from the conservatory, the dog leaped up from under the table and came after me. A black Labrador – a guide dog. I stare at the strip of light under the door and grip my sheets.

What is this? Where am I? Out there, beyond the door, horrors await. I feel it. A darkness. I can almost see it curling up from under the door like smoke – a palpable sense of wrongness. I need to go. I need to go, go, GO. But *where*?

In the quiet, I relive the incident on the Tube.

The sudden stop. Banging my forehead. I feel my head – the lump is still there. *Did we crash? Was it that? But then what happened to Bea and the other passengers? And what was that thing?* That hideous, bird-like creature thing crawling through the carriage like a . . . well, like a hideous, bird-like creature thing.

It's a dream. It isn't real.

Then I have an idea. My phone's still dead, and it won't charge, so I use the old eighties-style rotary landline Gad installed because he believes all mobile phones are brain-killers. One thing that I'm grateful hasn't changed.

I pick up the receiver and dial.

MRS G.: Hello? Sophia Gold.

ME: Uh . . . hi, this is . . . it's Ana, Mrs G.

MRS G.: Anna?

ME: Bea's friend . . . from school.

MRS G.: Who *is* this?

ME: It's *Ana*. Look, I know this is crazy, and I know you don't want her to see me right now, but . . . is Bea there? I really need to talk to her, Mrs G. I just . . . is she there? Tell me she is.

MRS G.: If this is a prank, it's not funny. I don't know who you are. This is disgusting.

ME: But, Mrs G., I –

MRS G.: What sort of person are you? Why do this?

ME: I'm sorry, Mrs G. It's just –

MRS G.: I'm not Mrs G. I'm Sophia Gold. And you are not –

ME: Please . . . just please put her on the line.

MRS G.: She's gone. Don't you understand? She died a year ago.

The line goes dead.

I stare at the receiver in shock. *She died a year ago.*

No. No, that can't be. I feel like vomiting. My throat closes. Fear turns, deep in my stomach. And it hits me like a bullet: I'm alone. Truly alone.

With trembling hands, I punch in another number.

LH: Lister Hospital. How may I help?

ME: Uh . . . this is . . . it's Ana Moon.

LH: How may I help you today, Ms Moon?

ME: I need to speak to my doctor. It's urgent. Dr Alice Augur. She's a psychologist.

LH: Psychologist, you say?

ME: Yeah. You know. Shrink.

LH: And you're sure it's the Lister you're after?

ME: Yeah. The Lister. Chelsea Bridge Road.

LH: OK. It's just . . . well, we don't *have* a psychology department.

ME: No, you do. Trust me.

LH: I'm sorry. I can assure you, we –

ME: Did you type in her name? Augur. A-U-G-U-R.

LH: I'm afraid we have no listing for a Dr Augur.

ME: But . . . I came in to see her today. You're making a mistake. Please. Just . . . try again.

LH: I'm afraid there's no mistake. There is no Dr Augur. Not at the Lister Hospital. Perhaps –

I slam the phone back in the receiver and try not to panic.

I'll call the police. That's what I'll do. I won't tell them about the creature, I'll just ... I'll say someone took her. My mouth is dry. I can't swallow. The thought of Bea out there somewhere with that thing makes me feel violently ill.

I lean over the side of the bed and retch into my bin, then recoil from the smell. I cough and spit, wipe my mouth with the back of my shaking hand and shove the bin under the bed.

And then I snatch up my iPad.

In the bright glare, I begin typing a Google search.

I think I've landed in a parallel universe.

I scroll down and stop when I hit a story about a woman called Lerina Garcia. She goes to bed one night, same as usual, and when she wakes up her sheets are a different colour. She brushes this off and heads to work, but when she arrives at her department she's told she works in another part of the building on a different floor. In a panic, she heads home only to find a man in her house who can't recall a breakup she believes they had six months before. Her new boyfriend – whom Lerina claims she was seeing for a month – is gone. No trace of him. No trace of anyone who knows him. Just gone. I feel the skin tighten on the back of my neck.

I turn off the iPad and lie down again, shivering. I'm confused – that's all it is. The Old Man isn't blind. Bea isn't gone. She's at home. She's fine. It's all fine. I begin to drift, convincing myself everything's right in the world and things are just as they should be, as they ought to be.

The room tilts and my eyelids close.

I fall into darkness.

I dream of winged things, pink and bony. They carve the dark outside my window, releasing blood-curdling screeches. One of them descends through the gloom, its eyes black and bottomless, so dense they suck in the light. It swoops towards my window, extends a pair of clawed talons and slams into the pane, scraping at the glass.

Snick . . . snick . . . SNICK!

I sit bolt upright, drenched in sweat, heart thumping against my ribcage. It's quiet. No light shines beneath the door. The house is fast asleep. I can hear Gad's snores through the walls, and yet . . . something isn't right.

I look around, take an inventory of the room. Everything – down to the precise angle of my bedside lamp, my John Green novel, open to the same page, my Aztec-pattern bedspread with its interlocking circles of colour – *every*thing is how it ought to be.

This is my room. But it's also *not*. There's something off about it. It looks the same but it feels – irrationally, at a deep, molecular level – *different*. A cold current goes through me. A pang in my gut. I feel a fierce and inexplicable sense of loss. An absence of something. Of some*one*.

And that's when I remember.

Bea.

Snick!

As clear as day, I hear it again, the sound that woke me – something hitting the glass of my window from the outside. I flip open my iPad on the bedside table: 4 a.m.

I spring out of bed and stumble, wide-awake now, to the window.

Snick!

I stand and listen. Motionless. Silent. But I heard it. I *know* I heard it.

Get a grip, Ana. It's the wind. Branches blown against the glass.

Then I think of Bea again. And my heart constricts.

I rip the curtains apart and leap back at the sight of the new moon and the crooked shape of the yew tree. Pallid moonlight turns the world two-dimensional. The garden looks like a kid's drawing, all flat shapes and rough lines. And no waiting creatures. But there *is* this: perched in the yew tree, cut out against the blue-blackness of the sky – a shadowy figure.

The floor drops out from under me. It just falls away.

It's him.

12

Dark-eyes. In *my* garden. At four o'clock in morning. Sitting in a tree. I'm not sure which of these facts is the more remarkable, since I'm still trying to make sense of a world just as messed up and upside down as it was when I fell asleep, hoping to wash all the weirdness away. He's cupping something in his hand. Pebbles.

'Will you let me in?' he says, opening his hand and letting them fall. They skitter down the trunk. 'I'm cold out here.'

'*You*,' I manage.

'Yup. Me.'

'You followed me.'

Course I followed you, he answers, as if it's the most idiotic question he's ever heard and, before I can get my head round this, I realize he didn't open his mouth to speak. He *thought* the words to me. *Again*.

'So?' he says, out loud this time. 'You gonna ask me in or not?'

I stare at him, gobsmacked.

'Well?' he says.

'You came after me.'

'That's more or less what happens when you follow someone, Ana Moon.'

'Wait . . . you know my *full* name?'

'As of tonight, I know a lot more than just your name.'

'But –'

'There's no time. If you want your friend back, you'd better let me in.'

I watch him move catlike across the yew branch, then step through the window past me, calm and unhurried, as though all this is an everyday, ordinary thing. Embarrassed, I snap my duvet over rumpled sheets and toe the sick bin further under the bed. He watches me. Dark-eyes. Malik. Just him and me, locked in my room. Equal parts terrifying and exhilarating and, because that's clearly not something I want him to know, I give him my most disaffected look, which fails appallingly and ends up a kind of grimace.

He's wearing the same outfit as before. White T-shirt, leather bomber jacket, high-top boots, faded jeans and a fat belt. Except this time there's a holster on the belt. And, in the holster, a matt-black gun. I mean, bloody hell.

'That's a pistol,' I say, flustered, snatching a look at my locked door.

'Nothing gets past you.'

'Why've you got a gun?'

'Protection.' He looks at me, grinning. He whips it from the holster in a blur, spins it in his fist, like a gunslinger, and then he extends it to me, butt first. I hesitate and he spins it again and replaces it in his holster, as fast as a bat's wing.

'Where are you *from*?' I demand, trying to look unimpressed, but my stomach is in knots and I feel a cold sweat coming on.

'Out there,' he says, waving a hand at the window, sauntering through the room, looking at my bookcase, tilting his head to examine the spines.

'Out there . . . where?'

'Many places.'

He moves on, scanning my shelves. He lifts a tome. Philip Pullman. His Dark Materials. He knocks it back between the others with a smile. He's calm, in control and cool, but not detached. Beneath it all, I sense a hum of raw energy. Here is someone who isn't afraid. Who doesn't know the meaning of fear.

'What's your deal?' I ask him. 'What's going on?'

'Finally. A question worth answering.'

'You got a ballsy attitude for someone who's just broken into *my* room.'

'Uh . . . you *let* me in, remember?'

'Look, I'm gonna call the police. If you don't –'

'The *police*?' He laughs. 'Gimme a break.'

'Keep your voice down,' I hiss. '*Please*. If they find you in my room . . .'

'They?'

That stumps me. What do I say? Who exactly are they, the Old Man and Gad?

'Look,' he cuts in, 'the police don't matter, Ana. Not now. Not here. They can't help.'

'The police don't matter?' I say. 'Really?'

'Nope. Let 'em go, Ana.'

'Let 'em *go*?'

'Everything you think you know. The world. All the things that seem so important to you, they're not what you think. Nothing is what you think.' He looks at the globe on my desk, spins it with a finger. 'Africa, Asia, Europe – they're not the same places you've known all your life. Similar. Not the same. So, yeah. Let 'em go.'

'You want me to let the continents go?'

He stops pacing, looks me dead in the eyes and my knees begin to shake. 'I'm gonna say some things to you right now that might sound crazy, OK? But stick with me. This place? This world? This is not your world. This is Lūna.'

'Lūna?'

'That's what I said.'

'OK,' I say, playing along. 'If Lūna isn't my world then . . . what's *my* world?'

'Sol,' he says, matter-of-fact.

'Right. And . . . where exactly has Sol gone?'

'Nowhere. It's still there. It just doesn't have you in it any more. Not *this* you.'

'You're doing my head in. You're crazy.'

'I've been called worse.'

'Look –'

'No, *you* look, Ana. You need my help. I was the nearest, and so here I am. That's the way it works, like it or not.'

'What are you talking about?'

'Your ears,' he says. 'They've been buzzing, right? Crackling. You've had a bad taste in your mouth for a while. Your teeth ache. And you've seen things.'

Seen things? What does he know about that? What *can* he know? Who does he think he is, telling me stuff like that?

'I don't know what you're talking about,' I snap at him, fed up. 'Who are you anyway?'

'Me? I'm about the only person you can trust right now.'

'*Trust?* I don't even know you or *what* you are.'

'I told you. My name's Malik. Malik Habib. I'm a Pathfinder.'

'Pathfinder?'

'Yup.'

'See, that's exactly the sort of thing that makes you come across as whacko. Let the continents go. A world called Lūna. Pathfinder. Just . . . stop messing with me. Stop all this madness.' I stride back towards the window. 'You need to get outta here. What was I thinking, letting you in? I was –'

'Acting instinctively,' he says from behind me.

I turn and look at him.

'You've landed in a strange new world,' he says. 'You've lost your best friend. What else can you do but be guided by instinct? And by someone who knows it. *Me.*'

I say nothing.

Malik snatches up my iPad. 'Tell me you haven't been googling alternate universes. It's the first thing everyone does. Nowadays anyway.'

'You expect me to believe in parallel worlds, is that it?' I grab the iPad out of his hands and slam it down on my desk, turning my back to him. I can feel his presence behind me. The weight of him in the room. The warmth of his body.

'I don't *expect* you to do anything,' he says.

'Are you always like this?'

'Like what?'

I turn and face him. 'Like *this*.'

Malik smiles. He paces, looks out of the window, into the night. 'What about her mother? Have you phoned her yet? What did *she* tell you?'

My heart snags. I think about Mrs G. . . . that call.

She died a year ago.

'We need to go,' Malik says, turning round. 'Right *now*. You need to come with me.'

'I don't think so.'

'Ana, trust me, you need to walk through this window with me. Your best friend –'

'Stop talking about her. You don't know her. You don't know *me*.'

'Here's what I know, Ana. I know your friend has gone missing. I know you haven't told anyone. Not even your father, or your mother, or your friend's mother.'

'How could you know that?'

'I know – I can see it in your eyes. And, trust me, I often know more than I'd like.'

I take a step forward. 'If you had anything to do with her being taken, I swear I'll . . .' I try to continue but I can't. I have nothing. No threats. No answers.

'Your anger is understandable,' he says. 'But misdirected. You're smart. You know I had nothing to do with her abduction. I told you, I'm here to help.'

'Oh really.'

'Lemme tell you why you haven't reported your friend missing,' Malik says calmly. 'Because you know – deep inside – that things are not the way they were before. Everything's changed. And calling the police is a waste of time. You know that. You *know*.'

I stand with arms pinned to my sides and say nothing.

'Look,' Malik says. 'It won't last, this feeling. It'll get easier. What you're going through, it happened to me. You and me, Ana, we're the same.'

'Oh, we're not the same,' I scoff.

'We are. Like it or not. We're Pathfinders.'

'Yeah. Right. Pathfinders.'

'When I saw you on the Tube, I recognized what you were. But I had the timing wrong. It was too soon. It hadn't happened yet. And then I felt it.'

'Felt it?'

'A vibration in the air. Like a distress signal. It happens when a Pathfinder Falls for the first time. Or when a Normal Falls.'

'What are you talking about?'

'Ever taken an Uber?'

'Of course. How is this even relevant right now?'

'When someone Falls –'

'*Falls?*'

This is getting ridiculous. I feel like laughing. Malik sits down on my bed, and I think about the bin of sick shoved underneath.

'There are weaknesses,' he says. 'Fault lines in the fabric between worlds. Sometimes, people Fall through them. And when a Pathfinder Falls for the first time, or a Normal Falls by some cosmic blunder, there's a disturbance – a signal – and we can feel it. The closest Pathfinder responds. Like an Uber. Count yourself lucky that in your case it was me. I'm a five-star.'

His eyes hold mine. Then he grins.

'And now?' I ask. 'What now?'

Malik pushes himself off my bed. 'Now we go,' he says.

Go? Together? Just him and me?

'Go *where*?' I say, willing myself not to leap across the room and smooth down the duvet, where he's left his bum-shaped indentation. Still warm.

'We're not alone,' he says. 'There are others. You'll meet them. It's your only hope. Your only chance of getting her back – your friend.'

'Her name's Bea.'

'Bea then.'

'And why should I trust you, Malik Habib?'

'Because, Ana Moon, what choice do you have? You've seen one of them, haven't you? It took your friend. It has her.'

Cold fear. A stone in my gut. I let my fist fall to my thigh and dig a knuckle into the meat of my leg until it hurts.

'So,' he says, watching me. 'You *have* seen them. Big and as ugly as sin. Eyes like black holes. We call them Reapers.'

'I don't know what I saw.'

'You're not listening,' he says. '*Listen* to me.'

'Why? You think I'm obliged to listen to everything you say? To hell with that. Welcome to the twenty-first century, mate.'

'What? No. I was –'

'You're damn right I'm not listening to your crazy *Matrix* mumbo-jumbo. I can –'

'You'd prefer to stay here, is that it? Those two men in the room next door, they're not your fathers. They may look like them, they may even behave like them, but they are *not* them. And there's something else too. Something you've realized.'

'Like what?'

'They suspect, Ana. They can sense you're not theirs – the one they love. To them, you've changed. *You're* different.'

And I realize something with a jolt. I might not belong here, but somebody does. A girl, someone Gad and the Old Man were expecting. A girl whose room we're standing in, who should be here right now.

Me but *not* me. Another Ana Moon.

'What have you done with her?' I whisper, fighting a tumult of thoughts. 'The other . . . the person that . . .'

'Don't worry,' Malik says. 'She's been taken care of.'

My jaw drops. 'Taken *care* of?' I make a gun out of my thumb and forefinger and point at my temple.

'No. Jeez. Relax. This isn't some film. I'm not the godfather. I mean the others have her, and they'll bring her back. Once we're safely out of the way.'

I stare at him, nonplussed. 'The *others* have her?'

'Just . . . trust me, Ana. OK? It's time to see the bigger picture.'

'What if I don't come with you, Malik? What then?'

'Not a good idea,' he says, straight-faced.

'Why?'

'Because Reapers don't just come to hunt. They come to *kill*.'

13

The night is cold and the new moon a silver sickle in the sky. We climb out of the window quietly, so as not to disturb the strange new occupants of 7 Underwood Lane. We clamber down the yew tree, Malik first, me following with my heart in my throat, and we drop on to a sodden patch of lawn – the garden. Last time I was here, it was as dry as a bone. Now it's wet and spongy underfoot. Another anomaly, but I've stopped counting. Besides, if Malik is telling the truth, that dry garden is a whole world away. I need time to process that, but time isn't something we have, apparently.

We jog to the road, the straps of my backpack digging into my shoulders. I threw it together in a few breathless minutes: a jumble of underwear, T-shirts, a second pair of trainers, socks, phone charger. I forget the rest.

Reapers don't just come to hunt. They come to kill.

I feel loose and wild. A kite caught in a hurricane. Frightened, but also reassured by the presence of this long-legged, gun-toting stranger. This Malik Habib with his dark eyes that speak of worlds beyond the known. Whose voice comes into my head uninvited. Who runs with an athlete's lope, as if he's never far off a sprint.

I turn and stare at our front door trapped in a pool of moonlight. Black not red. *My* home? Not so much.

That's when I hear the growl, low-throated and mean.

I swing round, half expecting teeth. But it isn't the dog that greets me and it isn't some mythic beast. It's a motorbike. Malik has swung his leg over a black metal beast and he's sitting at the kerb, holding out a jacket and helmet to me. The bike is big and sleek, like a shark's fin, all metal and polished chrome – not new but well looked after. And then there's this: it doesn't have any wheels.

It's hovering. *Hovering*. I mean. What. The . . .

'Forget it,' I say, shaking my head. 'No way in hell I'm getting on that thing.'

'*Thing?* This is a Dyson Thunderbird.'

'Are you taking the piss? Where are the *wheels*?'

'Why would a Thunderbird have wheels?'

'That thing's a monster.'

'No. The monsters are coming. Hop on the back, Ana Moon.'

'No.'

'Scared?'

'I'm not scared.'

'It'll be fine,' he says. 'C'mon. I'm not the bad guy here.'

Am I crazy? I'm following a boy I've just met into the night, away from the safety of my home. But like he said, what choice do I have?

They took your friend. They have her.

Malik is the only one who knows about the creature and, right now, he's my only link to Bea, my only way of finding her. And that's all that matters.

I'd go to the ends of the earth for you, Moon . . .

'Do you know what you're doing?' I ask Malik. I can't help feeling I'm directing the question at myself.

'Mostly,' he replies, nodding at the helmet in his hand.

An elemental, uncontrollable force takes hold of me and I grab the helmet from Malik and position myself behind him on the machine. Close. Right up to his body. A thrill leaps in my blood. I shrug on the black leather jacket. It's warm and, with my mustard hoodie underneath, a tight fit, but it'll do. The helmet is snug too, which makes me wonder for whose head it was originally meant. I fiddle with the strap. The bike's vibrations run through me.

Bea, they say.

Bea. Bea. Bea. Bea-Bea-Bea-Bea-Beeeeeeeeea.

Malik turns his head to the side. 'Ready?'

NO. How can I possibly be ready for this?

'Where are we going?' I shout over the engine.

'Soho!' he yells back.

Soho. Makes perfect sense.

'Ana,' he says, his voice gone quiet and sharp.

'Huh?'

'Are you holding on?'

I look from side to side. Where am I supposed to be holding on? My feet dangle either side of the bike. They find a pair of grooved footholds, but –

83

'ANA!'

'All right, all right. Take it easy.'

Malik reaches back, snatches my wrist and clamps my arm round his waist.

'Hey!'

'Both sides,' he barks. Before I can respond, the engine roars and the bike kicks. I bring my left arm round Malik's waist, as quick as a viper.

I hear it then. A demonic, bone-chilling cry.

SKRAAAAAAAAAAAAAAAAAAAAAAAAAAA-AAAAAAK!

The bike whines and up goes a pall of smoke. An acrid smell catches in my nose and something else. Something rotten.

We slide right, the nose of the bike tips, and we streak away. I flatten myself against Malik's back. We cut through the air and scorch up the black tarmac.

The wind roars and bites at us. I swivel my head to the side and my gut tightens. I see them. This time there are two of them – craving us.

Reapers, Malik called them. Seeing them now sends a jolt through my body, turns my stomach to knotted rope. It isn't just fear. It's more primitive – a revulsion from deep within – an ancient, inborn, chemical response.

And something else.

Hatred.

They come veering in, one from either side. A stink fills the air. A smell of landfill. Malik brakes hard and the Reapers dive-bomb us. A brutal gust of wind. A ripping noise, wings thrashing, beating the air. They streak past us, right in front of the bike's nose, and wheel up into the night. Malik explodes forward. I snap my head round and see the Reapers separate and turn. My heart shakes.

One descends. It comes hurtling towards us from a sheer height, at incredible speed. I shut my eyes, duck and scream. Too late. Something hooks my backpack and wrenches hard and my stomach drops. I'm being lifted off the seat.

'MALIK!' I yell, grabbing at him.

He hauls out his gun, one hand on the throttle, leans to the side and fires.

A flash. A loud *boom!* followed by a scream that flattens into a thin whine.

I feel a release and drop back into the seat. But before I can take a breath, I get another sharp tug. Drenched in fear, I pull my arms free of the straps of the backpack. As soon as I jerk out my left shoulder, the bag is ripped away.

Malik floors the engine and we fly onwards. He slams us into a tight bend and leans us so low I can hear a grinding noise, metal on tarmac. A shower of sparks. The bike makes a throbbing, *whumping* sound and we pop upright and swerve left. Everything merges. The engine. The wind. The screeches. My heart feels as if it's about to burst through my chest. We're going so fast the trees and the buildings blur into a wall of blue blackness. Four words repeat in my helmet, over and over.

We're going to die.

We're going to die.

We don't. We stay alive. Malik rides without fear, as though born to the bike, as though his body and the metal have melded.

I clutch him hard, fingers locked under his ribs, feeling his heart thump.

They follow. I hear their screeches ripping through my skull.

Malik swerves us into a network of narrow roads that slice between high buildings and, unbelievably, the terrifying sounds begin to fade, buried by the engine.

SKRRRAAAaaaaaaaaaaaaaaaaaaaaaaaaaaaaaaaaaaaaaak!

I squint up at a strip of sky – empty bar the new moon. They're gone. He's lost them. I feel exhausted, flooded with relief. But, when I look at the buildings flashing past us, I'm reminded of a terrible truth: this is not my London.

The night is blue madness. The road comes rushing.

14

Dawn. Monday. The sky in the west is still dark. In the east, a moonlike sun cowers behind skeins of cloud, turning the Thames molten silver and the spires of Parliament as black as pitch. We blaze over Westminster Bridge on the hover-bike (yeah, that's right, the *hover-bike*). The road is deserted, save for a few black cabs (they look like normal black cabs, but disturbingly these hover too, blasting jets of air downwards on to the tarmac, sending rainwater spraying).

My mind is torpid. I can't think straight over the drone of the bike.

I swivel in my seat and see the giant Ferris wheel – the Eye – watching over us, and beyond an unfamiliar skyline. Monolithic towers of steel and glass, each as tall as the Shard, appearing overnight. I scan the cold sky and see no movement. No Reapers.

Malik steers the bike up Parliament Street and we're immediately engulfed in shadow. The whumping sound of the engine hammers off the buildings and our blurred reflection races us in the windows. We hit Trafalgar Square and veer up a dark road and then duck right into Regent Street, St James's, which leads us to Piccadilly Circus.

The first image that assails me is a seven-metre-high silverback gorilla downing a Coca-Cola. *Just do it*, shouts the copy.

Before I get my head round this unholy brand mash-up, we blast right through the gorilla. I flinch and grimace. And, when I turn back, I realize that the hoardings of Piccadilly are now three-dimensional holographic projections.

So there's that.

We're blazing up Shaftsbury Avenue now and bank hard left into Wardour Street. The names are all the same, but the buildings, the cars, the *structure* of the place is different. Malik brings the Thunderbird to a thumping stop at a nondescript matt-black door. No doorknob. No letterbox.

Fixed over the door, a small gold plaque reads:

MEMBERS ONLY

Malik drops a gear and sends us down a ramp alongside the door. There's a flash, like a camera going off, and a corrugated metal door winds up and we slip under it and descend into an underground car park. Malik pulls up alongside several other hover-bikes and he cuts the engine. I hear a booming sound.

'Hell's that?' I ask, voice muffled by my helmet.

'Anchor clamp. Locks us to the ground.'

'Right. Of course.'

Malik pulls off his helmet, swings out of the saddle and his fingers are under my chin before I can say anything. He pulls the helmet from my head.

'C'mon,' he says, tucking it under his arm.

I traipse after him, dazed, the engine's vibrations lingering in me.

Malik walks up to a steel lift and pushes his thumb against a glass panel. The lift doors open and we step inside. It hums and clunks and my legs feel wobbly as it rises. We emerge with a *ping* into a stark white hallway. Malik strides up to a heavy-looking steel door and stares into a video screen to one side. A red laser flickers across his eyeball. Silence. Then a sequence of bolts thunk in the door and it swings open. The door is reinforced metal, thick and chunky. It looks bombproof. Malik steps inside. I linger a second, then follow.

From the futurescape outside, I now feel as if I'm stepping into a sophisticated members' club from bygone days. Our footsteps drum over polished wooden floors, the lighting is low and the temperature moderated. Dispersed through the room are discreet clusters of plush leather chairs arranged round dark coffee tables. A ceiling fan whirs. We choose a table and slip into leather seats wordlessly. Ensconced in the chair, I turn my gaze on the room. It's empty. Opposite us, I scan a curved serving bar, and I realize I was wrong. The club isn't empty after all. Behind the bar, it watches us.

'It' consists of a patchwork of gleaming metal panels bolted and welded together. Its eyes look like self-adjusting camera lenses. No mouth.

In any other circumstances, this would freak me out. It doesn't now.

'That's a robot,' I say.

Malik laughs. 'You really don't miss anything, do you?'

I look at him. His hair is coal-black and dishevelled. His eyes dark and brooding. His cheeks so carved he looks like he's sucking a sweet. He grins and raps the table with his knuckle and I watch the robot move out from behind the bar towards us. Its lower half is a solid metal block culminating in an exhaust that hammers an almost silent blast of air downwards. Like the Thunderbird, it floats.

'So?' Malik says. 'What would you like?'

I put my hands on the table, palms down, and look at him. 'I'd *like* answers.'

'I recommend the full English.'

I draw a deep breath and exhale. 'What are we doing here, Malik?'

'Eating.'

I shake my head. 'Not hungry.'

'Suit yourself.' Malik hands the robot the menus. 'One full English with everything and don't hold back on the sauce and . . . uh, two coffees.'

The robot clutches the menus between articulated fingers and floats back to the bar.

'So,' Malik says, looking at me. 'You want answers.'

'I think I'm entitled to them.'

'Looks that way.'

'Let me play this back for you, Malik. I see you on the Tube before Bea's taken. You follow me home. You almost get me killed on the back of a *hover*-bike. Then you bring me here to meet "the others", but all I see is a floating robot.'

'I know what it feels like,' Malik says. 'You think life is one way, then a door opens and you realize the world is bigger than you thought. I've been there, trust me.'

'You want me to *trust* you? I almost died back there.'

'But you didn't.'

'This is mad. Why am I even here?'

'You're here because you've Fallen. Through the space–time continuum.'

'The *space–time continuum*?'

'Yup.'

'So you're saying . . . wait, what *are* you saying?'

'I'm saying you Fell from your world into this one. From Sol into Lūna.'

'That makes no sense.'

'It will.'

I look away, take stock of my surroundings. Look back at him, rub the heel of my palm up and down my thigh under the table until my skin burns.

'My Old Man . . . this morning he could see, Malik. And now he can't. He's blind – just like that. I mean, it's not possible. Then, when I phone Bea's mum to see if she's there, she . . . she tells me my best friend's dead. *Dead.*'

'That couldn't have been easy.'

'*Easy?* Just . . . tell me what's going on. For real.'

'The dead Bea isn't the Bea you know,' Malik says. 'She was Bea's double, in Lūna. And maybe she *did* die a year ago, it's possible. But she wasn't *your* Bea.'

'You're blowing my mind right now.'

'Look, I'm no good at explaining this stuff.'

'No kidding.'

'You're better off asking Vidhan when he gets here. All I can tell you is that the Tube you were on crashed. A shock like that can trigger a first Fall. Later, you'll learn how to control it so you only Fall when you *want* to. But for now, you've got no choice in the matter.'

I shake my head and drive my thumb into a sharp corner of the table.

'You don't think it's possible?' Malik says. 'A world like your own, with the same basic physical laws, but existing in an entirely different cosmic realm?'

'Uh . . . no. I don't.'

'You've never experienced déjà vu?'

'C'mon!'

'No, it's true. That's a glimpse of another world. Just a flicker. A fragment. But we're far beyond flickers and fragments now. And you know it.'

'You presume a lot.'

Malik leans forward in his chair. 'This is how it goes,' he says. 'In the weeks before you Fall for the first time, you begin to experience strange things. Reality shifts. Lapses in memory. The air wobbles. Then *bam!* Something radical happens – an accident, a crash, something violent – and you Fall.'

Reality shifts. Lapses in memory. The air wobbles.

Was that *the shimmering?*

'But on the train ... I mean, I was *floating.* I was suspended – in the *air.*'

'That's how it works. First you lift. Then you float. Then you Fall.'

'None of this makes any logical sense.'

He crosses an ankle over his knee. 'You want a neat quantum physics explanation, is that it?'

'I want *proof.*'

'You're here,' he says, locking his hands behind his head and leaning back, entirely comfortable in his own skin. 'This is not your world. *There's* your proof.'

'That's not an answer. It doesn't explain *why.*'

Malik drops forward and sighs. 'You ask a lot of questions, you know that?'

I shove my hands into my pockets. The fingers of my right hand worry the edges of my phone. My *phone*! I haul it out and hit the power button.

Malik watches me. 'Who are you with?'

'What d'you mean?'

'Your carrier. Vodafone? O2? Orange?'

'What's the difference?'

He gives me a rueful smile. 'A network provider that offers reliable service across two universes? Good luck with that.'

I look at the black mirror screen. My reflection stares back, gaunt and hollow-eyed. So that's it. My only link to the real world is a dead weight of metal and glass. I'm cut off. Adrift in a world I know nothing about, and my only compass is *him*.

I spin the phone face down on the table. Malik watches me and says nothing. I draw my hands back, sit upright and look round the deserted club. The fan throbs. 'All this . . . it happened to you? You *Fell*, like me?'

Malik hesitates, gazes into the distance. 'Car accident,' he says. 'I survived, but when I woke up I didn't recognize the world. And my family . . . they were gone. Then, when the Reapers came for me, I ran. Been on the run ever since.'

I see it. The Reaper that took Bea. It crawls through the carriage. Naked and hairless. Sinewy legs. Black veins under pink skin.

'What *are* they?'

Malik looks hard at me. 'Reapers are a manifestation of everything wrong in the world. All the pain and suffering in all of existence.' He must clock a horrified reaction in my face then, because he adds, 'Don't worry. This place is protected.'

'You make it sound like a game. Like we're in the safe zone or something.'

This is a safe place, Ana. Nothing can hurt you here.

Dr Augur. Was that only last week? It feels like another lifetime.

'The club's a Haven,' Malik says. 'We're OK, for now. But, as soon as we walk outside that steel door, they'll come for us again, you can be sure.'

'And they want us . . . *dead*?'

'The ride over here didn't convince you?'

94

'I've never seen anything like them.'

'Stay in your own world and you're fine. But, if you Fall, they come. Reapers have been hunting Pathfinders for a long time and they're not about to give up now.'

It occurs to me then he's said nothing about *taking*. Hunting. Killing. Not abducting.

'The one on the train,' I say. 'It took Bea. It didn't kill her. It *took* her.'

Malik looks at me with a neutral expression. But his dark eyes can't hide the fact that he's working something through in his head. 'I know,' he says finally.

'Is that normal?' I ask. And then I think: stupid question. *Normal* is dead.

'We'll get her back,' Malik says.

'Do you think . . . that Bea's a Pathfinder . . . like you?'

'Like *us*?' Malik frowns and his mouth makes a tight line. 'I think so. Maybe. It felt that way on the Underground. But –'

'But why did it *take* her? And *where*?'

He shakes his head. 'I don't know,' he says. His dark eyes hold a well of secrets. 'But we're gonna help you find her, Ana.'

'Why?'

'Because we're Pathfinders.'

'What does that even mean?'

'There are pathways,' Malik says, sliding his hand over the table, brushing away invisible crumbs. 'Gateways from one world to the next. We find them. Keep them safe and free. We're not the same as normal people. We're a network of clans that follow two laws: one – guard the pathways that connect the multiverse, two – return Fallen Normals to their home world.'

'Whoa . . . hold up. Did you just say . . . *multi*verse?'

Malik remains silent. He looks hard at me.

'You told me there were only two universes,' I insist, breathless. 'Sol and Lūna.'

'I never said that.'

'But –'

'Ana, listen to me. You need to forget everything you think you know. There is not one universe. There are not two. There are seven.'

15

'Seven?'

'Yes. Seven.'

'A multiverse?'

'That's right.'

'Seven worlds?'

'Right again.'

'Actual *universes*?'

'Yes, Ana. That.'

'But *seven*?'

'Look, you can put it any way you want. Seven worlds. Seven universes. Seven realms. Seven Earths. It doesn't matter. It doesn't alter the facts.'

I try to come up with something intelligent or witty in response, but my mouth is dry and my brain feels woolly. I can't think of a single thing to say.

Malik falls silent and digs into his robot-delivered breakfast – two fried eggs, BBQ sauce, rashers of bacon, fried tomato, beans and black pudding – as if he hasn't eaten in a week. I take a sip of my coffee and watch him, feeling queasy.

When he's finished, he pushes the plate away, grabs his mug and eyes me over the steaming rim. 'You should eat,' he says.

I shake my head and watch the robot remove his plate. 'This is so . . . it's all so mad. I just want to get Bea and go home. Where is she, Malik? Tell me.'

He frowns, takes a sip and looks deep into the mug, as if all the secrets of life are held there. And when he looks up at me again I'm convinced he's going to shed some light at last. But then he says, 'Like I said, I don't know. Not yet.'

'Then what good are you to me?' I blurt.

He doesn't flinch. No flicker in his eyes. He's tough. But he's hiding something. I see it. In the darkness of his irises. It's there – the hurt.

'All right,' he says. 'Then, if you must know, I think it's the Order that's taken her.'

'The *Order*?'

'A group of Pathfinders that have gone rogue.'

'I don't understand.'

'Years ago,' he says, 'the Pathfinders split into two factions. The Collective, like us, and the Order. The Collective believes in a free, *connected* multiverse. Each world in charge of its own destiny. The Order wants to destroy the multiverse, so they can build a new world order. And rule over it.'

'Great,' I say. 'Extremism. The Order sounds like a riot.'

'Pathfinders are not always aligned,' Malik says. 'And they're not born equal. Some have limited abilities. Others – the masters – are powerful beyond measure. And some *elder* masters have been around longer than anyone can remember. There's one here in Soho, one of the few left. We call her Mother. Look, she knows things. If anyone has answers, it's her. After that, we'll try a Council Meeting in Ares.'

'So let's go then.'

He gives a gruff laugh. 'Hold your horses. We're waiting for the others.'

'Why?'

'Because there's a hundred ways to die in the multiverse, Ana. You need someone to watch your back. All the time.'

Before I can respond, the door blasts open and two figures enter the club.

'Ana Moon, this is Akuji Na,' Malik says, standing as they approach the table. 'She's one of us. Which is just as well.'

I stand too.

She?

Akuji seems androgynous to me. Neither feminine nor masculine – somewhere in between. Her skin is pale and her hair is albino-white and shaved to the bone. Even her eyebrows are white. I figure we're the same age, but she's all thin sinew and muscle. She wears a cut-off sports top, canvas combat trousers and a long jet-black jacket. Crossed and spiking from twin scabbards in her belt – fighting sticks. She gazes at me with steady, scrutinizing eyes. Eyes that seem to shift colour – opalescent, then silver. She looks nerveless, as competent as hell.

'And *this*,' Malik continues, 'is Vidhan Blue.'

Slim-shouldered. Spiky, truncated dreadlocks and skin the colour of hazelnuts. He looks of Asian descent and older than the girl, around Malik's age maybe. He wears a pair of oversized tortoiseshell glasses, jeans, a grey hoodie and a jacket. And, like the girl, he's armed. In his belt, in a scabbard, a short-blade knife.

He steps forward, pushing his glasses up the bridge of his nose.

'Akuji ain't long on words,' he says in what could be an Australian accent. 'Never says nothin. All telepathy. But, mate, can she dance with those sticks.'

'Akuji mightn't speak,' Malik says, 'but Vidhan does. Once he starts, he hardly ever stops. We call him the Professor. Most people think it's irony.'

Vidhan grins. 'Really, it's because of my giant brain. Almost as big as Malik's ego. But let's not go down *that* rabbit hole.' He cocks his head, considering me.

I look back at him and say nothing.

'So,' he says. 'We met before.'

'No. I don't think so,' I say, finding my voice. 'I'd remember.'

'Nah. Ya wouldn't. It wasn't really you; it was the *other* you.'

'What?'

'Your Lūna self. It's an ugly business, Falling. Plenty of loose ends. We had to keep her out the way until Malik here could make contact with you. But don't worry, she's home now, memory blunted, tucked safely back into her bed. Probably about to get woken by the dog.'

I look from him to Akuji in amazement and give a little half-hearted laugh.

Akuji ignores me and turns to Malik.

This is a bad idea.

Her words appear in my head, the same way Malik's words formed there. She thinks the words to him and, amazingly, I can understand them, as if I'm plucking them out of the air. More than that, I can understand their *tone*. The disdain in them.

Akuji swivels and shoots me a look of spectacular severity.

'That's right,' Malik says to her. 'She can read you.'

I try to say something but I can't. I feel edgy, uneasy. Can I throw back my *own* thoughts? The questions buzz, unanswered, in my head.

'I see it,' Vidhan says, watching me. 'In your eyes. You've got gifts. But you're as green as grass – a Noob. Anybody can bloody see that too.'

'*Noob?*' I splutter. 'What the hell do you mean by that?'

'Vidhan!' Malik says. He turns to me. 'You'll have to forgive him. Vidhan can be . . . well, Vidhan. But there's no one better to have on your side. No one faster. And, if you want answers, he's your man.' He glances at Akuji. 'But you need to understand that these are dark times. There are spies everywhere. Those that seek to undermine what we stand for. So everyone's on edge. When Prof. says you're a Noob, he only means you're new to all this.'

Vidhan watches me. He looks sensible and calm. But, for all his laid-back body language, I sense hidden reserves of energy.

'By all this,' I say, 'I take it you mean the *multi*verse?'

'It's difficult to process,' Malik answers. 'I get it. But –'

'Difficult?' I interject bitingly. 'Why would it be difficult? It's perfectly logical. There are seven worlds. Not two. Not one. Not five. *Seven*.'

I feel sweat gathering at my temples. Dots begin to float and spin. I need air. I need to get out.

'You OK?' Malik asks.

I shake my head, make an abortive attempt to say something, and then my knees give and I sit.

I grip the sides of the table and feel a light touch against my fingertips. A glass of water is put in my hand. I take a sip groggily. Then I cross my arms and drop my head on my forearms. The table swims and my eyelids close.

Words bloom in my head like ink on blotting paper.

She is a liability.

I know – I *feel* – it's Akuji again. *Her* thoughts. Telepathy, Vidhan called it. And then I realize I'm not really hearing her words, I'm feeling them, almost *seeing* them. They vibrate, and move, and form clear pictures in my head. Bleed into my thoughts as if they're my own. But they're not. Encoded in the words is a feeling of the person speaking – *thinking* – them.

She's in shock, Malik answers. His words float into the mix, as hers fade and drift away. *You remember what it was like. She'll be fine.*

AKUJI: *She fainted!*

VIDHAN: *She's only a bloody Noob.*

AKUJI: *Can she fight?*

MALIK: *She'll learn.*

AKUJI: *Does she have her weapon?*

MALIK: *Obviously not. But she will, once we find Mother.*

VIDHAN: *Think she's listening? Reading us now?*

MALIK: *Hard to say. She's quick and she's smart, like Issi. Stubborn and full of grit. It's uncanny. Only . . .*

VIDHAN: *Issi's gone, Malik. Ya know it.*

MALIK: *I know she's not Issi. But there's something about her. I can't put my finger on it. She's important.*

Malik's words distort. I feel a blur of emotions – pain, guilt. Feelings that seem to scramble the thoughts, make them indistinct. Suddenly, a crisp voice again.

AKUJI: *I do not trust her. She could be one of theirs.*

MALIK: *She's not.*

AKUJI: *How do you know?*

MALIK: *I know.*

A pause.

AKUJI: *One day, that is all. One day and already you take her side.*

MALIK: *Cut her some slack, will you? You know what it's like.*

AKUJI: *This is a mistake. Let her join another clan.*

MALIK: *Kuji, c'mon. One out. One in. That's how it works.*

No answer.

MALIK: *Prof? Where are you on all this?*

VIDHAN: *I gotta say, I'm with you, Malik. She's all right.*

A mumbled response, something else I can't catch. The air is heavy. The words blur again. They warp. Then darkness.

16

I wake slumped in the caramel-leather seat, a monster headache rattling in my brain, my tongue thick in my mouth. Things have changed. The club is humming. Small clusters of people – five or six per group – huddle at their tables, talking, eating, drinking. Vidhan is opposite me, ensconced in his own chair, grinning.

'How ya holdin up?' he says.

'I'm not.'

'Yeah. Figures.'

I look around, trying to get my bearings, to reset, but the windows are all blacked out, giving no indication of time. 'How long have I –'

'Two hours.'

I blink at Vidhan, groggy and confused, trying to banish the anxiety worming in the pit of my stomach. Across the room, at the bar, I see Malik and Akuji. They're locked in a debate and I get the feeling it's about me.

Malik glances up and our eyes meet. Akuji follows his gaze. I feel her suspicion like knives thrown across the room.

'I don't think she likes me,' I say to Vidhan.

'Kuji? Ah hell. She doesn't really *like* anyone.'

I pick up the salt cellar and begin rolling it round on its base, looking at the others in the room. Many of them seem younger than me, but only by a few years. Others are older, but no one looks over twenty. Yet something in their demeanour – a resignation, a steadiness in their gaze – tells me they've seen things and maybe even done things that have stolen their innocence.

'Pathfinders,' Vidhan says, watching me.

'Everyone's so young.'

'Falling takes a toll and the human body is bloody fragile. So, if ya see a Pathfinder over the age of twenty, most likely they're a master. Or they've Settled.'

'Settled?'

'They choose a world and stay there. Don't Fall so much.'

'Falling,' I say. 'Masters. Seven worlds. I can't get my head round it.'

'No kiddin. How much has Malik told ya?'

'Nothing that makes any sense.'

Vidhan shakes his head. 'Bloody figures.'

'I mean, look at you,' I say, pointing at the leather-strapped blade handle rising from his belt. 'You carry weapons. You've got these weird names for things and strange codes. How does it all work, Vidhan? The multiverse? Falling?'

'Whaddaya wanna know exactly?'

'Everything.'

'Thought as much.'

Vidhan snatches the salt cellar from my hand and, with surprisingly deft and slender fingers, unscrews the top and upends the contents on to the table. Dragging his forefinger through the salt, he sketches a circle. Linked through this a second, and another, and another, until he's drawn six overlapping rings and then, through the centre of them, he draws a seventh ring. The result is a beautiful design. A perfect, geometric, flower-shaped pattern, like a multiplying cell.

'Not doing it justice like this,' he says. 'The multiverse is more of a three-dimensional construct. But hey.'

He drags a dotted line round the image. Then labels each circle with a number and a name.

'You might've seen the pattern before,' Vidhan says. 'Some call it the seed of life. But really it's a depiction of the seven worlds – bound together. The multiverse.'

'It's beautiful,' I say.

Vidhan shrugs. 'It can be.' He rights his glasses and looks at me, eyes magnified. 'Seven realms,' he says. 'A current flows between them, an energy. All living things across all the worlds draw power from this energy. Anything in the wrong place and time damages the flow. See, it's delicate, the multiverse. Needs protection. Pathfinders are like guardians. We see to it things stay where they belong. Else everything collapses. We move between worlds to keep the multiverse alive. But . . .'

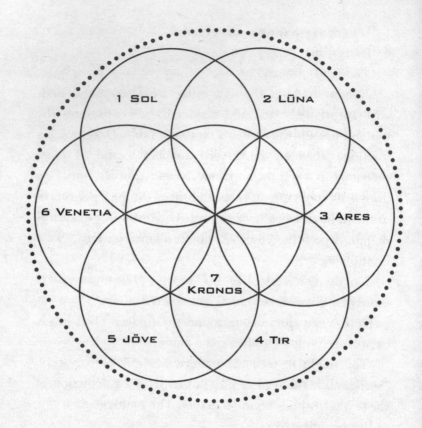

1 SOL
2 LŪNA
6 VENETIA
3 ARES
7
KRONOS
5 JÖVE
4 TIR

He hesitates, and I urge him on. 'But?'

'But some Pathfinders ... take a different view. Less concerned with protection, more interested in short-term self-gain. And power.'

I nod, remembering Malik's words. 'The Order.'

'Keep it down,' Vidhan hisses.

I snap my head round and look at him, shocked at the sudden change in tone.

'They're here?' I whisper.

'They're everywhere,' he answers. Then he points at the sixth ring. 'But mostly you'll find them in Venetia.'

The Order. The ones who took Bea.

I feel a spike of adrenalin. A reminder. This is the reason I'm here. I'm filled with a wild urge to get to her fast. To fly across the worlds to her.

'Vidhan, can we Fall between any worlds, whenever we want?'

He raises his eyebrows and looks at me as if I'm mad. 'Nah, mate. We move between worlds in order – forward or back. It's an immutable, multiuniversal law.'

Vidhan moves his finger to the top-left circle. 'Sol,' he says. 'This is where you're from.' He sweeps his finger clockwise into the next circle. 'Lūna's next, the universe we're in now. Then here's Ares. A warzone. Dangerous.' He slides his finger round and down into the adjacent circle. 'Tir, the most extreme of all worlds. Hot as hell in the day, freezing at night. Here's Jöve, the fifth, governed by massive tides. Half of the time everything there is a swamp – then *boom*, the whole world is underwater. And after that Venetia, the sixth, ugly to the bone. Normals there are superstitious brutes, the lot of 'em. Less time you spend there, the better. They know about Pathfinders and they don't like us.'

'Normals are anyone who's *not* a Pathfinder?'

'Exactly.'

'Do they *all* know about Pathfinders?'

'Depends on the universe. Take Sol. It's the least enlightened – and maybe that's a good thing. Normals there don't have a clue about any of this and those few that Fall by mistake are returned and have their memories wiped.'

'Wiped?'

He taps his forehead. 'Telepathy. We can use it to obliterate their memories of Falling. All gone in seconds.'

'Of course.'

'The further ya travel away from Sol,' Vidhan says, 'the more Normals are aware of Pathfinders. Ares wars aren't only fought between Pathfinder factions, but the Normals who hate them all. And, in Venetia, Pathfinders are vilified *and* idolized.'

'What about the seventh?' I ask, pointing at the epicentre, when he offers no further comment.

'Ah yeah. Kronos. Some say it's perfect, without fault. Others that it's as dark as oil and filled with horror beyond imagining. I tend to the former view. I reckon it's a panacea at the end of time.'

'What . . . like an *ultimate* universe?'

'Nirvana, the masters say. Valhalla. Avalon. Shambhala. Whatever name ya wanna call it. But nobody really knows.'

'Why not?'

He shrugs. 'There's no bloody way in. According to Pathfinder legend, the only way to access Kronos is through something called the Seventh Gate. But we don't know where that is or even what it is. There's an old prophecy that says one day a key will open the Seventh Gate and establish a pathway to Kronos and all the wonders and powers they say lie there. But nobody's found the key either.'

'But . . . if no one's been, how do people know it's perfect?'

'Science. Religion. Philosophy. Myth. Ancient Egyptian scrolls. They've all got an opinion. I mean, where d'ya think the phrase "seventh heaven" comes from?'

'C'mon!' I give the arm of the leather chair a futile thump. 'All these secrets within secrets. And why *seven* worlds anyway? Why not an infinite number?'

'Why is blue blue?' he answers calmly. 'It simply *is*. But think about it: seven is magical. Seven chakras. Seven colours in the rainbow. Seven days of the week. Seven sins. Seven seas. Seven continents. Seven layers of muscle in the heart . . .'

He licks the salt from his finger and falls silent.

I look at his sketch on the table. A vast multiverse straddling time and space. Seven worlds layered one over the other. Interlinked.

'So does that mean . . . are there *seven* versions of me out there?'

'Could be,' he says. 'If some of them ain't dead.'

'And these other versions of me – they're all *identical* to me?'

'Nah. Time ain't the same in every world. And time changes things.'

'I don't follow.'

'Lemme spin it this way then. Imagine you were cloned when you were ten years old, and your clone was taken away and, say, forced to grow up back in Oz. Today, she'd be seventeen years old, right? So you'd both have the exact same DNA, but different personalities, because you'd have experienced different things. And everything you experience changes ya, right? Leaves a mark.'

'So they're me . . . but *not* me.'

'More or less.'

'And, if *I'm* a Pathfinder . . . are *they* Pathfinders too?'

'Never,' he says. 'There can be only one.'

'And you had to hide me from my other self. Why?'

'Because two selves from separate worlds can't come into contact. It contravenes every rule of time and space going. You'd bloody disappear.'

I shake my head and say nothing. Vidhan reaches into his back pocket and produces a faded, time-yellowed booklet.

'Here,' he says, handing it to me, bending it back into shape.

I turn the booklet over in my hands. 'What's this?'

'Everything you need to know.'

The cover print is faded, but easy enough to read. A title – no picture, no author, nothing but text. I turn the book over. Nothing on the sepia back. I flip to the front again. The title and subtitle stand alone on an otherwise empty cover.

THE BOOK OF SEVEN
A PATHFINDER'S HANDBOOK

I turn to the first page, well thumbed and greasy, and read a few quick lines of dense, strangely worded text.

There have always been, and will always be, the Seven. At the dawn of the enlightened age, in the land of the pharaohs, came the first understanding of the **SEVEN WORLDS**. The Seven form a free-flowing ecosystem of independent universes in parallel. A **MULTIVERSE**. All worlds are discovered, but one. The seventh. By this author it is considered to be the perfect realm.

When I look up from reading, Vidhan is watching me keenly. 'So?' he asks.

'So it's bizarre. Who's the author?'

'No one knows. Me? I reckon it's a compilation – writings of all the masters. Especially the elder ones. Reckon Mother even wrote some.'

'Interesting style,' I say, handing it back to him.

'Keep it,' he says. 'You'll need it more than me. When ya get the chance, read the chapter on Falling.'

'Why *that* chapter?'

'Just read it.'

I sense the conversation is closed, so I thank him and stuff the book in my pocket. Over his shoulder, I notice Malik and Akuji walking towards us.

Malik glances at Vidhan and takes in the strewn salt, the empty salt cellar. Then he looks at me. 'You should've eaten. I told you.'

'I'm *fine*,' I say, standing. 'If that's what you're asking. So let's go and find this Mother of yours.'

Malik smiles and nods. 'Vidhan, you ready?'

'Born ready.'

'Kuji?'

She keeps her eyes on me, makes the faintest gesture with her hand.

'All right then,' Malik says. 'We go in pairs and –'

'Pairs?' Vidhan interrupts.

Malik raises an eyebrow. 'You got something better in mind, Prof?'

Vidhan grins. 'Just wondering when you became master of all our destinies.'

'Ah, quit your whining,' Malik says.

They eyeball each other, smirking. It comes off like banter, rather than genuine irritation, and suddenly I feel like someone who doesn't belong. I turn from Malik to Vidhan and then the bloodless Akuji. She's looking at me with the hint of a smile on her lips, as if she's taking pleasure in my discomfort.

Malik shifts his gaze to me. 'You should know,' he says, hand on the butt of his gun. 'Every step we take away from this building is a step towards danger.'

'Well, if you're afraid,' I tell him, 'you'd better stay close to me.'

Malik laughs.

17

A silver sun wheels across the dial of a new Earth. Lūna.
It's a cloudy, cold afternoon. We walk – Vidhan and me on
one side of the road, Akuji and Malik on the other – through
a futuristic London. There are echoes of Sol: St Paul's
Cathedral, the Houses of Parliament, countless other
limestone landmarks that look unchanged. It's a deceit, of
course. I know that now. And yet the idea hasn't quite sunk
in that I'm not in *my* world, that this is an actual parallel
universe.

A world apart.

With every footfall, I think of Bea – somewhere out
there, lost in the multiverse. And I know I won't stop until
I find her.

'Look,' Vidhan says, pointing.

A video newsfeed high on a billboard. Prince Harry
pressing Hillary Clinton's hand to his lips. Which doesn't
shock me, but the scrolling heading does:

WHEN HARRY MET HILLARY ...
US PRESIDENT CHARMS KING OF ENGLAND

A hover-car comes *whumping* past and we're hit by a hot gust of air.

'Trump lost,' Vidhan says. 'Slunk back to his golden tower.'

'And Harry's the king?'

'Yep. But just as a figurehead. A central computer system runs the show here – banking, traffic, tax, defence, NHS, immigration – *everything* is down to an artificial intelligence machine.'

'That's nuts.'

'That's Lūna. In many ways, the strangest of the seven realms. On the surface, she can look the same. More modern, yeah, but the street names are the same, some of the buildings, even the parks. See, she teases ya. If you're from Sol, you think you're home, but you're bloody not. She's like that on purpose, I reckon. To let ya know there are planes beyond the knowing. The other worlds, they can be a little intense. Way different to Sol. But Lūna ... she's deceptive. A soft landing.'

'Soft landing?'

'Pathfinders like us, we can usually remain hidden here,' Vidhan continues. 'In Sol, we're unknown and unseen. In Lūna, that's mostly true as well.'

I look at the unfamiliar (yet familiar) London around me. Doesn't *feel* like a soft landing.

The traffic doesn't seem to give off any fumes and the air is clear. Maybe it's because everything hovers, even the red Routemaster buses. A gleaming train of egg-shaped pods moves past, linked together without any sign of a coupling mechanism, as if they're magnetized. As I watch, one veers off, breaking away from the train, finding its own path. Each pod is seamless glass – some milky-opaque, others transparent, revealing passengers inside reading screens, dozing, watching the world go by. I wonder: do any of them know about the seven worlds, the multiverse, Pathfinders – with pistols and fighting sticks and knives – passing under their nose? Do they know theirs is not the real world, that it's a replica, an image in a cosmic mirror? How could they? They must be just as oblivious as me. As I was.

And then I realize I'm being an idiot. This is *their* world, not mine. To them, this *is* the real world. To them, Lūna is *home*.

'Hey, watch it!' someone barks, barging past me.

I step aside and watch the steady stream of pedestrians. The city is bustling, alive, packed with millions of souls, all caught up in their own lives. A young woman taking a dog for a walk. A man laden with shopping bags. A businesswoman in a suit. Ordinary people doing ordinary, everyday things. And yet . . . many of them sail over the pavement in boots that ride on cushions of air. But that's not the real surprise. It's the lack of mobile phones. It takes me a while, but, after bumping into about six people, I work it out, spot the little black chip on the side of their faces projecting a needle of blue light into a vague image in front of them. They're *communicating* with this projected image – like a screen but in the air – watching the news or speaking to their family, their friends.

I think about Bea and a lump starts to form in my throat.

Vidhan catches me staring. 'Blows your mind, right?'

'Feels like I've landed in the future,' I say, smothering the hurt. I try to keep my voice even, neutral, to hide my anxiety. But it doesn't work.

Vidhan gives me a sidelong look. 'You'll find her,' he says. 'You *will*. You've got me and you've got Kuji and Malik. And that ain't nothin. I mean, Malik's braver'n anyone I ever met. Sure, he's a hothead. But he's *our* hothead.'

I look across the road. Malik walks straight-backed, eyes narrow and steely. He glances left and right, then ahead again – full of purpose, like he's finding his way out of a maze.

I turn to Vidhan. 'Malik and you must have a theory, right? About why Bea was taken?'

Vidhan steals a look at Malik. 'Maybe.'

'So tell me.'

'There have been others,' he says. 'Normals and Pathfinders, from across the multiverse, that have been taken. Not just Bea.'

'And?'

'And . . . we think it's some sort of experiment.'

'*Experiment?*' I can't keep the shock out of my voice. An image of Bea strapped into a chair with electrical wires feeding into her flashes in my head.

'We think it's something to do with the prophecy,' Vidhan says. 'There are whispers, you see, that the Order has found the Seventh Gate and now they're trying to find the key to Kronos and the promise of unlimited power.'

'But what's that got to do with –'

'Word is, the key's not a thing,' he interrupts. 'It's a person. A Pathfinder.'

'And you think Bea's –'

Vidhan grabs my arm. 'Listen, you're better off finding out what Mother has to say. Everything I've told you, I got second-hand, third-hand. It's guesswork mostly. But Mother *made* that prophecy. She's got the only answers worth having.'

I stare at his hand on my arm until he lets go. 'Fine,' I say. Then I lift my chin in Akuji's direction. 'What about *her*? What's her opinion? Does she *ever* talk?'

Vidhan shrugs. 'Speaks with her sticks.'

'Right. And where's she from again?'

'Jöve. And Malik's from Sol, like you. London.'

I realize I haven't asked Vidhan anything about *him*. A whirlwind of questions about the multiverse and how it all works, but nothing about Vidhan Blue.

'And you?' I ask him. 'What's your world?'

'Same as you and Malik. Sol.'

'No kidding? London too?'

'Yeah, but originally Sydney, in Oz. Ever been?'

'No.'

'Travel,' he says. 'Only way to know who ya really are.'

'How long have you been doing this, Vidhan? Shunting between worlds?'

'Too bloody long, mate. Three years.'

We walk on. A cold wind whips between the buildings. I stare up at startling cliffs of glass and I think about origins and how things become what they are.

'Hey, Vidhan, who was the first Pathfinder?' I ask. 'Like the very first ever?'

Vidhan shakes his head, removes his glasses, polishes them on his shirt and replaces them. 'You ever stop asking questions?'

'How can I know what's going on if I don't ask questions?'

'That's another bloody question! Anyway, try *The Book of Seven*.'

'Hard to read and walk.'

'Try watching then,' he says. 'Try *looking*.'

'OK, so I'm watching. I'm looking. Uh . . . no. No good. I still have exactly not one freaking idea who the first Pathfinder was.'

Vidhan grins. 'The first was Thoth, an ancient Egyptian, revered as the god of knowledge. He was around about the same time they built the Great Pyramid. Which, depending on who ya believe, was about 2500 BC. In Sol.'

'Thoth?'

'One of his many names.'

'Any Pathfinders I might've actually heard of?'

'Da Vinci. Newton. Nostradamus . . . heard of them?'

'Of course.'

'Yeah, well, none of them were Pathfinders.' Vidhan laughs. It's a good-natured laugh – easy, unburdened. 'It's the ones ya least expect,' he adds, looking hard at me. 'Ya know. The nobodies. Like you and me'.

I feel a buzz in my skin. 'And Mother? Tell me about her.'

Vidhan stops in his tracks. Before I realize what's happening, he's snatched *The Book of Seven* from my back pocket and he's flipping through the pages. He bunches the book open in his fist and shoves it into my hand. 'Read this,' he says.

I take it from him and I stand in the middle of a mirror world and read the paragraph he's pointing at.

She sits right at the beating heart of the Collective of Pathfinder clans. Her name is one word. **MOTHER**. A pseudonym. A code name. She has been called – over the course of her long, remarkable life – many things. The Mantis. The Rider. The Dark Horse. None have stuck and none have a thing to do with her born identity; her real name left far behind in her first world, Lūna. She is the archetypal Pathfinder. Elusive. Hard to find, hard to know. A ghost. A prophet. And, if required, an assassin.

'An *assassin*!' I say aloud, looking up.

Vidhan nods. 'She's not just an elder master, she's a bloody *legend*. For a long time, she was a spy, working behind enemy lines inside the Order. She knows their secrets, front to back.'

A sharp whistle cuts through the air. Malik. He's shooting us a look, beckoning me to hurry. I shut the book, shove it in my pocket, and we fall silent and follow. Into the darkness – an alley.

The bright sheen of the glass-fronted buildings drops away behind us. Windowless brick walls enclose us now, either side. Our footsteps crunch over a stony ground littered with debris and shards of glass. So there's pollution in Lūna after all. In the shadows, eyes gleam. Furtive movements, figures shifting packages through their hands. Further in, we encounter tin-roof lean-tos and traders selling bootleg wares. Meat-sellers stringing up bloody carcasses jewelled with flies. The stink is godawful.

'Wait here,' Malik says. He steps up to a meat-seller and begins to barter. I look at Vidhan. He stops, without turning his head to see. Akuji, on the other side of the street, also halts. She watches me.

Malik returns. 'Let's go,' he says, without explaining.

We turn down a deserted alley. Metal bins line a sordid corridor of rubbish and rot. A dustbin clatters and I flinch. With a yowl, a black cat darts across our path, scrambles down an iron staircase and disappears. Malik pulls out his gun with a *shiffing* sound. My heart thunders. I shadow him, my steps in sync with his.

Behind us, Akuji follows, as silent and pale as the moon.

Vidhan stops ahead. He cocks his head, as if listening. Then he moves on.

A hundred paces later, I see a dog with a boxer's face and a terrier's scraggly body – a street mongrel. When it sees us, its tail wags and it whimpers and sidewinds to Malik, who crouches down. 'Hey, Bones. How you doing, boy?'

The dog sniffs and dances round him. Malik reaches inside his coat pocket and drags out a wrapped package smeared in blood. He tears it open and pulls out a strip of meat, and the dog snatches it from him. Malik scratches him under the chin.

'She here, Bones?'

The dog looks at Malik, scoffs the last morsel and barks once. Then it skitters away and turns and waits, watching us. We follow down the alley and turn into another, and then another. Finally, we come to a place filled with overturned bins and, against a wall, what looks like a one-man canvas khaki tent. Outside the flap sits a crumpled paper cup holding a few bronze coins. Malik scans the alley.

'This is it,' he says, nodding at the tent. 'This is where you'll find Mother. It doesn't look like much, I know, but that's the cover. In you go.'

'In *there*?' The tent is small and so battered and thin, I reckon a light breeze would lift it off the ground and send it jackknifing away.

Malik shrugs. 'The mind sees what it wants to see.'

'What does that even mean?'

'Don't worry,' he says. 'We'll be here. Waiting.'

I hesitate, unsure.

'You'll be fine,' Malik adds. 'In the multiverse, nobody knows more than Mother.' He jerks his thumb at Vidhan, grinning. 'Not even brainbox over there.'

'I don't know,' I say, hanging back, feeling anxious.

'You're not doing this for you,' Malik says. 'You're doing it for *her*. For Bea.'

He knows where to stick the knife.

I duck in through the doorway. The tent is dark and clammy, the air close. It smells of mould. I feel my way, heart thumping, head bent, eyes adjusting to the gloom. No movement. No sound of breathing but my own. I see a patch of pale light and crawl towards it. The light grows and the dark corners fall away, and now it feels as if the one-man tent has expanded into a much bigger space. I can't even touch the roof, which, seconds ago, was tight over my head. As I walk in deeper, towards the light, the darkness recedes and the space grows larger. I hear bubbling sounds and the air now tastes sweet and smoky. Above me, the tent roof is high and vaulted, supported on tall metal poles. Wreathes of smoke drift through the space and, ghosting beyond the smoke, I see a figure.

A woman.

18

She sits cross-legged on a seat of plush cushions and carpets, facing away from me, head raised as if in contemplation. She's dressed in a swirling blue wrap, like a Bedouin. She's not just old, she's ancient. Her skin is the texture of tooled leather. In her right hand, she clutches a hookah pipe. When I cough to get her attention, she turns her head and looks at me, eyes as narrow as slits.

I stand in the shadows, nervous, contemplating backing out.

'Mother?' I say, watching her take a deep drag on the hookah. She sits quite still and exhales, blowing a plume of smoke my way. She says nothing.

The ground tilts. The smoke floats.

'I've come a long way to find you,' I say, feeling light-headed. 'The Pathfinders brought me. They said you'd help me.'

She takes another drag, blows smoke out of her nostrils like a dragon and squints at me from under hooded eyelids.

Then she nods, but it's difficult to tell if she's understood a word. 'You,' she says finally. 'Huh! Who are you?'

'I'm Ana.'

'So, *Ana*, you think a name makes a difference?' She eyes me up and down, then flicks her hand impatiently. 'Look here, do you have anything to drink on you? I'm running short. Whisky's my preference, but I'll take whatever you have.'

'Anything to *drink*? I'm sorry . . . I . . . I'm confused . . . I thought . . .'

'You *are* confused,' she says. 'And, on top of it, lost.'

I let my fist fall to my thigh, but stop myself from dragging my knuckles up the muscle. 'I'm not from here,' I say, feeling marooned. 'This world . . . it isn't mine.'

'Is that a fact?'

'I don't belong here.'

'Oh? Where *do* you belong?'

My arms hang limply at my sides. I'm not sure what to say. It's a good question.

'You do not know,' she says – inhaling, exhaling. 'You will.'

'I need your help,' I insist. 'My best friend, Bea. She was taken by Reapers. I'm trying to find her. Malik said you'll have answers –'

'Malik Habib?' she interrupts.

I nod vehemently, feeling encouraged. At last I'm getting through to her.

'Never heard of him,' she says, and the spurt of hope dissipates.

'But –'

'Come,' she says, rising to her feet. A quick movement that belies her age, inexplicably fluid, as though ungoverned by gravity. Deep power emanates from her and I suddenly feel daunted and small. Without waiting, she moves away – a shadow within shadows – into the recesses of the tent (a tent that now appears to stretch well beyond the limits of logic).

'So you'll help me?' I call after her. 'Do you know who's behind Bea's abduction? Or where I can find her?'

She makes a grumbling noise and continues walking, moving quickly.

'Where are we going?' I ask, hurrying after her. 'And how big *is* this tent?'

No answer.

'This is *crazy*!' I shout after her. 'All of this. It's impossible.'

Without turning, she flicks her hand in the air. 'Hah! Impossible is nothing. Sometimes I've believed as many as six impossible things before breakfast.'

Somewhere, deep in my consciousness, a memory stirs.

Frankie, sitting on the edge of my bed, reading me stories.

Stories about Mad Hatters and White Rabbits.

I almost burst out laughing at the absurdity – the irony.

'That's Lewis Carroll!' I blurt. '*Alice's Adventures in Wonderland.*'

'A nom de plume,' Mother says, her back to me. 'I met him. Charles Lutwidge Dodgson was another of his names. Caused a ruckus when he wrote those books.'

'Hang on. You *met* Lewis Carroll? That doesn't . . . I mean, wasn't he like, from the nineteenth century?'

She doesn't answer. She keeps walking and I follow, until finally she comes to a standstill. We face a wall hung with a striking Persian wool carpet with seven geometric rings of woven red and dark blue medallions, worn to a shine.

'A dead end,' I say, looking left and right.

The old woman snorts. 'Look beyond the obvious, *Ana*.'

She grabs a corner of the carpet and gives it a sharp yank. There's a snapping sound and the entire thing comes tumbling down in a pall of dust. I cough and stagger back. And, when the dust settles, I see this:

A granite wall stretching from the floor to a gargantuan height and, on the wall, hundreds upon hundreds of weapons. Guns: bone-handled pistols, revolvers, what looks like a shotgun collection. Then swords: katanas and broadswords, a sabre. A crossbow, ninja weapons. Blowguns and throwing stars, a mace and spikes and hooks, and gory, unspeakable things.

'Well?' she says.

'Well . . . what?'

'Which one is yours?'

'*Mine?*'

'Are we not speaking the same language?'

I stare at her in stunned silence.

'You're a Pathfinder,' she says. 'Pathfinders carry weapons.'

'But –'

'I was under the impression you were searching for your friend.'

'I *am* but –'

'The path you are taking will lead to dark places and dark things. A weapon is not an option. It's a requirement. And, more importantly, it's the reason you are here.'

I look at the wall of weaponry in shocked amazement. And I feel it. My gaze is directed – *pulled* – by some invisible force.

Mother sees. She moves forward, unhooks a weapon from the wall and turns to me, the weapon laid across her forearms, polished leather strap and scabbard hanging below. The blade is fifty centimetres long. The metal is inlaid with seven white-gold and bronze symbols, so bright they seem to radiate their own light. The outside curve – the cutting edge – gleams. A sickle sword.

'This is Ra,' Mother says. 'The sun-blade. Take it. It is yours.'

I stare at her, dumbstruck.

'But . . . I've never used a sword. I wouldn't . . . I don't know how.'

'You will be surprised by what you do and do not know.'

I hesitate, uncertain. 'It's a *weapon*.'

'The sword is not the weapon. *You* are the weapon. The sword is merely a tool. It will clear your path.'

I feel like I'm floating, levitating, being dragged towards the sword. I take a deep breath, reach out and place my hand on the hilt. An electric current surges through me – from my fingertips, right up my arm to my shoulder and into my chest. Every hair stands on end. Ra, in my hand, feels dangerous. It feels alive.

'What now?' I ask, pulling the sword from its scabbard, moving it through the air, feeling the comfortable weight of it in my hands. 'Where must I go to find Bea?'

'You are not ready,' Mother says. 'Not yet.'

I bring the blade to rest. 'You're wrong. I don't have time to be unprepared. I'll do whatever it takes. I *will*.'

Mother looks at me. Says nothing.

'You think I don't mean that?' I say.

'I think you have no idea what *that* means.'

I throw the leather strap over my left shoulder and let the scabbard fall at my hip. I hold the blade in both hands, my fingers gripping tightly. 'She's my best friend,' I say. 'And I wasn't very nice to her the last time I saw her.'

No response.

'Help me,' I beg. 'Please. I'm all she has now. There isn't anyone else coming.'

'Kronos,' Mother says, stony-faced. 'What do you know of it?'

'The seventh world?' Vidhan's salt circles appear in my mind. 'Only that it's an ultimate realm.'

She nods. 'This is where you will find her. This is where she has been taken.'

My gut tightens. My palms feel clammy.

'But I thought no one had been there.'

'They have been,' she says. 'But not returned.'

'How do I get there?' I ask, breathless. 'What do I do? Vidhan said I need some sort of key –'

'Each world,' Mother says, watching me intently, 'must be crossed. One after the other. Lūna, Ares, Tir, Jöve, Venetia. There is a significance to this path. Here, in Lūna, you have found your weapon. In Ares, you will meet Gabe and learn a warrior's purpose. In Tir, you will be put to the test. In Jöve, your innocence will die. In Venetia, you will confront the darkness. It will not be easy and each time you will lose a piece of yourself to the Falling, but this is the path. Your path.'

'But . . . what do I do *now*?'

She shakes her head, clearly disappointed by my response.

'You have power in you,' she says. 'It has always been there. Waiting. But power is useless if you cannot understand what to do with it and when to use it. A Pathfinder is not a seed thrown on the wind. It is time to become who you are.'

She leaps forward and, with shocking suddenness, slams the heel of her palm into my chest bone and sends me barrelling backwards.

'What the hell?'

'Hit me!' she commands.

'What?'

'HIT ME!'

'No,' I say, confusion crackling through my voice. 'You . . . you're unarmed.'

She slaps me. Hard. A blow across the face, catching me on the cheekbone. I didn't see it coming, but I feel it sting and begin to swell.

'Stop doing that. Please, just . . . stop.'

She hits me again. I reel back in shock.

Slap!

I try to avoid it but I can't. She moves like a leaping flame.

'STOP! STOP IT! Why are you doing this?'

Whack!

Another blow. I try to duck, but it's impossible to move out of the way.

My cheek is pummelled raw. I feel a drop of blood fall from my nose. I wipe it away and plant my feet, grip the sword in both hands.

Let her do that again. Let her try.

Slap!

A stunning blow.

'There is a Pathfinder,' she says, advancing.

I watch her, wincing in pain.

'An elder master, once one of us, who became lost.'

My heart thumps. I stagger backwards, out of reach of her flying hands.

'Kei Shinigami,' she says. 'This is the name of the one you seek, the one who brought the Reapers back from the Between. The one who took your friend. First to Venetia, above Paris Nouveau, to the Seventh Gate.'

My fist closes on the sword's handle – tightly.

She comes at me and tries to hit me again and this time I move. Her hand whips through the air and I'm out of the way, and the sword slashes right to left from low at my hip to high above my shoulder. I stop the blade centimetres from her neck.

She looks at me impassively. I can't tell if she's pleased, or pissed off, or ambivalent. Then she snaps her head round and falls on her haunches, robes flaring. She presses a hand to the carpeted floor and listens.

'They have come,' she says now, looking up at me.

The light turns reddish. The air vibrates between us. It shimmers.

'*They?*'

'GO!' she commands. 'Find Gabriel. Now FALL!'

Before I can respond, she throws both palms towards me and I'm struck by a tremendous force and blown backwards. I lift violently into the air. The tent whips and snaps like a sail in the wind. Then I'm floating – weightless – my stomach in my throat, the air warping, bending. My hoodie billows and blows back.

I flip. Spin. Float.

Fall.

There is no up and no down. No north. No south.

The world unravels.

The third is **ARES**; known for its volatility. A world once famed for unparalleled beauty and abundance, now laid bare by avarice and savagery. And with these forces come divisions and insuperable walls. And war.

ARES

19

I'm on my hands and knees in a dark red muck, coughing and spitting. The sick explodes out of me, until all that's left is bile. When it's finally over, I hold my head in my hands and groan. It feels like my head is about to split open. There's a loud buzzing and crackling in my ears and my teeth feel loose. One more vomit and I'll be picking molars out of the mud. I try to organize my thoughts.

How did I get here? Where is *here?*

My body knows the truth. It remembers. Aching teeth. A persistent, locust-like noise. A feeling of wrongness. It can only mean one thing.

My brain churns. My body locks up in fear.

I've Fallen. And *that* means I'm no longer in Lūna.

I turn round, pushing down the panic, and get my bearings. It's colder. Much colder. Like a fridge. My breath fogs. Here in front of me is the tent – dismal, crooked and thin – nothing like the vast Bedouin marquee I'd lost myself in moments ago. The alley is different too. Darker. Rust-coloured. Huge flakes sift lazily down through the air, caught in strobes of crimson light. A thick carpet of red dust coats everything.

No footprints anywhere. I'm alone. No Mother. No Vidhan. No Akuji. No Malik.

And no Bea.

I lift the tent flap and this simple action brings the whole structure tumbling down. I leap back in disbelief. It's a ruin – shattered, reduced to sticks and cloth.

I try to picture Vidhan's sketch in the salt. Seven rings interlinked. Seven worlds. First Sol. Then Lūna. And the next ring along? I'm about to dig out Vidhan's pamphlet – *The Book of Seven* – when I remember.

Ares. Violent, war-torn and dangerous.

That's just great.

I traipse round the fallen tent, kicking up ash and I squint into the maroon shadows.

I listen. Nothing. A ghostly stillness. The ash falls. Then my skin prickles. I get a sense of eyes on me and I turn.

In a pool of gaudy light cast by a neon sign, a figure leans against the wall, watching me. All I can see is a smoky outline and the glint of eyes catching a strobe of light. I back up slowly, hand on the wall, heart walloping.

The figure doesn't move. Its eyes hold me.

I stumble over something hard. The sword! I bend and lift it, scabbard and blade, and keep my eyes on the silent figure all the while. My breath smokes.

Pathfinder? Normal? Something else?

The figure detaches itself from the shadows and strides towards me. A man in a dark jacket, moving fast.

No need to stick around to see what he wants. I plunge into seedy mean streets. Gone are the lean-tos, the meat-sellers and the drug-pushers. The alley is empty of people and the walls have massive chunks gouged out of them and are pockmarked with what look like bullet holes. Bricks and mortar are strewn in the road. I run hard, through flurries of red ash. No idea where I am, where I'm going or how to escape the labyrinth of alleys. Each leads into another, and yet another. I glance over my shoulder. Nothing. It's only me and the sound of my trainers scrunching through the muck and my heart booming in my chest. I skid round a corner and jog down yet another dark alley. Dead end. Brick wall.

I lean against the wall and catch my breath. On either side of me stand decrepit, bombed-out buildings – hunks of bricks, torn out of the walls, lie in scattered piles on the ground, all covered in a red frost. I listen. A bin clatters. A bottle breaks.

Something stinks here. It smells like a dead thing hidden in the bins. Far away, a rattling staccato sound, like fireworks. Distant, thunder-like guns and explosions.

Then quiet.

Now the crunching of boots and a shadow falls across the wall. For a second, I think I see a pair of wings. Then it's gone.

But the figure is here now, cloaked in the red mist. I look beyond him to the alleyway entrance, heart thumping, and see nothing but a ruddy murk. I take a shaky breath. I feel the roughness of the bricks behind me. I'm trapped.

The man is big and lit by flashing neon lights. He's wearing a dark suit and a black coat. Maybe I can make it past him. Maybe I can run up the wall and flick over his shoulder and somersault away like some free-runner. *Maybe.*

He advances, watching me. Blood pounds in my ears.

I guess he weighs maybe ninety kilograms. I weigh less than fifty. He's about thirty years old. I'm seventeen. He's about six foot four. I'm five five.

Still he says nothing. And *I* say nothing.

I click my neck and make a plan in my head, a map of where to hit him.

Throat – a good place to start. I'll smash him in the larynx with the back of my hand. But, if I miss and connect with his chin, I reckon the bones in my hand might break – so a fist won't work. Not on him. Groin – one punch. He'll feel it. Knees – a sharp side kick and he'll drop. It doesn't matter how big they are, a good kick to the knee and they all go down. My improvised plan will require speed and finesse, and a shit-load of luck. And I think: *Where is it from, this sudden knowledge?*

And then I think: *I'm an idiot.*

My fingers enclose the handle of the sword. Ra!

No hand-to-hand combat required.

He lunges.

But, instead of drawing the sun-blade, instinct kicks in – evasion. I feint left and spring right. Scooting low along the base of the wall, I use the bricks as leverage to propel myself forward and shoot past him. *I'm through. I've made it.*

I turn to gloat. He raises his head to look at me, panting, and I give him the finger, unfurl it really slowly, let him see.

It's a mistake. Run when you have the chance.

Run.

I feel a hard shove in the small of my back. Someone else. Behind me.

It sends me slamming into the man I evaded and he twines his arms round me, as thick as tree roots. I kick and squirm, but his grip is a vice. He grabs my wrist and bends it back and I let out a yelp and drop the sword. He clamps a hand over my mouth. I can't breathe. Through swirling dots, I see the second man, the one who must have pushed me, right in front of me now. He looks identical – same black coat and dark suit, same height and size and age – to the first man. Two against one. Not good.

I try to bite the hand over my mouth and my head is smashed into the wall. I feel a trickle of warm blood roll down my temple. I feel weak; my knees give way.

Stay focused, Ana. Stay awake. Stay conscious.

And that's when I feel their hands go slack. I drop to my knees and gasp, eyes watering. When I look up, I see the men have backed off, so far into the shadows they've merged into them, melted away completely. And, in their place . . .

A third figure – tall and thin – alone in the swirling red ash.

20

His eyes are obscured in the hooded shadow of a faux-leather coat with an ermine-fur collar, but I can see his mouth. He's a man. He's tall. Maybe six four and his skin is bone-pale, like Akuji's. Beneath his unbuttoned coat, he wears a suit of jet-black articulated armour. He carries a long hardwood staff in his hand and he advances towards me through the ash and it roils about him and smokes from his body. He seems a figment of the red dust and yet, somehow, also distinct from it.

'Good evening,' he says. His voice is sepulchral, familiar in a way that chills me. And I think, *Here is someone you cross and don't walk away from unscathed.*

I drag Ra to my body and, using the sword as leverage, I stand.

'Are you all right?' he asks. '*Bene?*'

'I'm fine,' I answer.

'*Fortunato,*' he says. 'A few more moments and your fate would have been sealed.' His accent is foreign. Italian maybe. But what world?

'I had the situation under control,' I tell him.

He smiles. With a flick of his free hand, he brushes back his hood, revealing white-blond hair cropped short. He's younger than I thought, pale-skinned and good-looking. His eyes travel over the sword and there is something brightly eager in his look, almost ravenous. I see him push this hunger forcibly away and the moment is gone.

'That is a handsome weapon,' he says. 'Meteoric iron, I suspect. Forged in Giza. It will slice through metal like butter. Perhaps *they* were the fortunate ones.'

I shiver and say nothing.

'You are cold,' he says. He leans his staff against the brick wall and brings his pale, slim hands together. He cups them one over the other and moves them furtively. A light appears, as if a burning coal is enclosed in his hands. With a quick movement, he releases his fingers outwards and the light leaps from his hands. A bright flame arcs to the ground. Now a fire without wood burns between us, emanating an immediate heat. Despite myself, I let go a breath of relief and shuffle in closer. He watches me without speaking and I wonder if his silence means he's less or more likely to try to kill me.

'So you're a magician,' I tell him, trying to sound unimpressed, but feeling a shock of warmth flood my body.

'Sì. Something like this.'

I edge closer to the heat, feeling my body unclamp.

'With whom do you fight?' he asks now.

'Fight?'

'You are a Pathfinder,' he says, raising his white eyebrows. Then he nods. '*Sì*. It is certain. But on what side, is the question. The Collective or the Order?'

A loaded question. I get a sense my life hinges on the answer.

'I'm not from here,' I deflect, thinking fast, pretending not to be scared. But my voice betrays me.

'I can see,' he says. 'You are new to this.'

'New. But not born yesterday.'

A flicker of a smile. He too now moves to the fire. I squint at him through the smoke. Entitlement pours off him, as thick as treacle. It takes an effort of will not to move away. But I stay where I am.

'Tell me,' he says. 'What are you doing here, on the front line . . . alone?'

The *front line*?

'I'm not alone,' I tell him, glancing beyond the fire. 'There are others.'

We'll be here. Waiting.

Silence. The flames gutter and twist.

'They'll be back,' I insist. 'Any second now.'

'Of course,' he says. 'But perhaps, if it does not trouble you, I will wait here with you, in case they are . . . held up.'

'Thank you but I'm fine.'

'No, no.' He glances at the sword again. 'I cannot leave you at the mercy of whatever foes emerge from the cold. It is not safe here.'

I say nothing.

He smiles. 'Might I have the pleasure of a name?'

Something about him – the way he moves and speaks, the way he looks at my sword – sends a thousand warning signals flashing up and down my spine.

'Fonzie,' I tell him.

Fonzie Rebecca Buckler, aka Tank Girl. I was obsessed with *Tank Girl* comics in my early teens, way back when the world was normal – and singular. I mean, what's not to love about an anarchic, goggle-wearing girl living in a tank in an apocalyptic desert, dating a mutant kangaroo called Booga?

'Interesting name,' he says.

'And you are?'

He bows elaborately. 'Rodolfo Graziani, at your service. In some circles, the Marchese di Jöve. A humble Pathfinder myself.'

Without understanding why, the name tightens my gut.

'That sword,' he says. 'Might I have a closer look? I am . . . an enthusiast.'

The request, and the ease with which he steers the conversation, frighten me. Despite every cell in my body screaming at me to run, I can't do anything but comply. He smiles sweetly, with an odd warmth, and I find myself holding the weapon out to him, hilt first. Perhaps I've been overly cautious. He *did* chase away those men. If they were even human at all.

But, as soon as he removes the sword from my hands, I feel it. I've made a terrible mistake.

'*Sì*,' he says, grinning wickedly. 'It is certain. You received the sword from Mother, did you not?'

An alarm bell peals faintly, far away.

'My sword,' I demand, holding out my hand.

'What providence is this?' he says, eyes alight. 'The one we have been hunting across worlds and years is finally at hand. She, who gifted you this weapon of weapons, is close. *Sì*, I feel it.'

'The sword,' I repeat.

'You want it?' An edge to his voice now. 'Then why let it leave your grasp?'

I look beyond him to the alleyway entrance, uneasy, pulse quickening.

'But the real mystery here,' he says, 'lies not in the sword, but why *Mother* would entrust a mighty blade to a girl with not one observable skill.'

I look at the sun-blade in his hand and say nothing. My brain runs through my options, but choices are few.

'So tell me,' he says. 'Who are you really? And *where* is Mother?'

'Before I answer,' I say, stalling, 'let me ask *you* a question.'

Graziani holds the sword horizontal to his face, shuts his left eye and, with his right flush to the metal, he examines the flat length of the blade. 'You believe your position is one of bargaining?'

'Those men,' I say, taking a step away from him. 'The ones from earlier, they weren't really . . . people, were they? They were Reapers.'

He smiles and swings the sword. '*Were?*' He points the tip of the blade into the dark. 'They are still here. In the shadows. Waiting.'

Fear pours over my heart.

'Then you work for *him*?'

'Him?'

'Kei Shinigami,' I say, dredging up from memory the name Mother gave me. *The one who brought the Reapers back from the Between. The one who took your friend. First to Venetia, above Paris Nouveau, to the Seventh Gate.*

Graziani cocks his head, assessing my answer. I can almost feel him reach into my mind, trying – and hopefully failing – to find my thoughts.

'*Sì*,' he says, dropping his arm. 'I follow Master Shinigami, Lord of the Order. The multiverse is in need of cleansing. Perfecting. Only Master Shinigami can bring order.' He stares at me, unmoved. 'But *you* are not of the Order. You are one of *them*, the Collective. So I will ask you one last time. Where. Is. Mother?'

I point over his shoulder, into the gloom. 'That way.'

He turns his head, keeping his eyes on me. 'Through the alley?'

'Yeah,' I tell him. 'You take a left there, then left again, then right, right again and left. Head straight for a bit and then that's it. You've arrived. It's right there, you can't miss it . . . right on the corner of . . . goscrewyourself and kissmyarse.'

He glares at me, his expression turning quickly from disbelief to fury.

My gut churns. False bravery. I don't know where it comes from, this instinct to hit back at him. Whatever it is, I go with it. And I realize something with a shock.

I *like* it.

Then everything changes.

21

A blur. Graziani's coat flaps open and a bright spit of blood arcs through the air and spatters the white-fur collar. He cries out and swings round. Whipping past him comes a shadow-shape – appearing, vanishing, then reappearing so fast it seems like a glimmer of light. It streaks across the space and another splash of blood flies up and Graziani howls and slashes down with the sword. He misses.

The glimmer flashes and stops and a figure blurs into focus.

I see now what it is . . . *who* it is. Vidhan.

'Holy hell,' he says, panting, switching his blade from hand to hand. 'Forgot how bloody cold it is here.'

I stare at him, amazed. I open my mouth to respond, but there isn't time.

Out of the corner of my eye, I see Graziani move again.

He lunges at Vidhan and Vidhan smokes out of the way – just blurs and vanishes. Then suddenly he's next to me again, grinning. 'Yeah!' he says. '*That* just happened.'

Before I can say a word, Graziani flies at us, sword cutting the air. And behind him – from the shadows – the others. The men in dark suits. Except they're not men. They're changing, morphing, becoming something else.

Graziani brings Ra slashing across at us. We duck and Vidhan, with uncanny speed, slides away and the Reapers follow him, bodies bulging and contorting.

Then a snapping sound, like a whip cracking through the air. It comes from the other side of the alley and I turn and see, standing in the red ash, a pair of fighting sticks in her hands, Akuji.

Vidhan glimmers past her, two Reapers in pursuit – grown taller, wings spreading. Akuji launches at them. Her sticks are gleams of light. She moves beautifully, fluidly, and the fighting sticks snap through the air. The Reapers try to evade her, but it's no use. She spins and brings one of the sticks chopping down from high over her right shoulder down to her left hip.

A clean strike.

She knocks one of them down and it wails and crawls back into the shadows. Akuji whips round and slashes the other stick from high left to low right. The second Reaper lets out a wild shriek and drops, curling and hissing. Pressing her advantage, Akuji stabs the stick right into the middle of its throat, using the heel of her palm to drive the point home. The Reaper makes a strangled, gurgling noise. It heaves backwards, dragging its wings, screeching. Then it's gone, into shadow.

Five seconds. Five jaw-dropping, mind-blowing, improbable seconds.

I stare at Akuji in wonder and awe.

And that's when I remember Graziani. I spin round and find him standing right in front of me – Ra in one hand, his long staff in the other – with violence-filled eyes. He raises the sword and I know things are about to go south, fast.

So I take the only course of action that makes any sense. I attack.

I don't know where it comes from. I can't remember ever doing anything like this before, but my brain is unexpectedly agile – adaptive and reactive, able to process the situation lightning-fast. It tells my body to move, to be the first one to strike.

In a heartbeat, I shift my stance – right leg forward, left back – and bend my knees. I stabilize myself. Then, immediately, I launch off my left leg, jump high, switch in the air and kick hard with my right.

The kick is ferocious. With the heel of my shoe, I find the dead centre of his chest with a thud. He cries out, eyes wide, and the sword is flung up out of his hand. I launch myself forward and somehow manage to catch it mid-air.

A current goes through me. Pure adrenalin. Electricity.

A gunshot booms through the air. A flash of shrapnel. And, when I turn to Graziani, I watch him hurl himself at the alley wall. Miraculously, he disappears.

It's as if he ran right into the wall – *through* it.

To some other side.

I turn to find Malik, gun smoking in his fist, striding towards me. He holds up his hand, motioning for quiet, and listens. Satisfied, and visibly relaxing his shoulders, he holsters his pistol.

Graziani's gone. And so are the Reapers.

Malik's eyes flick over me. 'Are you OK?'

'Barely.'

'D'you have any idea who that was?' he says, giving me a look that feels like a mixture of astonishment and maybe even respect.

'Yeah,' I say, trembling a little.

It seems to take him a moment to master his incredulity, and then he says, 'Rodolfo Graziani, the Marchese di Jöve.'

'I know. He told me.'

'He's only the leader of the Order's forces, second in command to Shinigami. And, more than that, a psychotic and mindlessly brutal assassin. He's an evil bastard and a real threat to the multiverse. You're damn lucky to be alive.'

Akuji comes towards us. Silently. She twirls her sticks once and then slams them home in their twin scabbards on her belt. She says nothing.

Vidhan, next to her, looks at the blood dripping off the ends of the fighting sticks and grimaces. 'Ya kill me, Kuji,' he says. 'Ya really do.'

He looks from Akuji to me and his face pales.

'What?' I say.

Vidhan takes a step towards me. 'That sword,' he says. 'It's Graziani's?'

I hold the sword tightly in my fist. 'No. Mother gave it to me.'

Impossible! a voice cries in my head. Akuji.

'The sun-blade,' Vidhan says, straightening his glasses. '*That's* the weapon she chose for you? *Ra?*'

'You know the sword's name?' I say.

All three stand in a semi-circle around me and their gaze, like heat, falls on the blade in my fist and it feels like a blend of jealousy and wonder.

I clutch the sword more vehemently and make a promise to myself: I'll never let it pass from my hands again.

'Why're you all looking at me like that?' I ask, locking eyes with each of them.

Malik is the first to answer. 'Something about you,' he says. 'I didn't know what it was, or why, but I knew you were important. And now this. The way you attacked him like that. Instinctively, without fear. And that sword, it's –'

'What are you talking about? It's just a sword.'

'Ana,' Vidhan says. '*That* is no ordinary sword. The sun-blade is an ancient Egyptian khopesh. See those seven symbols running down the blade? They each represent a world.'

'That sword,' Malik adds, 'was carried by Mother herself. It was *her* sword. And, before that, it was carried by the first Pathfinder. Thoth – the god.'

22

'God?'

'Yeah.'

'Do I believe in God!' Bea exclaims. 'That's your question?'

'Yeah.'

'That's a load of bull, Moon. I'm Jewish, you idiot. Course I'm supposed to believe in God. And of course I bloody don't.'

Bea elbows me in the ribs and I laugh. We're on the roof, lying side by side, watching the sun dip. Our way up was a wonky railing at the back of the Old Man's terrace. We climbed up when no one was around and lay across the warm terracotta tiles. Our second-favourite secret meeting spot (after the Circle Line).

'I'd like to be Jewish,' I say, staring at the sky.

'Oh yeah? why?'

Above us, blood-red clouds hustle over brightening stars.

'You get to have this whole community thing. Feel part of something bigger than you.'

155

'You've got four *parents and a brother, Moon. There's your community.*'

'That's different.'

'So you're saying what?' Bea flicks her hair and throws her hands behind her head. 'You wanna keep Shabbat?'

'Yeah. But . . . what exactly is Shabbat?'

'Day of rest. Memorial to God rescuing the Israelites from slavery in Egypt.'

'See, that sounds cool.'

'I mean seriously, Moon. Cut that out. You are not alone.'

'I know. It's just . . . don't you ever feel you're not really here? You're just observing all this. Like one of those stars in Orion's Belt, up in all that blackness.'

Bea laughs and rolls her eyes.

'You're laughing,' I tell her, annoyed, 'because you don't think I've got a legitimate claim to be screwed up. Unlike you.'

I regret saying it immediately, but Bea just looks at me. 'Moon,' she says, 'sometimes I swear your head is shoved so far up your skinny arse you don't see what's right in front of you, never mind what's thousands of light years away.'

I press my lips together. The roof smells of old leaves and tar.

'They used to fight, didn't they?' she says. 'Frankie and the Old Man.'

'All the time,' I whisper, watching the sun's curve burn to nothing. 'She'd come home and hammer at him. And they'd say all these hurtful things.'

'Yeah,' Bea says. 'Mine too. Sometimes it felt like the world was ending. And then, in a way, it actually did.'

We lie in silence, not speaking.

Bea turns to me. 'Look, you can be messed up if you want, Moon. Go ahead. Knock yourself out. I'm not gonna stop you. Because you know who's got your back?'

I look at her. A faint breeze lifts her hair away from her eyes. Her face is pale. Her eyes, bright and distracted. She smiles and my heart pings. 'Yeah. You.'

'Exactly. And whose got mine?'

'Me,' I tell her.

'Damn right,' Bea says. 'Wanna know why?'

'Why?'

'Because you love me more than anyone else in the whole entire universe.'

I reach out and grab her hand in mine 'That's kinda true.'

She laughs. 'So, you wanna know if I believe in God?'

'Yeah. I do.'

'I'll tell you this, Moon. If there is a God then He is a She. Hell, some days I wake up in the morning and I get a feeling maybe I'm God.'

'Jesus. That's taking things a little too far, don't you think?'

Bea smiles. 'No such thing as too far,' she says.

Stars blink at us. My head spins. I get a feeling of vertigo, as if the world has flipped and we're the ones looking down and the stars are below, looking up.

23

The red ash of Ares lies undisturbed ahead of us. We leave our footprints marching behind and stick to the shadows, making our way west through the city. Even under the cover of predawn darkness, I can see how London is transformed again. From a bright chill to a breathless bone-cold. From a spectacle of steel and glass and towers that climbed out of sight to the tumbling hulks of hollowed-out stone structures reduced to rubble, and always the floating ash, as red as blood – Ares is no Lūna.

'Hey, Malik,' I say, breath steaming, trampling after him.

'Yup?' he says, leaping over a pile of rubble.

'Where exactly is this place we're going?'

'The Collective Council Meeting.'

'I know, you said. But *where*?'

'Not far,' he says. 'West. A Haven near Kensington Gardens.'

'And *why*?'

'Because Gabe's there. All the clans of the Collective report to him. He'll be able to fill in the gaps.'

'Kensington Gardens,' I say, taking in the devastation all around us. 'I assume it won't look the same way it did in Sol.'

Malik smiles. 'It's basically a wasteland crawling with psychos.' He looks at the blade on my hip. 'Best keep that new sword of yours close.'

'How did you find me back there?' I ask him as we pass under the eaves of a shattered building.

'We're Pathfinders,' Malik says. 'It's what we do.'

Above us, I see a zeppelin shooting streaks of orange gunfire at some hidden foe. The cold is brutal. It turns everything numb. My fingers. My toes.

'Drink this,' Malik says as if he can hear my thoughts (and hell, maybe he can, which is worrying, to say the least). He produces a canteen from his backpack and hands it to me. The surface is freezing to the touch and covered in ice scales.

Too tired to argue, I tip back my head and take a long slug. Fire snakes down my throat. I try to take a breath, but all I can manage is a tight gasp.

Malik laughs. 'Ares Firewater,' he says, taking the canteen. 'It'll regulate your temperature.' He takes a sip and grimaces. 'Just gotta block out the taste.'

I cough and spit and we carry on. Crimson ash feathers down. The light is eerie. In the distance, I hear a thunder crack of cannons.

We arrive at a four-way crossing and Malik holds up his hand for us to wait as he scans the length of a deserted road, pistol drawn.

I feel the Firewater going to work now, spreading heat to my extremities.

'Where's everyone gone?' I ask Malik when we move off again.

'Hiding,' he says. 'They're at war. Pathfinders with Pathfinders. Normals with Normals. Normals with Pathfinders. All kinds of scavengers and war parties and bandits around Londra. People turn dangerous when they get desperate.'

'Londra?'

'That's what London's called here in Ares.'

I say nothing. Beyond him, I see Akuji watching us from across the road.

'So . . . the Reapers,' I say. 'You never told me they could shapeshift.'

Malik shrugs. 'Does it make a difference?'

I shake my head and look up and down the empty road. Vidhan and Akuji, on the far side, pick through the rubble. I think about how they moved before, during the battle. Vidhan, so fast he was a blur. Akuji, like a warrior trained to do only one thing: fight. And then I remember the way *I* fought. It was instinctive – *in* me.

The sword, Ra, pulls at my belt and chafes my hip bone. I realize that my hand hasn't left the hilt since we came out of the alleys and moved out on to bigger streets. I lift my hand self-consciously and feel Malik's eyes on me.

'This sword,' I say to him. 'It really belonged to Mother and Thoth?'

'Yup.'

'Then what am *I* doing with it, Malik? I'm nobody. It should be with someone like you or Akuji. It belongs to a warrior. Not me.'

Malik just nods. 'What did you think of her?' he says.

'Mother?'

'She can be tetchy, right? But she sees things in us. Where others see nothing.' When I don't respond, he adds, 'What did she tell you about Bea?'

'She said Shinigami took her to Venetia, to the Seventh Gate. And then . . . something strange. She told me Bea's in Kronos. But that doesn't make any sense.'

Malik stops in his tracks. He looks at me and his brow furrows. 'She really said that? *Kronos?*'

'Yeah. And then she said something like "some have made it there but none have returned". What do you think it means?'

Malik rolls his shoulders and frowns.

'Vidhan told me about the prophecy,' I continue. 'He said the Order's supposed to have found the Seventh Gate and been looking for the key that'll open it. But that the key's not a thing, it's a person. A Pathfinder. You think Bea's somehow mixed up in all this? That *she's* the key?'

Malik doesn't answer my question, because just then Vidhan crosses the road and asks Malik for his Firewater canteen.

'Hell's teeth,' Vidhan says, wheezing and coughing after taking a slug. 'That'll put hair on your chest any day of the week.'

Malik takes the canteen back, still frowning. Obviously mulling over this news about Bea being in Kronos. He takes a drink himself. Winces.

'Ares,' Vidhan says, looking at me and squinting. 'Not the worst universe, if you're partial to freezing your arse off. Man, why'd ya have to go and Fall?'

I don't bother telling him it was Mother's doing, nothing to do with me.

I take a deep breath and put thoughts of keys to bed. For now.

'All this is crazy,' I say, looking at the razed buildings, the urban rubble and the floating ash. 'This world, it's –'

'Broken,' Vidhan interjects.

'I can't believe it's London,' I say shaking my head in bewilderment.

'It's not. It's Londra.'

'Right. Fair point.'

'Tell me,' he says. 'Whaddaya know about ecosystems?'

I shrug. 'Only what I learned at school. A community of living organisms linked together. They depend on each other to survive.'

'All this,' Vidhan says, waving his hands over his spiky dreads, 'is part of a giant ecosystem, each universe woven into the other. And if ya introduce something into an ecosystem that doesn't belong –'

'It breaks,' I interject.

'Exactly. Ares wasn't always like this. Shinigami caused it by bringing stuff from the other worlds – technology, weapons, ideas, things that have no rightful place here. It's destabilizing the multiverse. And now they're telling everyone only the Order can fix things. Hell, they *caused* this.'

'So let's get outta here. Fall out of Ares. Into the next.'

Vidhan shakes his head. 'Way too bloody dangerous. The puking, the ringing in your ears, your teeth aching – these are all signs you're putting yourself through the wringer. Your body needs time to recover. Fall too often and too far and . . .'

'And *what*?'

'You get lost,' Malik interrupts.

'Uh . . . what I'm trying to say,' Vidhan says pointedly, 'is that Falling is not something you do lightly. Not every Fall takes you from one world to the next. Sometimes when people Fall – Pathfinders or Normals – they disappear: they get lost in the Between. Gone forever.'

Vidhan must see my stricken face because he hurries on. 'I mean, that's not what happened to Bea – she was taken, that's different. But every Fall is a risk, Ana.'

'The idea,' Malik adds, 'that passing from one universe to another is as easy as walking through a wardrobe is a joke – a lie perpetrated by literature.'

He freezes suddenly. Listens. Strafes the area with his eyes. And I only realize just how impressive his senses are, how in tune, when something – brown fur, bushy tail –

shoots across the road and disappears behind a building. Just a fox.

But I'm wrong about that. A pair of vagabond figures lurch from a side road into our path.

One is short and squat and grips a hunting knife in his fist. The other, tall and gaunt, carries a pocket revolver. Their masks are kerchiefs tied over their mouths and noses, and their eyes are red-rimmed and restless. They look high on something.

'Don't nobody do NOTHIN!' the short one with the hunting knife screeches, voice muffled behind his mask.

Silence.

'Your money!' his gaunt accomplice – the one with the revolver – yells, eyes scanning, twitching. 'Hand it over. Now. NOW!'

We stand and do nothing. Me in shock. The others calm. They don't seem at all concerned. Vidhan wears a lopsided grin. Akuji looks at them with casual disdain. Malik narrows his eyes. His hand drops to his hip.

'What are you, *deaf*?' the revolver-bandit barks. 'Your MONEY!'

'Look,' Malik says evenly. 'We might hand you the money. Only your mate over there told us to *do nothin*. So which is it?'

'Are you for real?' Revolver-bandit's eyes are full-on bulging now as he speaks. 'Hand it over. Everything you've got. RIGHT NOW!'

'Everything?'

'*EVERYTHING!*'

In the bat of an eyelid, Malik's pistol is in his fist.

'How d'you feel about lead?' he says, snarling.

Akuji removes a fighting stick, twirls it in the air. She looks lethal.

'You're Pathfinders?' the tall revolver-bandit says, watching her. I reckon he must be the leader of the two, since the squat one with the knife hardly speaks.

Malik turns his head to Vidhan, keeping his eyes locked on the bandits. 'Looks like you ain't the only genius here, Prof.'

The revolver-bandit sniffs and takes a step back. 'Collective?'

Malik just smiles.

The bandits take in the odds and back up further. 'Looks as if this mighta been a misunderstanding,' the revolver-bandit says, glancing at his companion.

'Might be,' Malik says.

'Reckon we'll be on our way,' the bandit says.

'Reckon so, fellas,' Vidhan says.

Carefully, very slowly, the two conceal their weapons and raise empty hands, their demeanour transformed.

'Wait!' Malik calls out. 'There's a price.'

The bandits exchange glances. 'What price?'

'Information,' Malik says. 'Where's all the heat? East or west?'

'East,' the squat guy says, all tics and nervous energy. 'The Order took down a few Havens over at the Wharf. So they say.'

'Like hell, they took out a few Havens.'

'Hey, pal, don't shoot the messenger.' He smiles toothlessly. 'I'm just repeatin what I heard. Them Reapers, they say they came by the truckload.'

Malik cocks his pistol. 'Look, man,' the bandit says, clearing his throat. 'S'all cool. We go our way, you go yours. No harm done.'

Malik indicates the alley with a sideways tip of his head. 'Fine. Get lost.'

The bandits turn and hightail it back into the shadows while Malik casually reholsters his gun. 'Normals,' he says under his breath.

'Really?' Vidhan says to him, smirking. ' "How d'ya feel about *lead*?" '

Malik smiles.

We keep moving, heading west. We walk silently, flanking each other, and pass buildings on fire that blaze with heat. Others are gutted and charred, like burnt skeletons. Eyes, gleaming, watch us from the shadows. Far away, behind us, a fading thunder of guns echoes across the annihilated city.

'Look,' Malik says. I follow his gaze and stop dead.

We've hit Piccadilly and there's a parallel statue of Eros, afloat on its green plinth, covered in graffiti, wings chipped and broken. But this isn't what catches my eye. It's the giant lumbering through the ash. I stare at it, speechless, half enthralled and half frightened.

'I'm dreaming,' I say. 'None of this is real. It can't be.'

'Oh, it's real,' Vidhan says. 'You're out in the great multiverse now. And, in the great multiverse, everything that can happen does happen.'

Crimson moonlight flutes down on an enormous machine, four storeys tall, with curved plates of steel and hanging wires and pipes. It stirs a dream-memory of *War of the Worlds*. Horrifying and mesmerizing. Carrying it through the desolation are eight spider-like, hydraulic-powered metal legs. I watch the behemoth in stupefied awe until, finally, it disappears into the gloom behind a building.

By rights, I should be terrified out of my wits. But I'm not. And maybe that's because I have a purpose – finding Bea. I will find her. I *will*.

That feeling courses through me, as bright as a blade.

24

As the word implies, A **HAVEN** is a place of safety, of refuge. All Pathfinders are, from time to time, in need of security. This is the purpose of a Haven: sanctuary from the many vagaries of the multiverse. A Haven is unseen to the Normal, their locations closely guarded, passed only by word of mouth. They are safe harbours. Sanctums. Protected by an elder **COMMAND**. A spell. The spell is absolute. It prevents Havens from coming under attack. Only were the multiverse to collapse would the spell fail.

'Get to the chapter on Falling yet?'

I look up from *The Book of Seven*, scraping damp curls behind my ears.

'C'mon,' Vidhan says, holding out his hand to me.

He hauls me up from my seat against a collapsed wall where we'd taken no more than five minutes of rest, and again we move.

Malik, Akuji, Vidhan and me. A Pathfinder clan in a dark world not my own.

We pass a bleak reminder of what I've left behind. A shrunken Thames, reduced to a muddy ribbon spanned by the buttressed hulks of collapsed bridges. On the putrid banks, I see vagrants picking their way through the ooze. On the streets, army units – in riot gear and hyped up – run helter-skelter, barking orders. A spit of gunfire. Shrapnel. Buildings ablaze and roaring in the dark. I see what must once have been Harrods department store, the ornate dome still standing but blown open on one side. Every window smashed and the hallways empty – gutted, nothing left to loot. Further along, the Natural History Museum: a skeleton, roofless, exposed to the elements.

The school had taken us once. We'd stood in the central entrance hall below the dark bones of the diplodocus in wonder.

'Well, Moon?' Bea said. 'How does it make you feel?'

'Small,' I remember answering. 'You?'

'Damn. I thought it'd be bigger.'

Bea. She never leaves my thoughts. Finding her, bringing her home, this is all that keeps me sane in a reality more bizarre by the second.

In a way, she was right. The dinosaur was nothing in comparison to the giant robot. We've seen more since, but always in the murky, dreamlike distance to the east, long, spider-like legs propelling them weirdly through the waste.

We turn right now, past the Science Museum, which is likely something else in Ares (half a dozen universe-sized holes missing in Sol's scientific thinking, I tell myself as we move past). As we head up Exhibition Road, the sword keeps hitting my hip bone, chafing me.

Here it stands, right before the wasteland of Kensington Gardens. I recognize the grand red-brick building, unbombed and still beautiful. In Sol, it was the Royal Geographical Society. The Old Man and Gad had brought me here to hear some explorer talk about his epic trip across the Arctic. I reckon when I get back, I might have a go at a speaking gig myself. Ah hell. Who'd believe me?

The grimy plaque mounted on the gate does not say Royal Geographical Society. It says:

MEMBERS ONLY

This time, Vidhan is the one who stares into the smashed video screen above the gate. A red laser flickers across his eyeball. Silence. Then comes the sequence of bolts and the gate swings open. Three stoic guards greet us on the far side. All in black. Silent. Armed.

Malik is the last through the gate and it shuts behind us.

We cross a short, curved driveway and the guards, without speaking, usher us into the main entrance, through an arched doorway and into a grand hall. The windows are floor to ceiling and have taken no damage. There's a huge limestone fireplace, lit. A drift of smoke rises from crackling logs that give the room a dense, expensive feeling. The ceiling is crossed with thick wooden beams. From the centre one hangs a wrought-iron chandelier fitted with low-wattage electric bulbs. Houseplants sit squarely against the walls, neat and trimmed. The walls have dark panelling, black with age, and the floor is worn flagstone. Ornately framed oil portraits hang on the walls.

Akuji paces the room, looking at the portraits, hands clasped in front of her body, down by her slinking hips. She walks lightly, almost on her toes, feet turned slightly inwards. In another life, she might've been a dancer. In another world, she probably is.

I look at the frames on the wall. Solemn faces stare back at me. Paintings of people I suspect are all masters. 'So the Collective has money,' I say.

'Why not?' Vidhan says, tapping his temple. 'Some of the finest brains going.'

Malik points up at an oil painting. 'Prof. here thinks *his* ugly mug will one day join these bad boys.'

'Ya better believe it, mate,' Vidhan says. 'But not unless they paint me in my board shorts. Whaddaya reckon, Kuji? I'd look bloody ace up there, no?'

'It'll never happen,' a curt reply comes booming through the air.

A tall man – dark and powerfully built – dressed in long robes. He strides silently across the floor to us, as if he owns every square metre.

'Gabe!' Vidhan cries.

The man laughs easily, full of charm. He puts a broad hand on Vidhan's shoulder, dwarfing him. 'Hell, it's good to see you. What's goin on?'

'I'm still alive, Gabe.'

'Well, that's what matters, Prof.' He looks at the others. 'Yo, Malik,' he says, turning. They clasp each other – a man hug, a little shoulder barge – warm and awkward at the same time. 'Still got the trigger finger?'

'Hasn't let me down yet,' Malik says.

'Look, you know I'm faster.'

'The hell you are.'

Gabe smiles. He looks slightly older than the rest of us, perhaps in his twenties. Beneath his sand-coloured robe he wears a holster sporting a gleaming six-shooter. He exudes natural confidence and charisma. But the dark rings under his eyes suggest he's on the edge of exhaustion. The kind of tired that only comes from months of unrelenting effort.

He looks at Akuji and gives her a nod. 'The silent one,' he says. She stays where she is on the far side of the room, gazing coolly – but respectfully – back at him.

'Ana,' Malik says, 'I want you to meet another master. Gabriel Savage. The real deal. You won't find a better Pathfinder in the seven realms.'

'The man's exaggerating,' Gabriel says, looking at me, smiling. 'So. This is Ana Moon.'

'You know me?'

'Heard about you. Through various sources. Been looking forward to meeting you.'

'*Me?*'

He unfures a finger and points at my waist. 'The mighty Ra. You and I, we need to speak. But first let's get you settled in. You must be hungry.'

'Bloody starved,' Vidhan says.

Other Pathfinders direct their gaze at us as we enter the dining room on the first floor, but after a quick once-over they quickly return to their discussions and their meals. The room is another elegant space, long and narrow. Polished wooden floors. A grandfather clock ticking against the far wall. More portraits and a long table running down the centre of the room with white tablecloth, candlesticks, gleaming cutlery and glasses. I try to look relaxed, like I'm one of them, but I don't *feel* like one of them. Gabriel excuses himself and we troop over to the table. I mimic Akuji and lay my weapon out horizontally on the wooden ledge on the side wall. We slide into seats and take in the well-stocked table. Bread, lean cuts of meat, potatoes and steamed vegetables. The others don't waste time.

'How do you get all this stuff?' I ask, picking up a stem of broccoli with a fork. 'I mean it's Armageddon out there. But in here –'

'It's a Haven,' Malik says, scoffing a slice of ham.

I watch him, waiting for more, but he offers nothing.

'What Malik meant to say,' Vidhan says, piling his plate high, 'is that a Haven ain't subject to the same rules as normal places. Plus, we stockpile food. Gotta love it. Grub *and* lodging. Rooms are on the second and third floors.'

He points to the ceiling with his knife, then across the table. 'Pass the salt, will ya?'

I hand him the shaker and watch him scatter salt over his food, then devour everything. To move the way he did in the alley must burn serious calories.

'Vidhan,' I say, leaning in to him. 'In the alley, with Graziani. How did you move so fast? I mean, it's not physically possible.'

He grins wolfishly. 'I know, right?'

'It was almost like you were . . . in two places at the same time.'

'Maybe I bloody was.' He taps his glass with his knife. 'See this? Look here.' He lifts the glass and the reflection from a ceiling light leaves two wobbling rings on the table. As Vidhan lifts the glass higher, the bobbing rings of light move apart and converge again when he lowers it.

'See? *Light* can be in two places at the same time. So why not me? Why not *you*?' He slams the glass down on the table, splashing the water. 'The glass, this table, *you*, everything might look solid, but it's all just atoms vibrating. Nothing is at rest. Everything moves. But the truth is, the way *I* move? Hell, it's one of those unexplainable Pathfinder things. It's mad magic.'

'It's mad all right,' I say.

'It's called superpositioning,' Vidhan says. 'All in *The Book of Seven*.' He points his knife at me. 'Read the handbook and you'll see.'

I slice into the ham on my plate and the knife screeches against the ceramic surface. I take a bite, chew and swallow. I feel like I'm losing it again. Do I really belong here at this table? Can I do all the things they can? Am I one of *them*? A Pathfinder. How can that be? I'm just Ana. But I know that isn't right. I'm more than that now. There's something inside me. Something I can't control. It's powerful. Violent even. And it's getting stronger. I realize, as I sit there, thinking, that I'm clutching the knife in my fist like a stabbing blade and Vidhan is looking at me, frowning.

'Excuse me,' I mumble, standing up and knocking over his glass.

'Hey!' he yells. 'What? What'd I say?'

I don't answer. I collect my sword and stumble back out into the corridor. I find a bathroom. Slam the door shut. Lock it. Lean against it.

Breathe.

I peel off my hoodie, then my shirt, and stand at the sink and stare at my reflection. A wild girl stares back at me – scratched and bloodied and bruised. Which makes sense. You don't cross three worlds and come away unchanged. My curly auburn hair is lank and lifeless, flat against my skull, and I scrape it back into an untidy bun. I turn and swivel my neck to look at the cuts and bruises on my body.

A sharp knock at the door. 'Ana?'

I freeze and say nothing.

'Ana, it's Malik. I just . . . I wanted to see if you're OK.'

I swallow, but the lump in my throat doesn't go away. *Am* I OK? It's hard to say. 'I'm not exactly sure,' I call back.

'Yeah,' the response comes from the other side of the door. 'That's to be expected, I suppose.'

A pause. My heart thumps.

I hear a sigh through the door. I can almost see Malik standing there. I imagine his hand on the door, palm against the wood.

'Listen, they want to talk to you . . . about Bea,' he says. 'Gabe and the others.'

'Fine. Just . . . gimme a second.'

I hear him run his hand over the door, then I hear him push away and his footsteps fade down the corridor.

I take a deep breath and think about Bea and the last time I saw her. On the Circle Line. And the Reaper coming through the carriage. I think about the Old Man and his yoga poses, about Frankie standing at her state-of-the-art espresso machine, then lifting Zig into the air, and something breaks inside me.

Is the world I left behind dead? Am *I* dead?

I feel dizzy, light-headed. I grip the sides of the basin and stare at my reflection, hollow-eyed.

Who am I? Is this *me*? Or is it a sheared-off version of me, a cutaway Ana Moon? A *new* Ana Moon. Reborn. I remember how I felt in that alley. The way my body moved of its own volition. I take a deep breath and compose myself.

The only thing I know with any certainty is this: nothing will ever go back to the way it was. Not really. This is me now.

The girl with the khopesh blade.

25

Gabriel – Gabe – is leaning against the wall opposite the bathroom door. When I emerge, he kicks away from the wall with a smile and asks if I'd mind following him.

Mother's final words come back to me.

GO! Find Gabriel. Now FALL!

We take a limestone staircase that's worn to a shine. It carries us in a tightening spiral to the roof and, when he opens the outside door, Gabe ushers me inside a conservatory. The air hits us like a wall, warm and humid. Multiple species of tangled plants climb eagerly to a curved glass roof and beyond lies the reality of Ares. Devastation. Ash. Fires like flickering stars in the distance.

'An oasis in hell,' Gabe says.

He guides me through a narrow path with ferns reaching for us on either side. The pathway leads on to a courtyard with an oval table. The table is bare save for a bottle of red wine and seven glasses. Round the table sit six people.

There are two free seats. Gabe pulls back one of these for me and takes the other.

I sit down and place my hands on the table. Polished rosewood. Frankie has something similar in the front room. Except carved into the middle of *this* table is an extraordinary etching of seven interlinked rings. The multiverse.

Three men and three women sit round the table. A young woman – I think in her twenties, like Gabe – with an aquiline nose and spiky black hair. An Asian man, older, jade rings on his fingers. A beautiful, fine-boned woman with high cheekbones and caramel skin. A silver-haired man, prim and upright. A bearded man, dark-skinned and barrel-chested, who looks as strong as an ox. And a heavily tattooed and muscled white woman swigging liberally from her wine glass.

All six wear robes identical to Gabe's. All six have eyes that express alertness and intelligence, but also sorrow.

'So,' Silver-hair says, leaning forward – first to look at the sword and then to eye me up and down (by his expression, I presume he reaches an unfavourable opinion of the latter). 'Ana Moon,' he says. 'It *is* a fine weapon.'

I swallow and say nothing. I feel tense but I won't let them see my discomfort. I sit with my shoulders back. Hands on the table.

'Gabe tells us Ra chose you,' Silver-hair says.

I look straight back at him, unsmiling. 'Yeah. I chose the sword.'

'No, no,' the young woman with the aquiline nose says, also leaning forward. 'The sword chose *you*, Ana. The distinction matters.'

I turn my head to her, keeping my body stiff. 'If you say so.'

'You felt it,' the woman says. 'The *pull*. It's the same for us all. The Pathfinder never chooses the weapon. The weapon chooses the Pathfinder.'

'You're all masters, is that it?' I look round the table, at each of their faces, and – determined to give off a cool, aloof impression – I lean back in my chair, loosening my shoulders. 'And this is a Collective Council Meeting,' I add.

'That's right,' Gabe answers, also leaning back. But, while *my* body language is fake, *his* is clearly genuine. He's utterly at ease and I get the impression he's always that way. Someone who doesn't panic – no matter what. Like Malik.

'Are you interviewing me?' I ask. 'An inquisition, is that what this is?'

Gabe laughs. 'Is that what you think?'

'It's pretty intense.'

'Well, I'm sorry. That's not our intention.'

'You treat her like a child,' Silver-hair interjects, all business. 'If she has the sword, she must understand what is required. We have no time to mollycoddle.'

'This is a mistake,' the Asian man says. 'It cannot be her.'

'Why not?' the tattooed woman says. 'You judge her on sight?'

'Man, look, there's no mistake,' Gabe says, placating them with his hands in the air. 'She has the sword, as you can well see. It's her. She *is* the one.'

'What's everyone getting at?' I demand. 'I mean, OK, I have this famous sword. But so what? I'm just trying to get my friend back.'

Barrel-chested beard-man grunts and says something under his breath.

Gabe looks at me evenly. 'Your friend,' he repeats.

'Yeah. My *friend*. Bea. Beatrice Gold.'

'Ana, don't you know what the sword means?' Gabe says.

'No. What does it mean? Tell me.' I keep my voice calm and steady, nothing to betray my nerves.

Gabe watches me, his expression preoccupied. Then he sits forward. 'It means that your mission, to find this friend of yours, has become our mission.'

'What?' All my fake calm disintegrates. '*Why?*'

Gabe glances at the others and settles back in his chair. The leather creaks. 'What did you think of Mother?' he asks.

I shrug. 'She's out-of-her-mind crazy.'

Gabe laughs. 'Yeah, that's a fact. And you don't know the half of it. I've known her a long time and . . . Well, let's just say –'

'Look, what's this got to do with Bea?' I demand, interrupting him.

Gabe strokes his chin, undeterred. 'We'll get there,' he says. He lifts his glass of blood-red wine, tilts it, rolls it in his hand and takes a sip. 'Mother's been a Pathfinder longer than anyone at this table. Than any other Pathfinder in the multiverse in fact.'

Murmurs of approval round the table.

I shift in my seat, feeling uneasy again. 'How long?'

Gabe puts down the glass. 'Long,' he says. 'Centuries.'

The idea should frighten me but it doesn't. I'm becoming inured to multiverse surprises. And I remember her comment about meeting Lewis Carroll.

'So you're saying . . . she's what? Immortal?'

Everyone smiles. Some laugh. Gabe shakes his head. 'She's no vampire, Ana. She's just old. Really, *really* old. And with that comes deep wisdom.'

'So, when she says something,' I murmur, 'you believe her.'

'You catch on fast.'

'She's been gifted with astonishing power,' the woman with the high cheekbones says. 'Abilities like no other. If Mother sees something in you, then it *is* true.'

'I still don't get what this has to do with Bea,' I say.

'Whoa, when you get the bit between your teeth,' Gabe says, eyes laughing. 'But don't fret, we'll come to that. First you need to understand some things.' His fingers toy with the stem of his wine glass, turning it absently. 'When I said before I'd heard of you . . . it didn't surprise you?'

'It did. But, when you consider everything else – you know, Falling between universes, almost getting murdered by Reapers – it wasn't exactly high on my "what-the-hell-is-going-on?" list.'

He smiles. 'The thing is we've known about you a long time, Ana. See, all this is linked to Mother's prophecy.'

'*Mother's* prophecy? About the key that will open a pathway to Kronos through the Seventh Gate?' I say.

'Almost,' he answers. 'That's the version of the prophecy in general circulation. The more accurate version is known only to a select few.' He indicates the others sitting round the table. 'What Mother actually said is that a girl from Sol would open a pathway to and from the seventh. A girl with a very particular name.'

All my attempts at being calm and composed vanish. I know what he's about to say. I can hear the words already.

'Beatrice Gold,' I whisper, my voice tight with excitement.

Gabe just looks at me and shakes his head. 'No,' he says. 'Ana Moon.'

26

I look from Gabe to Silver-hair and then at aquiline-nosed woman. My eyes travel to the others round the table, expecting them to react in some way. To fall about laughing. To tell me it's all bollocks. *Anything.* But they're dead serious. Every one of them.

I try to process what Gabe said but I can't. How am I supposed to feel about being the centre of some multiverse prophecy?

I look at Gabe. He stares back at me intently.

'What's so special about my name?' I ask.

'Well, Ana *is* a palindrome,' he says. 'And yes, that's interesting, but not all that *remarkable.* Then, of course, Ana Moon comprises seven letters. Coincidence? A link to the seven worlds?' He shakes his head. 'No. The real reason is that Mother made it plain. She told us a Moon girl from Sol was the key. A Pathfinder with powerful abilities. *You*, Ana Moon. So I'm sure you'll understand – and forgive us – we set about following you, watching you. Long before your first Fall.'

I grip the edge of the table, allowing his words to sink in. *Following you. Watching you.*

I'm back on the path into the woods with Bea. In my gut that familiar, nervy feeling. Something – hidden in the trees – following.

'It was *you*?' I whisper.

'Not us personally, you understand,' Gabe says, clearing his throat. 'Collective agents. Pathfinders acting on our behalf.'

'Stalkers!' I cry, standing up out of my seat, hand moving to my sword. 'You were *watching* me? Who do you think you are?'

'Sit down, Ana,' he says.

But I'm not listening. All I can think about is seeing things, figures across the street, and believing I was mad. But all this time it was *real*. It *happened*.

I'm breathing fast. My heart is racing. I'm tired of being turned inside out and upside down. I'm tired of reality twisting, shifting, dropping out from under me.

'Sit down,' Gabe says firmly. His tone is kind but commanding. Without being able to stop myself, I pull the chair in and retake my seat, pulse thumping.

'Listen, Ana, I know this is crazy,' he says. 'I get it. We all do. But we were looking out for you. Watching over you.'

'I thought I was going insane,' I mumble under my breath.

Someone's voice springs into my head, bold and clear.

There is no hiding behind a whisper here.

The Chinese man, I suspect. Then a different voice. Gabe.

You wanna say something? Speak your mind, Ana.

'You're lying,' I tell him. 'Malik, Akuji and Vidhan –
they didn't know who I was. *They* weren't following me.'

'Like I said,' Gabe says calmly, 'your importance is
known only to a few. The fewer people who are aware, the
better. Malik finding you first like that? Pure chance. One
in a million. But he knows now. I've told him.'

'And Bea?' I repeat.

'Look, here's the thing,' Gabe says. 'Sometimes, no
matter how careful you are, the watchers become the
watched. We think the Order got wind of our operation.
They might've been suspicious. Followed you too. Most
likely without knowing why, at least at first.'

I stare out of the conservatory glass at a city in ruins. I
feel hunted. Cornered. Caught in the middle between two
factions fighting a war I don't understand. Pathfinders.
The good and the bad. On both sides.

And me in between.

'What happened to Bea?' I demand. 'Just tell me.'

'We believe your friend Beatrice Gold was taken in
error,' Silver-hair says. 'We believe her abduction was a
case of mistaken identity.'

Silence falls on the room.

A buzzing sound. Swirling dots of light. The warping
glass wall of the conservatory seem to expand and contract.
Malik was right. *You think life is one way, then a door
opens and you realize the world is bigger than you thought.*

'Ana,' Gabe says, dragging me back to the present. 'Did you hear us?'

'Wait,' I say, head spinning. 'Just . . . say that again.'

'We think Shinigami learned, or guessed, that you're the girl from the prophecy and ordered your capture,' he says. 'But the Order got it wrong. Your friend was taken instead of you.'

'How . . . I mean, how's that even possible?'

'Reapers,' Gabe says. 'They're brutal and strong, but they aren't the brightest. You and Bea, you were always together, right? Inseparable? They mixed you up. It was a mistake.'

'But what did they want with *me*?'

'Haven't you been listening? You're the last piece Shinigami needs to access Kronos and its powers. We know the Order located the Seventh Gate some years ago. And we believe Shinigami has managed to use the gate, but only one way. People go in, but they don't come back. That's the significance of Mother's prophecy: that a girl from Sol would open a pathway to *and from* the seventh. Without you, Shinigami could enter Kronos but never come out.'

I take a deep, shuddering breath. 'Who *is* this Shinigami?'

'The Collective,' Gabe says, standing up and pacing round the table, resting his broad hand on the shoulders of the six masters he passes. 'We used to be the only way. Pathfinders moving between worlds to keep the energy flowing and the multiverse safe and free from harm.' He comes to a halt at the glass wall of the conservatory and looks out. 'But that all changed with Shinigami.'

Murmurs of discontent. Someone thumps the table.

Gabe reaches out, puts his hand on the glass. 'Shinigami was once one of us. Born in Lūna to Normal parents, rapidly ascending to become a master Pathfinder with abilities far outside the ordinary. Eventually becoming an elder and luring in susceptible followers like the infamous assassin, Rodolfo Graziani. Then, about fifty years ago, Shinigami began stealing from one world and selling to another for profit – weapons, technology, drugs, whatever – and, in the process, built up stupendous wealth. By the time the other masters understood what was happening, it was too late. Shinigami had formed the Order and started on phase two.'

Gabe paces again, round and round the table, in an ever-tightening circle. He stops at my chair and looks down at me.

'What Shinigami wants now is perfection. The Order believes the multiverse is in chaos and requires cleansing. They claim this can only come from destruction, from wiping out anyone perceived as weak or unsuitable for the Order's cause, perhaps even shutting down the pathways.'

'Which is destabilizing the natural flow of the multiverse,' I say. 'And *that* draws more converts to their cause, right? All looking for something better.'

'I see your mind is as sharp as that blade of yours is meant to be,' the tattooed woman says, downing her drink.

'Fear them,' says Gabe. 'Kei Shinigami is capable of extraordinary things, Ana. A master Pathfinder who went *deliberately* into the Between – the only Pathfinder ever to do so and survive. All those Fallen, previously lost, Shinigami found there, warped into Reapers. Somehow,

Shinigami brought them under control and led them back out – like an obedient army.'

A wing folds over my heart. A dark dread.

Gabe points to the conservatory's glass roof. 'This madness, here in Ares, is a direct result of all that unnatural interference. The Order grows stronger. There are even rumours of Havens being attacked, which means the energy safeguarding us, millennia old, has been compromised. Even without the power of Kronos, Shinigami will soon be strong enough to sweep the Collective away. The multiverse is collapsing, Ana. We *must* do something and fast.'

'Yeah, but what?'

He looks at me. Hard. 'A master like Shinigami can only be defeated by something truly unique. An exceptional, singular weapon.'

My heart sinks. All eyes round the table fix on me. The feeling of being cornered rushes over me in a wave.

I stand up, kick my chair back and put my hand on the hilt of my sword. 'That's not my problem. My problem is getting Bea back.'

'It's *everyone's* problem, Ana. If the multiverse goes, we all go.'

'Can she not see the gravity of the situation?' Silver-hair demands.

'She is headstrong!' someone else yells. 'She will learn. She *must*.'

'Enough!' I shout, drawing the sword, flashing it through the air.

'Whoa! Easy,' Gabe says, rising from his seat. 'OK, I get it. You're angry. And that's good. We need you to be angry. We need this Ana Moon.'

'You don't need me,' I spit back at him. 'You've got Mother. Go to her. Get *her* help, if she's so bloody marvellous.'

'We would,' Gabe says, 'but she gave *you* the sword, Ana. That means something.'

'This isn't my fight, Gabe.'

'Shinigami must be stopped.'

I pause. Breathe. 'What are you asking me to do?'

Gabe's eyes flick to the glass roof. 'There's a fortress,' he says. 'A pyramid. It floats above Paris Nouveau, in Venetia.'

'That's where they've taken Bea!' I say, remembering Mother's words. *To Venetia, above Paris Nouveau ... to the Seventh Gate.* 'Let's go. We'll storm the place.'

'I am afraid it does not work that way,' Silver-hair says.

'Why the hell not?' I demand, turning to him.

'Spies,' Gabe says. 'The Collective has been infiltrated in almost every part of every world. We could never organize an attack without Shinigami hearing of it. Every Reaper, every Pathfinder in the Order, would be waiting, and there aren't enough of us to face them head-on.' No one speaks. Gabriel bunches his fists. 'The Collective is being hunted. We're being exterminated. And, with every one of our Pathfinders killed, Shinigami becomes more of a god.'

'Not a god,' aquiline-nosed woman says. 'A devil.'

Gabe looks at her and then at me. 'So you see we must do this delicately.'

'Then what's the plan?'

'There's an object,' he continues. 'Ancient and coveted by our kind. We call it the Wraith. Someone in Tir is keeping it safe. You'll need this artefact before you can even think about going to Venetia. It's a vial of blood from the first Reaper ever killed, and its scent allows you to pass under their noses undetected. You'll be imperceptible – a clownfish hiding among the anemones, immune to their deadly poison.'

'A *clownfish*?'

'Yeah. You know, like Nemo. That little orange –'

'I know what a clownfish is. I just . . . it's a weird simile.'

He shrugs. 'Beautiful and smart,' he says. 'A survivor. Anyway, the Wraith-keeper's been briefed. He's to hand it to you, and you alone, on the Council's authority. He'll be waiting for you in Tir. Malik knows where. He'll take you.'

'This Wraith-keeper, is he a Pathfinder?'

Gabe shakes his head. 'No.'

'Then why would he care about your authority?'

'Because we funded his escape from persecution. But that's another story. All you need know is this: his loyalty is secure.'

'And after?' I ask, unconvinced. 'After I get this Wraith? What then?'

'We'll create a diversion in one of the other worlds,' he says. 'Draw the Order's attention away from you.

Meanwhile, your clan – Kuji, Malik and Vidhan – they'll take you all the way to the lion's den.' His smile fades. 'Getting inside, finding Bea – and the rest – that's down to you. You'll know what to do, and how, when the time comes.'

'The *rest*?'

'Malik told me about your . . . *exchange* with Graziani. The way you managed to retrieve your sword. No easy feat from that bastard.'

'I shouldn't have let him have it in the first place.'

'Look, man, you made a mistake,' Gabe says. 'You won't again.'

I sit there, saying nothing.

'You were given that sword and your powers for a reason, Ana. You'll need to discover them – *all* of them – and learn to use them. Not just for Bea but for all of us.' Gabe strokes his chin and looks at me. 'Your situation, this thing with Bea, it presents an opportunity. They wanted to snatch you before you knew who you really are, but they messed up. And, because of that, you're a ghost. You can be anywhere and everywhere. So now you will go to them unseen. On your terms. On our terms.'

A knot tightens in my gut. 'Just say it. What are you expecting me to do?'

'Isn't it obvious?' he replies.

'Tell me. I need to hear the words.'

He pauses. Holds my gaze.

'Ana,' he says. 'We want you to kill Shinigami.'

27

I stand in a room that's square and tidy. The floors are varnished wooden parquet and the four beds are neatly made with white linen. We're on the first floor and there are two windows, which give on to a red dystopia. Beyond the glass, flakes of ash swirl in a gaudy, atomic light. My bed – the bed I'm ushered to by Malik – is next to a window and a few paces away from Akuji. Vidhan and Malik move to the other side of the room. I sit on the mattress in silence, trying not to think about what Gabe told me. Instead, I think about the person – the *girl* – who might have slept here before me.

There are worse places, a voice says in my head.

Akuji.

She sits on the edge of her own bed and watches me coolly. Behind her, Malik and Vidhan exit the room, towels in hand, and the door clicks shut.

Akuji falls to her knees and turns to face the bed, like she's about to pray or something, but instead she pulls out a drawer. In it she places her fighting sticks and slams it shut. Then she stands up and drops her clothes. She's nothing but muscle and bone, and the split second before I turn away I see a tattoo – a line of secret symbols driven into her bloodless skin that travel up the side of her ribcage.

I strip down to my underwear as fast as possible, feeling self-conscious. When I turn round, pulling down my cotton vest, I find her gazing right at me. She's barefoot, wearing a pair of grey tights and a white V-neck T-shirt. Ironic words, in black, are emblazoned across her chest.

SLEEP WHEN YOU'RE DEAD

What did they tell you? she demands. The shape of the words snaps through the air. The fact that I can hear them – *feel* them – still throws me.

'No big deal,' I say. 'Just that getting my friend back is important or, you know, the whole multiverse will end.'

She stares at me, no expression in her marble-pale eyes.

'Can I ask you something?' I say.

You just have.

'Can *you* hear what *I'm* thinking? Like I can hear you?'

She shakes her head. *You must isolate the words first. Free them.*

'How do I do that?'

Choose the word. In your head.

'Any word?'

Think of it. Think of nothing else. Take all the noise in your head, everything that is not the word, and black it out. Leave only the word.

I focus. I take a deep breath and I think about a word. One word.

Akuji stares at me and I stare back at her. The room is still and the word is bright in my head. A jewel. Nothing else. Just the word.

Simple, Akuji thinks to me, without hesitation. *Issi.*

I nod slowly, impressed and more than a little scared. 'She was Malik's girlfriend, wasn't she?'

What makes you say that?

'Intuition.'

Akuji smiles. I run my hand through my hair, feeling exposed. A bar of red light falls across her jawline. Her eyes sink into shadow.

'I'm taking her place,' I say. 'And you don't like it.'

Akuji just looks at me.

The air in the room feels thick. Outside, the ash floats down unabated. A neon light flickers.

'Something bad happened to her, didn't it?'

She became lost, Akuji thinks to me.

'Lost?'

Between.

'How?'

It happens. Some Fall between worlds. They do not return. Not the same. Falling . . . it can break you. Make you into something else.

Akuji turns, climbs into her bed and rolls on to her side away from me. Like hot breath on cold glass, the moment quickly fades. Her voice vanishes from my head.

I crawl into my own bed. Weary, tired to the bone. The sheets are stiff and cold.

I don't see Malik and Vidhan re-enter the room, but I hear them. Drawers open and close and then the light dims and I hear a few mumbled words and clothes being shed. Then someone comes pattering over in socks to my bedside and murmurs my name.

'Ana? You awake?'

I roll my head on the pillow. Malik. Murderously beautiful in the garish red light. 'I spoke with Gabe,' he says. 'He told me everything.'

I look at him and try to speak. My body is lead. My eyelids are heavy.

'I'm tired,' is all I manage, voice fading.

Truth is, I'm way beyond tired. I'm shattered. Every muscle in my body hungers for that dark descent. That annihilation of my senses.

'Good,' Malik says. 'Sleep. We've got a long journey ahead. We'll wake early, head south towards France and meet the Wraith-keeper along the way. In Tir.'

28

I'm floating. Flying! I throw out my arms and shout at the cobalt sky and the high moon, then break through a bank of clouds and see land below. Great swathes of white sand and dark mountains. Desert. I slam into another wall of cloud and spin out of control. When I blast out the other side, the land has changed. A forest now, thick and green. I'm drifting over the canopy where wreathes of mist flow between the branches.

I crash through another cloud and I'm whipped by the wind, flipped upside down. Then I'm out the other side again, and here the land is menacing and nightmarish. I fly over scorched earth, over skeletal trees and scree. Freezing air cuts across my face. A river snakes through the cinders and I see an island in the middle of the river. Above, a giant pyramid looms, shining gold in the sun. From the mouth of the pyramid extends a ramp and here I see a circle of Reapers, pink and bony, their wings torn and frayed and folded to their backs. They enclose a figure in a hooded white cloak, their eyes and face in shadow. The figure lifts something to the sky and the Reapers rock and screech and I see the offering now – pale skin, near luminous against the ash-blackness.

Bea!

The figure in the hooded cloak turns its head, as if listening, sensing a disturbance in the air and I know – I *know* – it's *me* it feels. Its head swivels towards me. I can't see the eyes but I know they see me.

It points and the Reapers let out a wild cry. *SKRAAA-AAAAAAAAAAAAAAAAAAAAAAAAAAAAAAK!*

They launch into the air, beat their wings and come for me.

It's just a dream. They won't reach me. It'll be OK. It will.

I'm wrong. They keep coming and coming and I shout in fear and horror. It's no use. When they slam into me, I feel their hooks and their teeth and their claws, ripping, gouging, tearing me to shreds.

29

'Wake up, Ana. We gotta go.' The voice is far away.

'Ana!'

All right. OK. Lemme alone.

Someone's shaking me. Hands on my shoulders.

Lemme go!

I try to throw them off but they hold me tight. I open my eyes and see Malik's face close to mine. His dark eyes wild and fierce.

'Ana! We gotta go. C'mon. Now!'

I sit upright, blinking, trying to get my bearings. The window lets a stream of red moonlight into the room. The door is closed. I see the four beds arranged round four walls and I can see Vidhan sitting up, putting on his glasses, and Akuji, nearest me, already out of her bed and half dressed. Outside, someone shouting.

'C'mon!' Malik urges, throwing my yellow hoodie on the bed.

'What's going on?' I ask groggily.

'Reapers,' he says. 'They've found us. Quick, get your gear. Hurry.'

Tiredness curdles into bright fear. I remember the dream. The claws and hooks ripping into me, tearing me apart.

I leap out of bed, high on adrenalin, not even caring I'm half naked. But he's not looking. No one's looking. The tension in the room is palpable. I hear a scream from down the corridor. Doors slamming, footsteps drumming on floorboards, people yelling. Crashing noises. Thumps and bangs. It's as if the place is being ransacked.

'We can't use the front door,' Malik hisses when we're dressed and ready. All four of us alert and wide-eyed. 'We'll have to go up to the roof,' he says. 'There's an emergency ladder back there. We can climb down. C'mon!'

Vidhan, Akuji and I grab our weapons and follow. Malik opens the door a crack, scans the landing and waves us through.

'Move. Go!'

We jog down to the end of the corridor and thunder up the limestone staircase. The noise behind us is frightening and close. Blood-chilling screams. A carrion stink in the air. We haul ourselves up another flight of stairs to the third floor.

Malik throws open a fire exit at the end of the corridor and we step out into the freezing pre-dawn air. Malik is last through. We slide and skim along the icy cement, outside the conservatory this time. Chimney stacks rise black against the sky.

I can see other figures struggling across the flat rooftop, ducking and diving for cover. And then I see why. Reapers.

Two of them, circling. One turns in the sky, heaves upward, checks and dives towards us.

'Hit the deck!' Malik yells. His breath is smoke.

We throw ourselves down in the red shadows and freeze. The Reaper gusts over us.

That's when I see a man standing upright and tall on the roof, pistol drawn. With fluid ease, he turns and follows the Reapers in the sky and, while turning, unleashes a hail of gunfire with absolute precision. I see who it is now.

Gabe.

'Go!' he shouts at us. 'Get to the bikes below!'

Then disaster. In slow motion, I see it. A third Reaper, unseen by Gabe. It hammers down out of a pall of red ash and, in a violent gust of wings, swoops.

'GABE!' Malik yells. Too late.

Gabe turns at the last second, off balance. Then he runs, explodes full tilt across the roof – across the ice.

And he slips.

His arms windmill desperately. The Reaper cries out, extends its claws in front of its body – an eagle on a rabbit – and plucks Gabe off the roof, jerks his kicking body into the air. Gabe cocks and fires his pistol, but the Reaper knocks it from his hand with a wild slash of its wing.

Malik drops to one knee and shoots. One. Two. Three shots.

Blam! Blam! Blam!

The slugs pummel the Reaper – it screeches and flails and its claws retract.

Gabe drops. As he falls, his robe flaring, Malik fires off round after round. The Reaper shudders and wallows in the air. It shrieks and plunges over the side of the building.

Gabe – with an awful *thunk* – slams into the rooftop.

He doesn't move.

'Go! Go! GO!' Malik yells at us, pointing to the edge of the roof.

We race to the edge of the building and throw ourselves behind a low parapet.

Malik skids away from us.

He slides up to Gabe. He puts his hand to his wrist – a second, two seconds – then presses his ear to Gabe's chest. He jerks himself away, then punches the ice.

'No!' he screams. In one movement, he stands, raises his gun, slams back the hammer with his palm and begins firing shot after shot at the other circling Reaper. I watch in amazement as the Reaper is hit again and again and again. It bellows in pain and turns and comes at him. My heart constricts. I get up to go to him, but Akuji throws her arm in front of me. I struggle against her but it's no use. The Reaper, searing in, gives a terrifying wail and crashes into the rooftop, coming to a sliding stop centimetres from Malik, who levels his gun at its pink head and fires the fatal bullet. Then he turns and, without looking at Gabe's supine body, joins us at the roof edge. Wordlessly, sweat pouring from him, he unbolts a black ladder with Akuji's help and slams it down the side of the building.

We leap on to the ladder, one after the other, and scramble down. Three storeys below, on the roadside, we steal through the shadows, hugging the walls. We find an iron gate and Malik waves his hand over a screen and the metal slides open. We slink past him into the gloom of an underground parking space.

The screams die. All we hear now is the squeak of our shoes on cement.

There's a row of hover-bikes, just like the Dyson Thunderbird. Malik jumps on one, Akuji commandeers a second and Vidhan a third. He points to the bike next to him. 'This one,' he says. 'It's automatic.'

I snatch a leather jacket from a hook on the wall. Then I leap on to the saddle and turn the key already in the ignition. I grab hold of the handlebars. The bike shudders, makes a guttural, throaty sound. Then it slides a little and settles on a cushion of air. I pull on the helmet hooked over the handlebar. Immediately, the sound is muted. Far away.

The others streak off and I pull back the throttle with my right hand and the motor *whumps* and a hot blast of air slams out behind me. I belt after them. We slam through the parking space, thump up the ramp and blast out on to the road, fishtailing across the tarmac. We pull low through corners and bomb fast on the straights. I turn my head to my shoulder and see no sign of Reapers following. I hold on with everything I've got, feeling the solid strength of the bike under me. Malik flies ahead. Then Akuji, followed by me and Vidhan. Fear hammers a frantic urgency into the way I ride. But the bike goes easily, smoothly, the gears shifting automatically. All I need to do is brake, accelerate and steer through the wrecked city of Londra.

We hit the waterless Thames and throw ourselves left on to Embankment. We follow the river east, past Waterloo Bridge, Temple and Blackfriars.

The names are the same, the buildings aren't. On the opposite side of the river, I see the Bankside Power Station, which in Sol is the Tate Modern art museum. Here it's a hard-working power plant, pumping giant clouds of white effluent into the air. We skim past the Tower of London, reduced almost to rubble. Tower Bridge is a wreck. Parts of the structure have sheared away and lie mangled in the putrid waters below. We blast onwards, past a stinking dump with seagulls wheeling in the sky, then sink into a deserted tunnel. In the dark, the engines roar and the tunnel walls make a cocoon of the sound.

Soon we're up and out on the other side and we fly away from the city. We hit a two-lane road that skirts a bleak series of grim suburbs. We're heading south now, towards the Channel – and France – far away.

We float over warped and buckled cement. Frozen weeds thrust up from fissures and cracks half a metre wide in places, but we glide uninterrupted over the broken surface, leaving eddies of mist in our wake. We pass few other vehicles, some clusters of tents on the roadside – refugee camps, I imagine. People fleeing the fighting. I duck my head lower, out of the freezing wind, and push my body up against the bike for heat. I think, *We've made it – we're home free.*

And then the bike's engine chokes.

Malik rises off his haunches and kicks my bike's undercarriage as he blows out his cheeks. They're smeared with grease. His eyes are so dark, they're almost black.

'Kaput,' he says, not looking at me, a grim expression on his face. He works his jaw as if he's clenching his teeth. 'No damn Thunderbird,' he says.

'So we share,' I tell him. 'Two on one, like before.'

Malik clicks his neck. He looks at the road. He looks at the bikes. He arches his neck and scans the sky. The ash has stopped falling. His eyes travel to the horizon, across a frozen field of wind-beaten plant stalks. He takes a deep breath and exhales.

'No,' he says finally. 'They'll be looking for us on bikes anyway. We ditch 'em here.'

'Malik . . .' I say, searching for words. But I'm robbed of them.

Gabe is dead. He was alive an hour ago and now he's gone. The irreversible truth of it cuts into my gut. I see him falling, smacking into the roof. The appalling sound. The stillness after. Everything in the multiverse, until this moment, has seemed unreal – a dream. But now it's something else altogether.

No one speaks. Above us, the clouds gather.

Vidhan polishes his glasses. He stoops to lift a stone and hurls it across the road, jerking his skinny arm. He gathers more and throws them. *Thwack! Thwack!*

Every stone hits its mark – the trunk of a dead tree.

Thwack! Another ricochets away.

He stands still and lets the stones fall from his hand. They scatter over the broken asphalt. 'Those fuckin Reapers,' he says, staring at the road.

'They're Reapers,' Malik says. 'They don't care about us. They don't care about Gabe. There *is* no damn revenge. Not against them.'

'Shinigami will pay,' Vidhan says, wiping the corners of his eyes with the heel of his palm. 'Graziani too. They'll taste my blade, those bastards.'

Malik pulls out his pistol. He shakes his head – violently, as if he's been caught in the rain – and points his weapon at the broken bike. Gives it a hard, thousand-yard stare. He leaps in the air, wheels, hammers the bike with a crunching reverse-kick. It crashes down, parts flying.

Malik shouts, letting loose a gut-wrenching, despairing sound from a deep well of pain.

He drops his arms and takes a long breath. His chest rises and falls.

Then he reholsters his unfired gun, ice-calm again, and he points south-east across the fields. 'That way,' he says. 'To the pathways and to Tir.'

30

We cover the bikes – camouflaging them with dirt and leaves and branches – and set out across the field. Rows of hollow plant stalks rise to my midriff, covered in rinds of ice that shatter when kicked. The air is brittle. We cut through the field at a swift pace. Malik leads. Then me. Then Vidhan and Akuji. The frozen mud underfoot makes it slow going. My teeth clench against the cold.

Above us, apart from clouds, the sky is clear. No sign of Reapers. I switch off and let my feet carry me. I run my hands, palms down, through the stalks and they come away wet. I follow Malik's flattened trail, without speaking, without thinking.

Vidhan walks up alongside me. He slaps his hands together, cups them and breathes into them. His breath smokes. The cold is to the bone. We trudge side by side, wordlessly.

Malik is far ahead, out of earshot. Akuji flanks us, scouting out wide to the right.

'Whatsamatter?' Vidhan says to me. 'You ain't askin questions no more?'

'I'm done asking questions,' I say.

Vidhan sniffs and spits. 'Bloody Gabe,' he says. 'He was one of the good guys.'

'He was trying to protect us,' I say, flipping up the collar of my leather bike jacket. 'Making sure we got away.'

'He was a Pathfinder,' Vidhan says. 'Doing what was he born to do.'

'It's my fault, Vidhan. If it wasn't for me –'

'Don't,' Vidhan says, looking at me. His eyes are magnified behind his glasses. 'Don't get swallowed up in that blame game. Ain't nobody's fault. Got me?'

'Yeah,' I tell him, listening to my feet crunch. 'I got you.'

'Gotta stay sharp, Ana. Keep it together. Only gets harder from here.'

Gabe's disembodied voice hammers in my head. Six hard words.

We want you to kill Shinigami.

I take a deep breath. The cold air hits my chest like a hammer. I stare at Malik up ahead. His head swivels from side to side, endlessly scanning the field and the sky.

'He's different round you,' Vidhan says, observing my gaze. I say nothing. Keep walking.

Vidhan shrugs. He lifts his glasses and cleans them on his shirt. 'I always thought his heart was gone. That, if ya cut him, you'd find nothin inside. He'd be hollowed out. But now . . . with you . . .'

Vidhan falls silent.

'Bad things have happened to him,' I say. 'I can see it. Terrible things.'

Vidhan pushes his glasses up the bridge of his nose and sniffs. 'Hell. Terrible things have happened to all of us. Me? I choose to forget.' He quickens his pace and marches away.

'Vidhan, wait!' I breathe hard and hurry after him, but he doesn't break stride and so I let him go.

A lone oak tree – around which a farmer has ploughed concentric circles, now frosted and hard – stands like a sentinel in the field. Isolated. Nothing else into the distance. We decide to rest here, to rehydrate. Akuji stands away from the tree, stone-silent, eyes sweeping the horizon. Vidhan, hopping from foot to foot, disappears into the field of stalks. I slump down with my back against the tree's rough trunk and pull my knees to my chest. Ice particles swirl through the air. My legs and feet ache. I'm wrung out, exhausted from the walking. It feels like I've been slogging through this field for hours, but it could easily be minutes. Time has lost all meaning.

Malik leans up against the tree. He slides down next to me, roots through the backpack he's been carrying and pulls out his canteen. He hands it to me. I throw back my head and drink. Instantly, I feel the Firewater do its warming work.

'Thanks,' I mumble, wiping my mouth, pressing the canteen back into his hand. Malik doesn't respond. I listen to his breathing, feel the heat steaming off his body. He takes a slug of Firewater and swallows. Sets the canteen down.

Silence.

I stare at the toes of my Stan Smiths – battered and brown and sodden.

'Two years,' Malik says, breaking the quiet. 'That's all. That's how long I knew him. But that's a lifetime in the multiverse.' He puts his hand flat on the ground, close to his hip, and the tips of his splayed fingers almost touch mine.

The sun shines down on us, but I can't feel its heat.

'I liked him,' is all I manage.

Malik sucks his teeth. 'He was a mentor,' he says. 'An older brother.'

I nod and look across the field. 'I'm sorry, Malik. I really am. And . . . about all the others too. People like Issi.'

Malik gives me a sharp look and then his eyes slide away. 'What do you know about Issi?'

'I know I've taken her place,' I say.

'Leave it,' he says. 'She's gone, Ana.'

'I know. But –'

'But nothing. There's nothing we can do about it. She's gone and so is Gabe. *Gone.* All we can do now is fight. Because, if we don't, their deaths mean nothing.'

He falls silent. The cold knifes into my chest. Malik blows out a breath and coughs. I look at his profile and I see, in the tight line of his jaw, the pain.

Without thinking, I put my hand over his. It just happens. He doesn't move.

I look away, feeling self-conscious, heart in my throat.

We watch Akuji. She's hauled out her fighting sticks and is practising her moves fluidly, faultlessly. A warrior-dancer.

I don't see how anyone stands a chance against her. We sit like this a long time, not speaking.

My hand on Malik's. His under mine.

Malik makes no move to shift away, nor does he take my hand in his. I feel the moment requires me to say something profound. But the words I find are banal. 'So, uh . . . you're from Sol's London.'

Pins and needles spike and burn in my hand. I feel the sweat on his skin, on *mine*, the heat between us. Skin on skin. The strangeness is dizzying.

'Yup,' he says. 'I'm from London.'

'Whereabouts?'

'The wrong side of the tracks. Didn't go to some fancy school or own a pony.'

'A *pony*?'

'You ride. You're good at it. I saw the trophies.'

'You do that a lot? Snoop round girls' bedrooms?'

'Not so much. And you let me in, remember?'

'I don't *own* a pony. I muck out a stable outside the city, that's all.'

'Either way,' he says. 'I'm sure you know what you're doing.' He coughs again. My hand throbs. I swear I can feel the blood beating under his skin.

'Maybe I'll take you there one day,' I blurt.

He looks at me. His eyes are as dark as gunpowder.

'Well,' he says, 'maybe I'll let you.'

Then he moves his hand from under mine and runs it over his jaw.

Damn it.

'So . . . wrong side of the tracks,' I say, trying to salvage the connection, pulling my hand back to my side. It feels like a dead weight.

'Life was good and bad,' Malik says. He glances at me, glances away.

'Well, you can have mine,' I say, curling my hair behind my ear.

'You don't like your life?'

'You haven't met my stepdad. His name's *Dave.*'

'What's wrong with that?'

'Are you serious? I mean, c'mon. He wears corduroy, for chrissakes.'

Malik laughs and I make a mental note to make that happen again.

'And then there's my *other* stepdad . . . Gad. He's a hippie. Not your common-garden-type either. Top of the range. A nudist.'

Malik pauses, then softly asks, 'But does he love you?'

'Gad? Well, yeah. I mean . . . I suppose so, but –'

'You don't get it, do you?'

'Get what?'

Malik looks at me and the humour snuffs out in his eyes and his smile fades. And the whole feeling of the conversation wheels from light to dark.

'My father's dead,' Malik says. 'I watched him die. I watched them both die.'

It stuns me. And I think, *I'm an idiot.*

Malik rolls his neck. I hear the bones click.

'Malik, I . . . I didn't –'

'You wanna know how?' he says.

'Only if –'

'That car accident I told you about? When I Fell for the first time. I didn't really Fall *because* of the accident. I Fell *after* the accident. After I saw.'

He takes a breath. Lets it out.

'I was in the back,' he says. 'Mum and Dad were up front. Mum was driving.' He smiles bitterly. 'Dad . . . he hated being a passenger. He was hassling Mum, same as ever. Slow down, Nayla! Get in the left lane, Nayla! The road's wet, Nayla!'

Malik picks up a stone and chucks it into the field.

'He could be a real pain in the arse sometimes.'

He pauses and I become aware I'm holding my breath. And when I suck in the air and blow it out, it sounds unnatural – makes a loud roaring in my ears.

'They didn't see the lorry until it was too late,' Malik says. 'Too busy arguing, trying to be right. By the time Mum saw it, she had seven seconds left to live. And, the worst of it is, I should've died with 'em. But I didn't. Know why?'

I shake my head, despite knowing the answer.

'Because I'm a Pathfinder. I Fell instead,' Malik says. 'That's why.'

I can't speak. I don't make a sound. I'm numb.

Eventually, after what seems like an age, I turn to him. 'Malik,' I say. 'They want me to kill Shinigami.'

Malik squints into the distance. 'I know. Gabe took me aside. He told me.'

I drag my hand through the dirt. 'I don't think I can do that.'

Malik nods, considering my answer. 'Pathfinders like us,' he says, 'we're the ones that run. We run away from the past and we run away from Reapers. We're nomads and wanderers. Misfits and outsiders. I mean, look at Vidhan. His foster-parents chucked him in an asylum for a year. And Kuji? She's been through enough juvenile-detention centres to last two lifetimes. What they did to her in those places, it'd break a Normal in a day.'

I watch Akuji pace up and down, straight-backed, her fighting sticks in their scabbards again, spiking at her belt. I look at Malik side-on and I realize that what I knew about him – about *them* – I could've written on the back of a postage stamp.

'But the thing of it is this,' Malik says. 'We're part of something much bigger than ourselves. We do things and see things no Normal could ever imagine or believe. We have a job. It makes a difference. It matters.' He turns to me and we look at each other. 'The good and the bad,' he says. 'It's a gift, Ana. And it's a curse.'

Vidhan reappears out of the bushes and the moment breaks.

Akuji fake lunges at Vidhan and he sidesteps her in a blur of speed. He laughs and then comes and leans against the tree and looks down at us.

'Ready to go?' he says.

And I feel it then. The burn of Malik's name tattooed on my heart.

31

'Pathways,' Vidhan says, jerking his thumb over his shoulder. 'I was takin a piss back there and saw 'em. Not far to go.'

I recall something Malik told me, a long time ago, in Lūna.

There are pathways. Gateways from one world to the next. We find them. Keep them safe and free.

But, when I squint in the direction Vidhan's pointing, I see nothing.

Vidhan laughs and shakes his head. 'Mate! Ya still bloody haven't read that chapter on Falling, have ya?'

'You tell me when I've had the time, Vidhan.'

'Falling,' Malik says, standing, using the tree as leverage, 'doesn't happen for no reason. When you first Fall, the pathways are invisible, but afterwards you begin to see them. And, when *that* happens, you'll never un-see them. They're like the Northern Lights – they come and go, never in exactly the same place. And they move, like air currents. And, like currents, we feel them pull.'

I grab hold of his extended hand and he jerks me to my feet.

'Come on,' he says 'You'll see.'

Malik stands with his arms by his sides. He closes his eyes and tilts his face to the sky. Akuji and Vidhan do the same. We're standing in the middle of the field. All around us the stalks lie flattened. A single flake of ash whirls down from somewhere far above and lands on Malik's cheek. He brushes it away absently and, when he opens his dark eyes, they burn with intensity.

'There!' he says, pointing above. I follow his gaze.

The Ares sky is apocalyptic, the colour of rusted metal . . . and it's empty. A faraway bank of storm clouds, that's all. And a crimson smudge of rain.

Do you see it? Malik's voice blooms in my head.

'I don't see anything,' I say, scanning the sky.

'A shimmering,' he says aloud. 'Like heat waves.'

'It's freezing!'

'Look with your mind,' he counters. 'Close your eyes and *feel* them.'

So I stand the same way he does, arms by my sides. And I close my eyes. I concentrate on the velvety darkness behind my eyelids.

Nothing.

Then a change. Suddenly I feel a density in the air – a weight – tugging and swirling around me. And it's not the wind. I begin to realize I'm able, if I concentrate, to isolate – to *feel* – each particle of air vibrating and moving. *Pulling.*

215

'Now look,' Malik says. 'Open your eyes and see.'

I flick them open and I see a shimmering. Heat waves. A blurry current flowing upward like a vertical river rising into the sky, so clear now that I wonder how it's possible I never saw it before. And, woven through it, a trembling blue light.

An urge to run and leap flutters in my stomach.

And then Akuji does just that.

She sprints forward and hurls herself into the air, and I stare in shock and wonder as she keeps rising. It's as if an invisible wire is attached to her back, hauling her up. She's high in the air now, arms outflung. The air quivers around her. She floats, hair fanning out, clothes loose. Then she begins to disintegrate.

She breaks into a million particles that whirl upward and away. And disappear. Akuji is gone.

Vidhan laughs and then *he's* running, so fast he's a blur.

'Catch ya on the other side!' he cries.

He leaps into the air and shoots up into it, a kite pulled on a string. Then he's floating. And then he's falling apart. Spirals of him, like dust, swirl up from his body. He's coming undone, becoming smoke. And he's gone.

Malik turns to me. 'Your turn,' he says.

'But –'

'Don't worry,' he says. 'I'll be right behind you. We'll Fall through and land in the same location ... just in a parallel world. Tir. It's like running out of a sauna and diving into a freezing lake. Except more or less the other way round – Tir is as hot as hell. I'll pick you up on the other side and we'll find the Wraith-keeper. You can do this, Ana. One state to another. That's all.'

'One state to another,' I repeat. 'Piece of cake.'

'Exactly.'

'Except I've never run from a sauna into a lake. I mean, I'm not Finnish. Can't you think of anything more –'

The scream cuts me short.

SKRRRAAAAAAAAAAAAAAAAAAAAAAAAK!

Malik squares his shoulders. His hand flies to his hip and he draws his pistol. A shadow passes over the sun and dread runs in my blood.

RUN! shouts a voice in my head. I don't stop to ask where. I run.

Fear. It guides me low and quick through the field. I don't look back. I run. It's a crouching, stumbling, awkward kind of run. I forget to look up at the sky. I forget to fling myself upward. I simply keep moving.

A shadow ripples over the field. I feel the heavy beat of wings, a gust of air. Then I catch a root and slam into the ground. My shoulder crunches into hard ridges of ploughed earth. I reach for the sword, roll on to my back – steel myself for whatever comes.

A shape looms. The plants are thrust aside and . . . It's Malik, brandishing his gun.

'Get up, quick!' he yells. 'There's a burnt-out barn back there.' He hauls me to my feet and points straight ahead. 'C'mon! Go! GO!'

He runs. I follow. We explode through the plants into a wide firebreak, long and straight between two rows of wind-hammered stalks. Ahead, I see the charred hulk. The wreck of a hay barn maybe. Its slate roof shattered, ash-black beams naked to the sky.

I feel a stitch in my side, like a broken rib. It's screaming at me to stop running. I steal a look back over my shoulder and I see it.

Panic slices through me.

The Reaper wheels – and, oh God, it comes.

'MALIK!' I yell.

'Go! Go! GO!' Malik shouts over his shoulder.

We sprint along the firebreak towards the burnt-out barn. Malik streaks ahead. He runs lightly, on his toes. I'm losing ground, falling back. I know the Reaper's gaining on me. Then I feel a pull, a weight tugging me backwards into oblivion.

There's a putrid smell. A stench of rot. It descends. I feel it. And I know – I *know* – I'm not going to make it.

Malik must sense it too, because he stops running and turns, wide-eyed.

My fingers reach for the hilt of Ra, but it's too late. It feels like a ton of bricks slams into me, and I face-plant.

I can't move. I'm pinned to the ground, squashed under a massive weight. My face is mashed into the ice and dirt. Stones cut into my cheeks and I taste coppery blood in my mouth. Lightning pain shoots down my back. Something burning-sharp pierces skin and muscle.

So this is it then. This is how I die.

My body slumps. I'm numb. In shock. The world begins to spin and blur. I hear a voice far away, down a tunnel.

'Let her go!'

I'm plucked off the ground and jerked into the air – a savage pull.

I try to block out the pain and narrow my focus to one thing: getting rid of the Reaper on me. I force myself to breathe.

Stay calm, Ana. Think!

Heat pumps round my body. An energy surges through me, fingertips to toes. I clench my fists and, at the top of my voice, I scream. Then I twist my shoulders round. The Reaper screeches and I feel its hooks ripping out my skin.

I fight through waves of agony, and I feel the last hook tear out of my flesh. Then I drop, but something clamps round my ankle and I jerk and swing.

The Reaper's claw. Like a vice.

Ana, the SWORD! Use your sword.

I'm upside down in the air, dangling, arms hanging. The sky is above.

Ra clatters against my chest in its scabbard. I try to pull it out, but it spins away. The blood rushes to my head and pounds. I kick and I shout but it's no use.

A rough yank at my ankle triggers a fresh wave of panic and I hook one leg over the other to stabilize myself. I know what's happening. It's carrying me. It's flying me away like some roadkill snatched up by a vulture.

I have a vague sense of someone below charging after us, but I'm spinning, losing consciousness. Over a buzzing in my ears, I hear the double blast of a gun.

Blam! Blam!

Something cuts through the air with a sharp whine. A wet *thunking* sound and I feel a spray of blood. I hear the gun firing again and again and again. The Reaper screams and beats its wings, and I jerk violently.

It's freezing. Flakes of snow swirl round me. The light is silvery and the air seems to wobble. I'm thrown about like a ragdoll. And, incredibly, that's when my hand bangs into Ra.

Focus, I think to myself. *Focus on surviving.*

I grab hold and pull it from the scabbard in one clean move. Using every ounce of strength in me, I stab it hard upward into the pink-skinned, black-veined underbelly of the beast. Hot blood gushes over me.

The Reaper howls. And, as I feel the claws retract, the world turns dark.

Gravity pulls, sucks me down. And then releases.

I lift.

I float.

I Fall.

It is the mercurial nature of **TIR**, the fourth realm, that confounds Pathfinders Fallen into this world. First located by the Persian mathematician, philosopher, poet – and Pathfinder – **OMAR KHAYYÁM**. Many say his poems invoke the multiverse, Tir in particular:

Oh threats of Hell and Hopes of Paradise!
One thing at least is certain – *This* Life flies;
One thing is certain and the rest is Lies –
The Flower that is once blown forever dies.

TIR

32

Pain. White-hot. It shoots up and down my back. My teeth throb in their gums and there's a buzzing in my ears. It feels like every bone in my body has been broken and reset wrong. And it's hot. Furnace-hot. I tear off my jacket and my hoodie and gasp. I try to stand, but the ground spins and I thump back down and lie there, stunned in the sudden heat, watching my breath blast up puffs of dust. The ground is chalky and white. I gaze at a crack splintering, forking away from me and try to organize my worming thoughts.

Malik – his gun firing. The Reaper – its pink, bony wings. I remember being jerked into the air. A vile stench. Then blankness. A blur. I lose the field and the sky and the Reaper and Malik below. The red sky, the freezing cold – everything goes. My head pounds.

Keep it together, Ana. Don't lose it.

I know where I am. Sol, then Lūna, then Ares. And then . . .

Tir.

I feel ill. I push myself up on to my knees and vomit. My back is raw and hot.

I see my bloodied sword in the dust and crawl to it, then rise unsteadily and tie the scabbard to my belt and thigh with shaking hands. I take my time with it, fighting waves of pain and nausea. Then I look up and blink in the sun's glare.

A white desert stretches away from me, boundless and bare. The ground is the colour of bone, like a salt pan. There isn't a tree or blade of grass anywhere. Far in the distance, a range of black-boulder mountains heave up to meet a gunmetal-blue sky.

I shield the sun's brightness with my hands and stumble towards the mountains. Soon there's no line between the land and the sky. The two merge in a watery blur – an infinity. I'm lost in a cloud.

I think about Mother's words.

Each world must be crossed before you reach . . . Kronos. It will not be easy and you will lose a piece of yourself to the Falling, but this is the path.

A sudden swirl of a dust – a mini tornado – and here, rising out of the wilderness, come a pair of lean figures warping in the heat haze. One with two fighting sticks, the other with a knife.

'Jesus,' Vidhan says, jogging towards me. 'What happened to you?'

'Where's Malik?' I ask, head spinning.

'Search me,' Vidhan says. 'The hell went down back there?'

'Reaper,' I say, finding it hard to breathe in the hot, thin air. 'It came after you Fell.' I turn, show them my back, swaying on my feet.

'You're bleeding,' Vidhan says, eyes swimming with concern. 'Gotta get that poison out fast.'

'I'm OK.'

'Nah, mate. You are *not* OK.'

Vidhan glances at Akuji and when I stumble they each grab one of my arms.

'Malik,' I whisper.

Akuji's voice snaps into my head. *He'll find us. He's Malik.*

I try to protest, but I can't find my voice. My legs are jelly.

'Come on,' says Vidhan.

The desert swims. Mountains, like colossal black bones, bear down on us. We weave between thick trees with fat, beet-coloured trunks and branches that fan like roots into a mercury sky. We pass under flat-topped umbrella trees, as tall as houses, like something out of an ancient, prehistoric land. They cast pools of pale shade. We stumble through the torrid heat. I feel blood, sticky on my back. The sun is a ring of white fire in the sky. I'm half awake, half dreaming, shuffling through a vast emptiness like a zombie. Floating in and out of consciousness. Here. Not here.

'There!' Vidhan cries, his voice swirling, rising from afar.

I squint into the warping distance. A light blinking in the sands. Jagged shapes – reflecting the sun – like mirrors.

*

We draw close to the wreck of what looks like a crashed aeroplane. The sun glints off its curved surface. Mangled seats – forgotten occupants long dead – lie strewn across the desert. The plane is sunk into drifts of white sand. Its windows are cracked and grimed. One wing has been sheared off. A wide hole is ripped in the side of the fuselage. I stare into the dark within, tense and guarded.

We step through the tear together, into a maw of blackness and hanging wires. The floor is a tip of debris and chunks of metal. And, between them, boot prints.

'HELLOOOOOOO!' Vidhan cries, cupping his hand to his mouth.

Helloooooo, Helloooooo, the empty space echoes back.

I slump down in a wrecked aeroplane seat with an exhausted grunt.

'Sit tight,' Vidhan says. 'It'll get cold soon. Gotta build a fire.'

He leaves me sprawled in the seat and starts sifting through the wreckage. Akuji, a silhouette against the twilight, stands guard at the hole in the side of the plane. The darkness reels.

The ground tilts.

I black out.

Fire. A blaze of orange. Sparks tumble up into the cold dark. Beyond the fire, faces. Huddled figures, wrapped up in cloaks and ponchos. A crown of feathers. Eyes gleaming. Weird shapes and the spit of the fire. Then darkness again.

*

Malik's face appears in front of me, lit amber by the fire. I can't tell if it's the fever playing tricks on me or if it's real.

Tell me it's you, Malik. Tell me it's not another dream.

He puts his hand on my wrist and I let him. I feel the warmth of his skin.

'It is you,' I whisper, my voice hoarse. 'It's really you.'

'Thought you could get rid of me?' He smiles. His eyes are dark pools, as dark as the far side of the moon.

'The Reaper,' I say, sitting upright.

'Dead,' he says.

Sparks are thrown up from the fire. They swirl through umbilical loops of wire, and out into a black night and the stars beyond. I see that I'm wearing my hoodie again and that it's dry now, trapping heat from the fire.

'We've Fallen into Tir,' Malik says. 'Not far from the nine runways of Gatwick Airport. It's a sea of discarded planes out here, for miles and miles.'

'And Vidhan? Akuji?'

'Went for more firewood. They'll be back.'

I find my sword leaning up against a chair. Clean of blood, as far as I can tell. I reach out and grab the handle, pull it to my side.

'Not bad,' Malik says, watching me. 'The way you gutted that thing mid-air.'

I turn the sword in my hand. I can still smell it – that awful intestinal stink. I can feel its claws and its hooks digging into me. A part of me wishes it wasn't dead. Wants to go back and find it, watch it suffer. A smarter part – the survivor – never wants to see a Reaper again.

I stab the sword into the ground and haul myself up out of the chair. Immediately, the ground lurches beneath me. I stumble into Malik and he tries to take my elbow, but I pull away. I'm tired of being helped. I rest my hands on my knees and wait for the spinning to pass.

'You were delirious in the night,' Malik says, watching me.

'Everything hurts,' I say, stretching upright.

'It will,' he says. 'Mind if I take a look at your back?'

I turn round and feel his cold fingers roll up the edge of my hoodie. Gently, he peels up my shirt. The air hits my exposed skin and I get goosebumps.

'What's it look like back there?'

He lets my shirt fall. 'It'll heal,' he says. 'But it'll take a few days at least. We'll have to stay here. To recover. And to train.'

I pull my hood down and step up to the rip in the side of the plane's hull. Outside, in the moonlight, through bent metal shards, I see a graveyard of planes and between them, huddled round fires in ponchos, fugitive figures.

'Hermits,' Malik says at my shoulder. 'Don't worry. You can trust 'em. I've been here many times before. They got the best medicines going. The one you'll meet, AM-41, he took a slug out of my leg once. Hardly left a scar.'

'They're with the Collective?' I ask.

Malik shrugs. 'They're mostly on our side. When they can be bothered.'

'I thought I dreamed them,' I say.

'They're real,' he says. 'Normals drove them out of the cities, claiming like should live with like.' He shakes his head. 'Different world, same old hate. But they're the right sort to hide something important.' Then he shakes his head and his eyes darken. 'I've known AM-41 for years, but even I had no idea he had the Wraith until Gabe told me. Hermits know how to keep a secret.'

I shiver and say nothing. Sword at my hip, I return to the fire. Then there's a blast of cold air and the dirt spins.

I look up to see Akuji and Vidhan, caked in dust and filthy, enter through the hole in the fuselage, carrying firewood bundled in their arms.

Behind them – in shadow – a tall, outlandish figure.

A hermit.

He wears a crown of what looks like crow feathers and a torn maroon poncho, long to the ground. His face is in shadow, but his eyes shine like lit blue torches in the gloom. And, through the poncho's tattered V-neck, I see metal against his skin. At first, I think it must be a suit of armour. Then I look closely at his face when he moves out of the shadow. *Metal.* All of it, metal.

'Ana!' Vidhan says, dumping the wood, laying his hand on the shoulder of his startling companion. 'This here's AM-41. He's a cyborg, but don't let that bloody scare ya. He saved your life. Best medicine man this side of the Seventh Gate.'

AM-41 presses his metal hands together. 'She be the one seeks the Wraith?' he says. His voice is clipped, impatient, run through with static.

'She's the one,' Vidhan says.

'On account of?'

'She's got the sword, 41. You can see it right there. She's carrying Ra. Gabe told you about her. He did, right?'

AM-41 nods. He makes a whirring, clicking, machine-like noise deep in his mysterious body. 'Know how to use that there blade?' he asks.

'She cut a Reaper out of the sky,' Malik says.

AM-41 drags a metal finger down his metal arm. Slowly. 'You got poison in the blood,' he says. 'Weren't for 41, you'd be six-foot deep, pushin' daisies.'

He's watching me, assessing me – deciding.

'I'm alive,' I say, sheathing the sword. 'And, if that's down to you, I'm grateful.' I look at him, then the others. 'I'm not ready for death.'

'No?' AM-41 says. 'Well, then I have something you're gonna need.'

33

'"There's one true thing you gonna need to know about the world, Buttercup," my dad always said.' I've heard this story countless times, but I let Bea continue anyway.

With twelve quid apiece, we're making our way to Cineworld. A horror movie we've been waiting for is finally here. But I'm beginning to think it's a mistake. Bea was in a mood at school, over a fight with her mum that culminated in Bea announcing she wished her mum had died and that her dad was the one alive.

That kind of hurt – delivered or received – sticks.

'What did he always say, your dad?' I ask.

'He said, "You come into this world alone and you go out alone".' Bea laughs ruefully. 'God, he was a miserable bastard.'

The conversation is growing bleaker by the minute and I'm starting to wonder whether we should cancel the film, head to the Old Man's roof and let the night slide. But *then maybe the movie will take her away, throw dark thoughts to the wind.*

'He's right, though,' I tell her. 'I mean, you know, technically.'

'Technically? *Say it ain't so, Moon. Say you don't believe that crap.*'

'But he is right. It is true.'

'It isn't even half true.'

'Bea –'

'No, listen. He was wrong. About everything. I mean, I loved him. I did. I'd give anything to see him again. Just for one minute. A second. I adored him. He could be wickedly funny. He took up so much space. But Dad . . . he saw monsters and shadows everywhere. And he never once faced them.'

'I feel like that sometimes,' I whisper. 'Like I'm . . . being closed in, chased by shadows.'

Bea stops walking, swivels, grabs me by the shoulders and turns me to face her. Her eyes, under the wedge of hair, swim with brightness. 'You're nothing like him,' she says. 'OK? Nothing. You're brave. Braver than me –'

'No. I'm not. I'm –'

'You're not like him, Moon. He was afraid. And, in the end, he deserted us. But that's not you. You'd never do that. You face your monsters. That's you.'

34

AM-41 wears the Wraith barely concealed under his poncho, looped on a simple chain round his neck. I had assumed an artefact of such legend would be under severe lock and key. Not so much. But it occurs to me, as he dips his head and unhooks the chain, that this is perhaps the best way to hide something rare – in plain sight.

He releases the clasp and drops the chain and the vial of blood – black in its tube of glass – into the palm of his metal hand. Then he extends it to me. His blue machine-eyes bore into me.

I step forward, reach for the vial, enclose it in my fist.

Deep in my body, the heat begins. A swirling, burning feeling from head to foot. It happens the moment my skin touches the vial. I slide the chain over my head and draw a sharp intake of breath. My heart thunders. My pulse roars.

Compelled by a sudden desire for open space, I step outside the plane, into the dawn. The world is different outside. Brighter. Stars burn like lit bonfires and the waxing moon is so fierce I can't look at it without a sharp pain in my eyes. And, low to the curving Earth, a ball of amber fire rises.

Malik comes to my side. Wordlessly, we climb up on to the wing of the shattered Boeing and walk to the end. We stand there and watch the sun climb, my eyes adjusting to the brightness.

Something inside me is waking up.

'Ana?' Malik says. 'You need to know something.'

'Oh?'

He sucks his cheeks. Looks away. 'I lied.'

'Lied about *what*?'

He turns to me again. 'That Reaper. The one you stuck. It's not dead.'

My stomach shrinks to the size of a fist. '*What*?'

'We caught it,' he says. 'And we brought it back here.'

'*Who* caught it?'

'Me. Kuji. AM-41. Some of the hermits.'

I wheel round. Look back at the fuselage of the plane.

'It Fell through with you,' Malik says. 'It happens sometimes. They can't see the pathways. But occasionally, they get close and Fall by mistake. That's how it happened with you. When I came through, you were gone. But that thing was there.'

'And *you* brought it here? You're out of your mind.'

Malik looks me at me, matter-of-fact. He points at the vial of blood on my neck. 'All I've got to go on about that Wraith is myth. I've never seen anyone wear it. I've never seen it work. But I'd like to. Now more than ever. Wouldn't you?'

236

He's got a point. From here on in, I don't see Reapers getting any fewer. So, if the Wraith works, I need to know. Same as Malik.

'Where is it?' I whisper.

In his hand, AM-41 carries what looks like a long cattle prod. The tip surges with a crackling pulse of electric current – bright blue. 'One touch'll stun an elephant,' he'd said, and I believe him. Vidhan, next to AM-41, moves his short-blade from fist to fist methodically, slowly. Akuji, alongside Vidhan, has both her fighting sticks in hand. Malik, pistol drawn, stares across the space . . . at the cage gate.

The air is close and putrid. The space is cramped. We're somewhere inside the dark belly of the plane. I look at Malik. He holds the heavy latch of the gate, poised to release the lock.

'You don't have to do this,' he says. 'I'd understand if you didn't.'

I glance down at the vial of blood on my neck. Back up at Malik.

'I'm doing it,' I say. I look at the iron-barred cage. The thing inside. Freakishly big. Abominable. Nobody speaks. The atmosphere in the room is thick.

I feel a confusing mix of emotions. Fear. Revulsion. Even pity.

The Reaper gives a strangled cry and twists its head from side to side. In its gut, I see the garish cut. An ooze of dark blood trailing. Cords of muscle pull tight on its neck. I watch it make a futile attempt to unfurl pink and bony wings, now bound to its body with wire. It moans and stalks the cage, a thing of teeth and sinew. All I feel coming from it is dumb hate. But I keep vacillating, switching between thinking it's a beast without sentience to feeling sorry for the brute and wanting to set it free.

'You're sure about this?' Vidhan says.

'No,' I say. 'But I'm doing it anyway.'

Then I do something driven by instinct. I lean down and untie my sword.

'The hell are you doin now?' Vidhan cries.

'I don't need a weapon for this,' I say, swinging the blade off my hip. I leave it leaning in its scabbard on the curved inner wall of the plane.

'Ana,' Vidhan says. 'That's ... I mean. If the Wraith doesn't work –'

'I'm dead. But it will.' I don't know how I'm so certain of this, but I am. Then the Reaper, as if on cue, rocks its head towards me. Now it seems to stare right at me.

Am I wrong? Can it see me? Sense me?

'Ana,' Malik says. 'Gimme the word.'

'Do it,' I say.

35

I step through and every muscle in my body seizes up. Malik slams the gate shut behind me and my world reduces to the cage. And the monster.

Fear gives way to white noise. I know I'll never feel fear again. Not like this.

Close up, the Reaper is nightmarish. It swivels its head mindlessly, muscles bulging and contorting. The stench of it is enough to make me hurl, but I don't. I don't move a muscle. Not even an eyelid. I don't breathe. The Wraith is a weight on my neck. The Reaper drags a trail of blood. It's dying, I can tell. But it's not dead yet. A raw, untamed power still beats off the thing. Its nostrils flare. It staggers towards me and my heart pumps. Then it stops. Centimetres from me. So close I see my bent reflection in those black eyes sunk into its pink head.

Eyes that roll . . . and focus . . . beyond me. Slowly, it dawns. It's the others, over my shoulder, that it hungers after. Not *me*. It's blind to me.

A drop of sweat runs down my spine. I feel it traverse every ridge of bone.

'NOW!' Malik yells. I drop to the ground like a lead anchor, just as we planned, and clamp my hands over my ears. Malik opens fire.

BLAM! BLAM! BLAM! BLAM! BLAM! BLAM!

My ears ring. The smoke hangs.

I take a step . . . and bump into hard flesh.

The Reaper. Dead.

36

The sword makes a chopping sound through the air and I focus on it, and the positioning of my feet, and the weight of the blade. The four of us are high above the graveyard of planes in the black-boulder mountains. It's late in the day, my third straight day of training, and the moon has risen. We train where the atmosphere is thin, high on a flat spit of rock that juts out over the plain like a tongue. When the air is cool – early mornings and late evenings. We rest only to sleep, eat and drink.

And we begin again.

Every day we train and every night I'm inside the cage in my mind. That moment, standing alone with the Reaper, stays with me. It never lets go. We burned the thing. We built a pyre and torched it, watched the black smoke rise.

It makes me stronger – remembering.

Every day, I feel the wounds in my back healing and the muscles in my body transforming, lengthening. The sun tans my skin nut-brown. I've seen quantum leaps in my fighting ability. Hand–eye coordination. Speed. Footwork. Reaction time. Range. I'm changing, evolving so rapidly it's as if these abilities were always in me. Lying dormant. Waiting. Which Malik says they were.

I widen my stance and bend my knees. Plant my left leg forward and grip the sword with both hands. Right hand at the hilt and my left at the blade to generate torque. Then I start swinging the blade again, pushing and pulling as I whip Ra down from high over my head. I slash diagonals, up from my left hip to right shoulder and down from my left shoulder to right hip, cutting an X in the air, concentrating the force of the strike on just the first five centimetres of the blade.

Faster! a voice commands in my mind. Akuji.

I bring the sword back horizontally to my right side, pointing the tip behind me, parallel to my hip . . . and then I whip it across on a horizontal plane from my right to my left, lethal-quick, raise it high over my head and then step forward and slam the blade down. The sword slices the air as though I've practised these moves over a thousand days instead of three. Up. Down. High to low and low to high. Nothing tentative or faltering. A flow.

Akuji – elemental, as pale as alabaster – leans on a jutting rock, one leg bent at the knee, watching me, slow clapping. Next to her, Malik and Vidhan.

Akuji pushes away from the rock face and draws her fighting sticks.

The air is sharp. My chest heaves. I watch her come.

We circle each other, maybe two metres apart. I feel the edge of the rock ledge behind me, a drop to certain death. The planes are toys below.

That was halfway decent, Akuji thinks to me. *Now let us play for real.*

She dances forward. Strikes. Her fighting sticks scythe down and I manage to parry them with a cross sweep and leap back and out of the way. She smiles, spins her weapons and we circle again. Her sticks are lethal, made from a wood that never chips or breaks. I'm beginning to think maybe they *aren't* wood, that they must be some type of metal. I watch her and steel myself for whatever comes.

Akuji steps up to the rock edge and glances over. *Some drop that.*

I look at the edge. A dead tree hangs over the precipice, clinging to the rock, its branches like arms clawing at the sky. Akuji watches me, waiting for a reaction. When I offer none, she feints forward and I skip sideways.

She attacks for real again, hard and fast. A bright flash of pain. I'm hit. On the shoulder. I stumble back, white-knuckled.

'Chrissakes, Akuji!' I yell breathlessly. 'We're on the same side!'

She laughs and comes at me, as fluid as mercury. I slink out of the way, panting hard. Akuji leaps at me and I bring the blade slashing down, but she blocks it effortlessly. She's toying with me. She wheels and attacks. I don't know how, but I manage to sidestep and chop down the sword in time and the metal clangs against her sticks. She advances furiously. A whirlwind assault, one blow after the other, and I defend as best I can. Then she connects to Ra with a powerful blow and the sword flies from my grip and skitters across the ledge, lodging itself into the rock face. I stand with my back to the drop, weaponless, breathing hard.

Akuji mock-thrusts and I sway back. My stomach drops.

I feel a hollow pull of gravity. I'm at the edge.

Panic. My arms windmill.

Akuji, watching me, calmly resheathes her fighting sticks. I see it in those cool, serene eyes of hers – indifference. I'm tipping. I'm going over.

And there's nothing in the seven worlds I can do about it.

37

A hand. It clamps on to my wrist and my fall is arrested. Akuji holds me, keeps me hanging, letting me know it's by her power alone I'm granted a second life. Then she hauls me back up and I fall to my knees, coughing. She stands over me and I look up at her, ashamed. Unable to do anything but gasp.

Without speaking, still in shock, I retrieve my weapon and return it with shaking hands to its scabbard. I turn and look at her.

She looks back at me, expressionless.

'You forgot the most important lesson of all,' Vidhan says, coming to join us, Malik at his shoulder.

'Oh yeah?' I say, annoyed.

'Yeah,' Vidhan says, taking off his glasses, blowing on them.

'Well?' I say.

He gives his glasses a quick polish and replaces them. 'Never trust Akuji.' He looks serious for a second and then he bursts out laughing and slaps me on the shoulder – the painful one – and I grimace. 'You were good,' he says. 'Hell, ya made Kuji break a sweat and I ain't never bloody seen that.'

I fumble with the straps on the scabbard, keeping my eyes averted. I take my time over it, saying nothing. After a while, I realize Akuji and Vidhan have moved away. Only one person remains with me on the rock ledge now. I stare down at his boots, his black jeans.

'Vidhan's wrong,' Malik says. 'You did far more than make her sweat. You gave as good as you got.'

I shake my head, pull the leather strap tight on my thigh and look up at him. 'No. He's right. She was close to killing me, Malik. If that had been a real fight . . .'

'You're ready,' he says.

'I can do better. One more day and –'

'You're *ready*,' he repeats.

That night we build a bonfire and watch the sparks whirl up and merge with the stars. It's cold and the hermits, taciturn and watchful, join us at the fire. AM-41 sits on a flattened hunk of metal, maroon poncho falling loose off his shoulders, metal hands on his knees.

Malik hooks a stick under the lid of a black, three-legged pot on the fire. Peers inside. Rabbit stew. At least that's what Vidhan assures me. I have a bad feeling rabbits are an unlikely inhabitant of these salt-coloured deserts. But tell that to the saliva in my mouth. The smell is intoxicating and strong. So rabbit stew it is. Again – *the mind sees what it wants to see.*

AM-41 unrolls an ancient map, dog-eared and faded, from the folds of his poncho. He flattens it on the ground and points.

'Here's Gatwick,' he says. He slides his metal finger to the south. 'We're here.' He moves his finger across. 'Main road's here, ten clicks to the east. Runs to Doverville on the Channel. From there, reckon you can buy passage to Gaul.'

I lean over the map next to him.

'You think we should take the road? And then a *boat*?'

AM-41 shrugs. 'In this world,' he says, 'why not? You got guns. You got swords. Ain't nobody gonna stop you boostin a ride.'

'What's that?' I say, pointing at a faint black line on the map running north to south alongside the highway.

'Goods train,' he offers. 'Carryin parts and supplies for them off-world ships they're buildin in the port towns.' He takes a slug from a brown bottle and makes a weird grinding noise. He sways a little in his seat and hands the bottle to Vidhan.

'That would've been the Eurostar, back in Sol,' I say. 'London St Pancras to Gare du Nord. Crossed right under the Channel. Two hours fifteen minutes.'

'Might've been so in Sol,' AM-41 says. 'But that goods train'll run dog-slow. And there ain't no hope of it goin under any Channel. Not in Tir.'

'You've been there?' Malik says, looking at me. 'To Paris?'

'Been there? I'm *from* there.'

'You're French?' Vidhan says. He takes a drink and his eyes pop wide open.

I shake my head. 'I was born there, in Paris. Been back many times.'

'Can you *parlez*?'

'*Un peu.*'

'Well then, you're one up on us,' Malik says, shifting the coals under the pot. 'None of *us* have been.'

'We should take the goods train south,' I say. 'Doesn't matter if it's slow. If it's carrying supplies, like you say, 41, we can hide in the crates.'

'Freight-surfing,' Vidhan says. 'Hell, I'm in.'

Next to him Akuji gazes into the flames, saying nothing. I watch her while nursing the callouses on my fingers and my palms. She lifts her gaze and her eyes find mine. I look straight back at her through the smoke. I feel certain she's about to offer some sly remark about falling over ledges, but she doesn't. Instead, she does something entirely surprising. She stands, walks round the fire and sits down next to me.

You are thinking too hard, she says into my head.

'About the *route*?' I say, turning to her.

She shakes her head. *About your mistakes. Your poor footwork, your bad strikes and defences. You get stuck in your mistakes. It is why you lost. Put them behind you. Let go. Find a way to win, from inside.*

For Akuji, it's an epic speech. And it strikes me as a fair comment, which makes it even more unusual. Akuji lives with such visible intensity it's hard to imagine *her* ever letting go. She's a walking contradiction. An enigma. One thing and then another.

'You're right,' I tell her aloud. 'I'm forcing it. But I *will* get better.'

She holds my gaze. Her eyes don't waver. *Yes*, is all she says.

'Speaking about getting better!' Vidhan yells. 'Have a swig of some of this stuff.' He hurls a bottle over the flames and I snatch it cleanly out of the air.

'Firewater?' I ask opening the cap.

'Nah, mate. Home brew. I call it the Doctor. AM-41 keeps a stash for me, in case I ever need it. Which I do. A lot.'

I take a sip and feel the burn sear my throat.

'Hoo-haa!' Vidhan shouts. A log snaps and collapses and sparks swirl up into the night. On the far side of the fire, Malik watches me. I feel light-headed and woozy. My skin tingles. I throw back my head and take another long slug.

We sleep on our bedrolls in front of the glowing embers, long into the late morning. When we wake, bleary-eyed, we pack our gear and, with the gift of a poncho each, we leave the graveyard of planes and the cyborg hermits with their metal faces and their quiet intensity. We trek east across an unremittingly bleak desert. AM-41 accompanies us, leading the way. After about five miles, we see the train blinking in the sun.

AM-41 swings his poncho over his metal hip and looks at me.

'Thank you,' I tell him, hand reaching instinctively for the Wraith, fingers rubbing the bevelled edges of the glass vial.

He watches me and says nothing.

'Will we see you again?' I ask.

'If you must, you will,' he says. 'In this world or the next.'

I squint at him. My mouth is dry. I feel a monster headache coming on.

38

The train comes at us at an angle, surging towards us in a cacophony of noise. Wagon after wagon – most shuttered closed – hammer past, thumping over the tracks. I can just make out crates and boxes in the dimness between flat steel bars. But some of the wagons are empty, just steel boxes on wheels.

'Aim for that one!' I shout, running alongside the tracks, heart pumping.

Vidhan – in a smoky blur – flashes ahead and, without visible exertion, he's up on the goods train and looking down at us, yelling something snatched by the wind. Ahead, I see Akuji haul herself up. Malik turns his head to the side, looks behind, waits. Then he sprints. He reaches out and grabs a steel-pipe ladder at the wagon's edge. With an effortless, animal grace, he leaps off his feet and swings into the air. And then he's up and next to Vidhan – just like *that*.

I'm the last.

Malik crouches on one knee, hair blown back in the wind. He holds on to the steel ladder with his left hand and reaches out to me with his right.

'C'mon!' he shouts.

No sweat. Just a massive jump into a moving train. Easy.

I stare at the tracks, trying to focus, watching the sparks fly from the wheels. I imagine my legs getting caught and twisted, being pulled under, bones crunching. I watch the wagon arrive. I see Malik urging me on – oh God, he's beautiful.

I reach out my arm . . . retract it just as a tree comes rushing between me and the train. I fall back. Then sprint to catch up, reach out again.

My fingertips graze his.

Here goes nothing. I jump. I sail through the air . . . high and impossibly far, as if I'm strapped into a jetpack . . .

. . . and I'm in the train.

Whump! I slam into Malik and we tumble over each other and crash up against the back of the space, smashing legs and arms. I end up sprawled on top of him.

I blush and roll off and leap to my feet. Malik sits up on his elbows, grinning.

'Some jump,' he says.

I take a deep breath and feel the hot air blasting me. The train rattles and sways. It has a blood-iron smell of machines. My head spins. I swivel round and look for the others.

'They went up,' Malik says. He points to the ceiling.

Right. So . . . just me and him then.

'Tell me something,' Malik says. 'That jump. Did you think about it, before it happened? I mean, did you focus, let everything go? And then *wham*?'

'I dunno. I jumped. Why are you suddenly so interested?'

'Like I said, it was some jump. Seems like your abilities are really kicking in.'

'*You* did it,' I say, trying to remember if I *did* think hard about it or if it just happened. 'The others too.'

Malik grabs hold of the metal ladder and swings into the wind and throws out his arm and then he swings back in again. 'Yeah,' he says. 'But we've had practice. And you just picked it up. Like *that*.'

'I jumped on a train, Malik. I didn't cure cancer.'

He laughs. Runs his hand through his hair. 'Combat and sword-fighting . . . that's level one of your Pathfinder skills, Ana. There are layers to your abilities.'

'Like?'

He looks at me, rubbing the stubble on his chin. 'I want you to try something.'

'What?' I ask suspiciously.

'I want you to dodge.'

'Dodge what?'

'This.'

He spins out his pistol and, instinctively, as he lifts the barrel to my face, I slip sideways and turn my shoulder. The next thing I know, and with a blast of panic, I'm teetering forward over the edge, tracks running beneath me, and then I feel a hand grab my hoodie at the small of my back. Malik yanks me to safety.

'Are you *testing* me?' I demand, slapping his arm away.

Malik reholsters his gun and smiles. 'You're quick,' he says, eyes dancing. 'I thought so. That's good news. But I'm still faster, so you'll need to improve.'

A conversation I had with Vidhan, at the Haven in Ares, flashes back to me. I see him lift a glass off the table and I watch the bobbing rings of light move apart, and converge when he lowers the glass. *See? Light can be in two places at the same time. So why not me? Why not you? . . . Nothing is at rest. Everything moves.*

'C'mon,' Malik says. 'We'll talk about this later. Let's have some fun.' He tips his head at the open door. 'Follow me.'

'Why?' I ask, red-faced and irritable. 'Where?'

'Up,' he says.

We climb the steel-pipe ladder outside the door, ponchos swirling, the bare desert rushing below. We climb to the train roof and splay ourselves out on the hot metal. The wind screeches and hammers at us. Malik stands and leans forward, then turns and shouts something at me I can't make out. I get to my feet and we stumble forward, up the length of the wagon, leaning into the wind. Each step an effort of will.

I watch Malik's broad back, feeling unhinged by him. Angry. And, at the same time, excited. Wild.

At the end of the wagon, we clamber down another steel ladder, step over the coupling joint and climb up the other side and on to the roof of the next.

The train rockets into a black tunnel and we fall flat in the sudden dark. The tunnel releases us, and we shoot out into bright sunlight. Malik laughs into the wind. We hit another tunnel. And slam out the other side. And another.

Dark. Light. Dark. Light. One after the other.

Ahead now, at the front edge of the forward engine, I see the familiar quiescent shape of Akuji, sitting perfectly still, her back turned to us. Next to her, Vidhan. He's standing, shouting into the wind. Malik throws up his arms and lets out a whoop.

Despite myself, I can't help grinning. I lift my arms, like Malik and Vidhan, and they see me and we howl at the sky. I'm feeling reckless now. Elated.

I start laughing. An uncontrollable, manic laugh. Here I am, freight-surfing across an England that isn't England. So what if Reapers are hunting us? So what?

Malik grins at me, hair flowing back. Then he does something so unexpected it stuns me. He kisses me. A shock goes through my body.

Malik laughs. The train pulls us hard into a bend and the wagon tilts. We hammer over the tracks and, in my bones, I feel every dent in the metal and, like a silver thread woven through every bump, is a single unstoppable image – Malik's lips on mine.

We descend from the roof when the bitter cold arrives. A pale moon floats and the open side of the empty wagon frames a night sky cloudy with stars. Akuji and Vidhan stake out claims in two corners of the space and fall asleep, deep under their ponchos. Malik and I, untired, sit with our legs out straight and our backs to the cold metal wall and rock with the train's motion.

My blood zings. I stare into the restless night, into the vastness of space, and all I can think about is that kiss – unprovoked and so sudden. How would Bea have reacted? She would've made conversation. She would've kept it light and cool. She'd know how to flirt, to make him kiss her again.

Think of something, Ana. C'mon.

'D'you know how many stars there are in the galaxy?' I blurt.

Nice. Light and breezy. Epic.

Malik looks at me. 'Which galaxy?'

Right. Good point. 'Let's just say ours. Sol.'

He shrugs. 'No idea.'

'Over two hundred billion. I googled it. And now there's not just one, and not two, but *seven* universes and who knows how many billion stars in each.'

'I suppose that's right.'

'Right. Well, doesn't that make you feel small? Like a speck of dust.'

'No.'

Perfect. You're blowing this, Moon. The train rocks. I wrack my brains for something meaningful to say. Something *personal*. 'I feel like that sometimes. Like a speck of dust. Just . . . floating. And now this . . . all this Falling. It's mad.'

'It's not *that* mad when you think about it. Falling from one world to another. It happens to us all, Pathfinder or not, at least once in our lives.'

'Oh yeah? When?'

'Birth. A day before you're born, you're just as conscious as the day of your actual birth, did you know that? You're as completely developed. The only difference is you're still inside your mother's womb, and the womb is everything – your universe. Then out you come and take your first breath and the world you knew vanishes and here you are – in a new one.'

My heart drums. My hands feel clammy. The stars feel close enough to touch.

'Something Prof. told me,' Malik adds into the silence.

'I like it,' I say. 'It actually makes sense.'

'I mean, what are the chances of being born at all?' Malik says. 'Basically, zero, right? But here we are. You and me. All of us. We've won the lottery, Ana. That shouldn't make you feel like you don't matter. It should make you feel you *do*.'

I clam up. The night is bright and freezing. I have goosebumps, but not from the cold. Here we are. Malik and me, centimetres apart. Worlds away. *You kissed me*, I want to say. *We kissed*. Lips on lips. All that mad electricity, that closeness.

'That Reaper,' I say, scraping the barrel for conversation to cover my lameness. 'It was a human once, right?'

Malik nods, says nothing.

'But then it Fell into the Between and changed forever.'

'It happens,' he says.

'And it happened to *her*. To Issi.' The words leave my mouth before my brain can stop them.

I watch Malik's profile. His jaw tightens. When he looks at me, his eyes are almost black. 'You wanna talk about that?'

'Not if you don't. I just thought –'

'She was beautiful,' he interrupts. 'Like you. And, like you, she had this wild streak. Didn't care about rules. I suppose I liked that about her.' Malik pauses, runs his fingers over the stubble on his jaw. 'The day it happened was nothing special. Routine search-and-rescue mission for some lost Normal. But Issi . . . she'd been Falling on her own for weeks in a row. So the Fall we made that day . . . it was one too many.'

I stare out at the night, unable to speak.

'I should've seen it coming,' Malik says. 'I should've seen the signs. But I didn't. And then she was gone. Out of my life. Like everyone else that . . .'

'Malik –'

'You shouldn't get close to me,' he says, rolling on to his side, away from me. 'It's a death sentence.'

His words sting. The moment – whatever moment it might have been – is lost. I put my hand on his shoulder and he shrugs it off.

My heart breaks. And breaks.

'Get some rest,' Malik murmurs. 'You'll need it.'

I close my eyes and hunger for sleep. But it doesn't come. My mind is whirring. He loved her. Does he still? I try to shake off the hurt and focus on Bea instead. And our journey – to France and the Seventh Gate.

'Malik?' I whisper into the darkness.

'What?' he groans.

'You think the seventh is a perfect world?'

He says nothing for a long time. Then, just when I think he's asleep, he answers. 'No such thing as a perfect world,' he says, voice low in his throat. 'A *real* world, with crap bits and good bits all mixed together, that's about the only thing makes any kinda sense.'

The train shakes and rolls, carrying us into the night.

I lie awake. And, by moonlight, I read.

THE SEVENTH

What is the seventh? This question has long enthralled Pathfinders of the Collective. Why is one world unreachable when others are not? Why do many pathways span six worlds when, it is believed, there is only one Path to **KRONOS** – the Seventh Gate? Answers to these questions are as arcane as the origin of the multiverse itself. Indeed, a hunt for the seventh has sustained generation after generation, bent on a powerful idea: that perfection is attainable. And that immortal power lies beyond the gate.

However, it is an empirical, unshakable truth that corruption of our values occurs most insidiously when the quest for the seventh overrides an inborn Pathfinder inclination to protect and serve the multiverse. It is bitter irony then that a search for perfection may well deliver annihilation.

The words float and blur in front of me. Then drift away.

39

I wake before dawn, confused and startled. For a moment, I'm unsure of my whereabouts. Then I feel a hard rocking motion and I remember. I turn and look at the sleeping shape next to me – Malik, his chest rising and falling. I get an urge to stroke his cheek, to feel his skin's heat.

But I don't. I stand and stretch. Roll my shoulders to ease the ache out of them. I step past Vidhan and Akuji, still sleeping, and move to the open wagon door. I grip the steel ladder, plant my feet and look out. The air is hot. The sky the colour of lead. I watch light seep into the world and sharpen the edges of things.

Behind me, Malik rouses himself. I turn and see him sitting up, blinking, scratching his head. He comes to join me, clicking his neck, standing close.

I let my hand fall near his and I look away, ashamed of my body's eagerness.

'Where *are* we?' I say, surveying the bleak landscape.

He yawns and stretches. 'Northern Gaul by now, I reckon.'

'Gaul?'

'France.'

'So we've crossed the Channel?'

'There is no Channel in Tir.'

'Right.'

I stare out over the alien land, feeling the wind on my skin and the coming heat. Then my gut tightens. Something pulls my gaze upward.

A smudge. Up high in the sky, between the last fading stars and the Earth, it moves – convulses, pulses and throbs. It looks alive, like a murmuration of starlings. But these aren't starlings.

Malik makes a grunting noise in his throat. His hand flies to his hip and he flicks out his pistol. His face is pale and stern and his jaw clamps tight. He turns and gives Vidhan a sharp kick in the legs. 'Vidhan!' he shouts. 'Kuji!'

Vidhan's head pops up over his poncho. He blinks at us, finds his glasses and put them on. Malik points at the sky and Vidhan follows his gaze.

'Oh crap!' he cries, scrambling upright.

I watch the shape grow and I begin to see individual creatures, pink and bony. They come like buzzards to roadkill. A seething mass, more than I can count.

'That's a *swarm*,' I say.

'Actually,' Vidhan counters, 'the collective noun for Reapers is pod.'

'The door!' I shout. 'We have to shut it.'

A chain hangs on the door and we take hold of this and pull. It yields. Then sticks.

I smell them now. A stink of rot on the air.

'Again!' I yell.

We heave . . . and it moves. Agonizingly slow. Sliding. Then sticking.

A shape comes hammering at us out of the sky, claws first.

The door gives – unsticks again – and slams shut just as the Reaper crashes into it from the outside. The sound is violent. A thundering echo, like the pounding of a massive sledgehammer into metal.

BOOM!

We fall back in shock. The boxcar shudders and the metal door warps inwards. A wild scream comes from outside.

SKKRAAAAAAAAAAAAAAAAAAAAAAAAAAAA-AAAAAAAAAAAK!

Then another hit.

BOOM!

And again.

BOOM!

And twice more.

BOOM! BOOM!

My back hits the opposite wall. I lean into it. It rattles with every blow from the other side.

I wheel round. The wall behind us is another sliding door.

Together, we lunge for the hanging chain, grab and pull. This time, the door slides open easily. We reel it all the way back and a gust of hot wind slams into us.

Nothing in the sky. Not a single Reaper. They haven't come round to this side yet. Which gives me a hit of courage . . . that vaporizes when I look down.

Down.

Down.

Into thin air. A void.

We're crossing a bridge over a ravine so deep the bottom is obscured in murk.

BOOM! BOOM!

'We have to jump!' Malik shouts.

BOOM!

SKKRAAAAAAAAAAAAAAAAAAAAAAAK!

I turn and see the far door begin to buckle. A claw, sharp and long and black, cuts through from the other side – a *metal* door. A bolt explodes out and, with a whine, shoots past my head, out into the vast ether. I figure we've got about a minute left. Sixty seconds before iron-hard talons eviscerate us.

I look out of the open side again. 'I can't see any pathways,' I say.

BOOM!

Malik spins his smoking gun. 'They'll come,' he says. 'They *have* to.'

We stare into the sky, waiting. Nothing comes.

SKKRAAAAAAAAAAAAAAAAAAAAAAAAK!

The screech is close this time – *inside* the car.

I turn and see that a Reaper has broken through enough of the metal to shove part of its head into the space. Malik points his weapon and fires point-blank.

The muzzle flash is close. The sound ear-splitting. Then no sound at all, as if a wodge of cotton wool has been stuffed into my ears. I look at Vidhan. He's shouting something.

Finally, his voice reaches me, tinny and faraway. 'Look!'

I turn and seem them – wavy lines, like heat rising. A dazzling, vertical river rushing up into the sky.

We step back together. Three. Four. Five paces. We stand in a line and face the open side of the carriage. I look out at the bottomless void. I look at the sky and I see Reapers. They've circled round and now bomb in towards us.

'Ready?' Malik says.

I nod and say nothing. Vidhan gives me a two-fingered salute. Akuji tips her head at me – a fleeting gesture, beyond any recognition I've seen from her yet.

See you on the other side, she thinks into my head.

'There's just one thing,' Vidhan says.

'What's that?' I ask.

He gives me a lopsided grin. 'I bloody hope ya can swim.'

Akuji laughs. A sharp sound. It's the first time I've heard her laugh. And then I realize it's the first time I've heard *any* sound from her at all.

'Now!' Malik shouts. And we run.

And we leap.

40

This happens as soon my toes leave the edge of the boxcar:

First we lift. We're not hammered by the fierce sideways wind I expect or sucked down by gravity. We fly upward. *Upward.* I see Vidhan wielding his knife, stabbing, hacking at Reapers. Malik firing his pistol.

Then we float. The air becomes jelly and the Reapers blur and vanish. Here it is: the weightlessness, my stomach in my throat, the air warping. I look at Malik and grab his hand. His hair is a halo around his face. Time slows.

Then we Fall. We drop with frightening violence. Spinning. Tilting. Turning. I feel my fingers rip away from Malik's hand. I lose my bearings. Lose sight of the others. Malik, Vidhan and Akuji disappear. Everything unravels, becomes a blur. And then my bones disintegrate, turn to dust. I'm breaking apart.

And then I'm gone.

'Jovial' is not, ironically, a word used to describe the character of the people of **JÖVE**, the fifth realm. Jövians are, by nature, malcontent. Pathfinder masters believe the tides – governed by the two moons of Jöve's Earth – are the likely cause. The tides and a pathological, Machiavellian quest for betterment.

But, if ordinary Jövians are dissatisfied with their lot, then the elite of Jöve (especially those residing in the ancient underwater cities of Europe) are the apotheosis of discontent. In addition, they are renowned as fierce warriors: loyal but often devious.

JÖVE

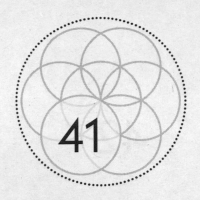

41

Boneless. A squid ripped inside out. That's how I feel. My head pounds and my ears buzz and my aching teeth chatter. I try to shake off a feeling of doom, but I can't. I see things: a claw raking up my stomach . . . gutting me like a fish, hauling out my worming innards, sprawling them out, pink and steaming.

Get a grip, Moon. Think!

How did I get here? What happened? Where was I?

On the train. With Akuji and Vidhan and Malik. The pod of Reapers came. We jumped. We Fell. Malik's hand in mine – ripped away.

I remember nothing after that. Nothing . . . until this. But what *is* this?

Where am I now?

A silky thickness runs over my skin. I'm suspended. I'm floating. But I'm not in the air. And I'm not breathing. And I *can't* breathe.

This . . . is water.

42

Salt water. The realization hits me hard. I swing my head from side to side. Bubbles stream up from my mouth, up to a surface I can't see. I kick my legs and spin round. Malik isn't here. Neither are Akuji and Vidhan.

I'm alone. I'm underwater. And I'm drowning. And yet I'm weirdly calm.

This is it, I think. *Bea's lost. And so am I.*

No! Focus!

I'm alive.

I remember the sword then and realize its weight must be dragging me down. I look below me. Down into the blue murk. And I remember something Malik said: *You're out in the great multiverse now. And, in the great multiverse, everything that can happen does.*

Far below my feet lies a submerged city. Strange lights beam up through the dark from pod-like buildings that rise out of the depths like giant mushrooms, lit from within. Skimming over them, schools of shimmering fish and weird pillars of floating kelp and, between them, driving back and forth, otherworldly vessels throwing up bubbles like stars from their spinning turbines. A city. Underwater.

Mind. Blown.

Then a voice. Far away. A whisper. Something I can feel more than hear. My name spoken into my head.

Ana.

And I know who it is. Malik.

Ana, are you OK?

Malik! Where are you? What's going on?

First tell me you're OK.

I'm underwater, Malik.

Listen to me, is Vidhan with you?

Did you hear me? I'm underwater. I'm drowning.

Ana, you need to . . .

He doesn't finish. His voice fades. And – like *that* – he's gone.

Malik?

No answer.

MALIK!

Still nothing. I don't feel so calm any more. My lungs are burning, bursting. I thrash my legs and look around frantically.

Then I get a sense of movement, of something in the water with me. I look up (what I think is up – I can't see the surface, but I follow the stream of bubbles) and I see a figure diving down to me, pulling through the water, hair floating.

My heart gallops. But it's not Malik. It's Vidhan.

Ana!

Vidhan! Need air. Drowning.

Breathe, comes his insane reply into my head. *Just breathe.*

Breathe? He's out of his mind. I'm seeing dots now. Spinning circles of light. My chest convulses. I thrash in panic. I can't hold my breath any longer.

I *can't.*

I watch Vidhan in horror. His mouth is open. He's shouting something at me. Bubbles explode around him.

Can't hold ... must breathe ... can't ... hold ... must ...

I open my mouth – it's involuntary.

I choke in a breath ...

The water surges into my lungs ... and flows out again. In ... out ... in. Smooth and fluid and – staggeringly – I'm breathing. I'm underwater ... and I'm breathing. It's not possible. I look at Vidhan in amazement.

I'm breathing underwater. Like a fish!

I'm not sure what I expect from Vidhan. One of his grins maybe. A laugh. But instead he looks strained.

I'm breathing, I think to him.

I know.

Underwater.

I know, he thinks to me. *That's Jöve for you.*

He winces, clutches at his side. And that's when I see it. A red cloud floating around him. It can only be one thing. Blood.

What happened, Vidhan?

It'll be OK, he thinks back to me. *It's nothin. A scratch.*

A brief glance at his belt confirms his short-blade has gone. And the red cloud blooming from under his hand is unrelenting.

I swim towards him, but a sudden strong current rips through the water. It yanks me away from him and I flip upside down and tumble away like I'm spinning in a washing machine. When I'm finally upright again, he's further away, being pulled away from me by the second.

He points down, below his feet.

Down there, he thinks to me, his voice fading. *Get help.*

No. Not leaving you.

No choice, Ana.

I swim as hard as I can towards him, kicking and pulling, screaming with the effort. But it's no use. He's spinning away.

Stay with me, Vidhan. I won't leave you. I'm right here.

He floats away. Becomes a shadow in the water.

No. *Nononono*. Please no.

But I can't reach him. I *can't*. I float in the water and watch him go.

I tread the water, alone. A pang of despair in my gut.

Then, behind Vidhan, a shape looms. A colossal thing emerging from blue darkness. A whale? It slides effortlessly through the deep and I realize it's not some frightening beast – it's a ship, a submarine, but unlike anything I've seen in the movies. Not grey and tube-like, but an elegant, organic-looking thing, starkly beautiful and streamlined. Whale-shaped in design, with a criss-cross pattern of white metal curves like the striations of a humpback and blue-tinted windows between.

A metal mouth opens, a portal, at the front of the submarine. The monster-ship glides up to Vidhan and swallows him whole. Like that, he's gone.

Then it turns in the water and comes at me.

I backpedal frantically but there's no escape. It's close now, steaming in at me. The door opens – a dark mouth. I'm engulfed.

Gulped up like a fleck of krill.

43

I swirl into a confusing space, upside down, spinning. When I manage to swivel upright, I see the hydraulic door close. Now a series of clanking noises vibrate through the water and I see a surface above, sloshing. The water recedes rapidly into an enormous floor grate and I spin round violently until I'm dumped on the grate, driven flat by gravity. My body convulses and I roll on to my hands and knees and vomit streams of water from my lungs.

The next thing I'm aware of, I'm lying on my back, staring up at a metal ceiling. I can hear the loud whirring sound of an engine close by, and a fan somewhere below the grate, blasting up hot waves of air. I groan. Roll my head to the side.

And I see Vidhan. Not moving. Bleeding.

I crawl to his side and press my ear to his lips. Nothing. He's not breathing.

Moving fast, I tilt back his head, link my thumbs like I learned in first aid at school and pump hard on his chest with the heel of both palms. I count it out.

One ... two ... three ... four ... five ... six ...
seven ...

He spasms. Flaps his arms. Rolls to his side, coughs and
throws up.

Finally, he chokes a long, rattling breath and he slumps
back, eyes staring.

I look at the blood leaking from the side of his body and
his pale, waxy face.

'You're OK,' I tell him, heart thumping. 'You're gonna
be fine.'

He nods. Blinks at me.

I look up. The space we're in is a metal rectangle. The
floor beneath us is the grate. The walls of the room are
featureless. The door to the dark water beyond fits
seamlessly into rubber strips. It looks pressure-sealed. A
succession of thumping noises and hollow moans come
from the metal walls. The blast of a turbine.

On the other side of the room is another door with an
opaque portal window.

I stand and walk to the door. Five strides.

It's closed. Locked. The window is too grimed to see
through. I bang on the door with the heel of my fist. No
response.

On the wall is a red button. I hit it and the door on
the opposite side ratchets open, sending in a wave of water.
I slam the button again and the outside door closes.

I walk back to Vidhan, dripping, and crouch on my
haunches.

He looks at me with eyes unmoored, his glasses gone.

'The darkness,' he whispers, wide-eyed, like he's going into shock. 'I feel it, Ana. It's all around us. D'ya see it?'

'Nothing's gonna get us, Vidhan.'

He takes a shuddering breath and releases it. Then he sits up on his elbows, lucid suddenly. 'Ana?' he says.

'Vidhan. S'all right,' I say. 'It's OK.'

'Got bushwhacked,' he says, groaning, holding his side. 'Soon as I came through the Fall. Before I even hit the water.'

'Reaper?'

'Yeah.' He shakes his head. 'I mean . . . I dunno. Maybe.'

'Did you see Malik?' I ask. 'Akuji?'

'They'll be OK. Always are.' He coughs and groans.

'Just . . . take it easy, Vidhan. Rest.'

'Yeah. Could do with that. Reckon it's time for old Vidhan Blue to Settle.'

Vidhan sweats and shakes and I bunch his grey hoodie and press it down on the wound, staunching the blood. His body clenches.

'You could've told me, by the way,' I say to distract him.

'Told ya what?'

'The breathing underwater thing. A minor detail.'

He smiles. 'Ah yeah. Your first time. Never easy, that.'

' "I bloody hope you can swim?" *That's* how you chose to warn me?'

He laughs, coughs and grimaces.

'Mate, there's no real way to prepare for that kinda shock. Best to be *un*prepared actually. Let the body take over.' He laughs again and that triggers another fit of coughing and he clutches his side.

'Vidhan, you shouldn't –'

'I'm fine,' he says. 'Just don't make me laugh.'

We listen to the thumps and groans of the ship. 'What is this thing?' I ask, pulling off my hoodie, wringing it dry.

'Jövian submersible, I reckon,' he says, wincing.

'Looked like a whale from out there.'

'Rather be taken by a bloody whale.' He coughs and holds his side. 'Ah man, I need 41, some of his meds. That'll sort me out.'

'Jövian submersible,' I repeat, trying to divert his attention. 'It was like they were waiting for us. Like they expected us. Do you think it's the Order?'

'Could be,' he groans. 'Or just your average Jövian. Normals or Pathfinders, it doesn't matter. All Jövians are bloody combative and almost entirely unreasonable.'

'Wait a minute . . . Akuji . . . you said *she* was Jövian.'

'Exactly.'

I look at the door, feeling light-headed. I'm beyond exhausted, I'm shattered. Every bone and muscle in my bewildered body aches. 'There was a city out there,' I say. 'In the water. It was incredible. They live like that, down there?'

'They do and they don't. Two moons hang in the sky above the Earth in Jöve. The moons pull the tides back and forth, like nothin you've seen before. They change everything. Jövian cities are underwater one day and stuck in a swamp the next.'

'How do they deal with that?'

Vidhan snorts. 'Dealing is easy. Not letting it get to you and make you bitter, that's the hard part.'

I look at him. Brush his damp hair away from his eyes. 'Malik told me you had it rough as a kid,' I say, unsure if I'm overstepping the line. 'He said . . . once, your foster-parents dumped you in an *asylum*. That true?'

Vidhan laughs and coughs. 'Who's to blame 'em? Tell someone who ain't your blood you're seeing creatures like Reapers and . . . well, shit happens.'

'They sound like world-class jackasses to me.'

He smiles. 'Hell, they were OK. Least I got to spend my time doing two things I loved. Surfing and getting lost in the corner bookshop. Guess I liked to escape.'

'Yeah. Me too.'

'You surf?'

'No. I escape.'

'There's this beach,' Vidhan says, nodding. 'Back in Oz. Locals only, cos of the riptide. But we used the rip, let it take us out to the swells and rode the waves back. I'd steal my foster-dad's board and I'd surf all day and go home to the strap. It was worth it, though. Ah, mate, ya shoulda seen that water. Clear to the bottom and warm as blood. Didn't even need a suit. I'll take ya there one day. Teach ya how to drop into a barrel and come out the other side laughin. Nothin better in the seven worlds.' He snatches my wrist. 'Promise you'll go, when all this is done.'

'All right. All right. I promise.'

'Nah, like ya bloody mean it.'

'I promise, Vidhan. I *will*. I'll go to that beach.'

He smiles and lets go of my arm.

'That's the seventh, I reckon,' he murmurs. 'Miles and miles of perfect swell. An endless yellow beach to the moon and back.'

Before I can respond, hydraulics whine. The door hisses and slides open. I stand up off my haunches, hand on my sword.

A backlit figure appears. Tall and thin. His eyes obscured in the hooded shadow of a coat with an ermine-fur collar. A long staff in his hand.

'*Benvenuto*,' he says. 'Welcome . . . to *my* world.'

44

'You,' is all I can muster.

'Indeed,' he says. 'Me.'

Rodolfo Graziani, the Marchese di Jöve, steps into the confined space with us. His boots clang on the metal grate. Threat pulses off him – in the economy of his movement, his coiled energy. He's tall and lean and strong. His skin is as pale as the moon and his hair is almost peroxide-white. Beneath his long, unbuttoned coat, he wears the same suit of jet-black articulated armour, etched with patterns.

Beyond him, I see movement. Someone in the shadows. My gut tightens.

Graziani looks at me and then at Vidhan. His hand travels to his throat. He brushes aside the ermine collar and reveals a long pink scar.

'*Guarda*,' he says, still looking at Vidhan. 'A *testamento* to *your* skill.'

Vidhan shrugs. 'Skill? Nah, mate, I was bloody aiming for your eyes. But gimme another go and we'll set it to rights.'

Graziani smiles. 'And you,' he says, looking at me. 'The girl with the sword. Fonzie, was it? Or is it Ana Moon?'

I glare back at him and say nothing.

'Ah, look. She is changed. Not the girl I met in the alley. Someone new.'

He moves further into the room confidently. The door behind him remains open. An invitation? A challenge? He stops. Looks at the door. Looks at me. Smiles again. 'You think you can escape? You cannot. Even *if* you were both fully fit, I would still cut you down. This is as true as the tides.'

'I don't think so,' I say.

'Have you forgotten how effortlessly I acquired the sword from you last time?'

'Come and try again.'

He shakes his head, looks at the doorway again. In the darkness, I'm certain I see a shadow-shape. Someone waiting there.

Who?

'And something else,' Graziani says. 'Have you so easily forgotten being defeated on the black mountains in Tir?'

I open my mouth to speak, but no words come.

Beyond the doorway, the shape detaches itself from the shadows and moves into the light.

My heart leaps. And then it sinks.

'Kuji?' Vidhan says.

45

She has the same skin as Graziani – that alabaster-pale tone. And the eyes – the same startling opalescent colour. And I recognize them now – the symbols running down Graziani's armour are identical to the tattoos I saw stamped into Akuji's body back in Ares. Akuji – wearing a black, armoured-weave suit, just like Graziani – strides into the confined space, looking as self-possessed as when I first met her. But colder.

'Kuji, what is this?' Vidhan asks.

And that's when I'm hit with another surprise. She answers back. Aloud.

'This?' she taunts, spitting the question back in his face. 'This, Vidhan, is the end of the road.'

Her voice is cool and controlled. Emotionless. But the pitch of it is different. She has an accent. *Italian?* So she was hiding that too.

'Ya gotta be kiddin me!' Vidhan roars. 'You *speak*?'

'Never heard of subterfuge?' she says. 'Misdirection?'

I stare at her with mounting anger and Gabe's words come crashing back: *These are dark times ... There are spies everywhere ... The Collective has been infiltrated in almost every part of every world.*

I know what this is. I know what it means.

Betrayal.

I open my mouth to speak but I can't. I feel like throwing up. Vidhan stands clumsily, holding his side.

'But, Kuji ...' His voice is breaking. He glares at Akuji, who watches him warily, but I can see she's reached the same conclusion I have: he won't be able to muster any of his usual speed. And, when I see Vidhan's short-blade knife tucked into her belt alongside the fighting sticks, I realize what happened.

'*You* did this,' I say. '*You* ambushed Vidhan.'

She looks at me evenly, says nothing.

'You sold us out!' Vidhan cries. 'You're a bloody spy.' His voice is hoarse, thick with pain. 'Chrissakes, Kuji. We're *mates*.'

'Nothing personal, Vidhan,' she says. 'That is how it goes in the multiverse. Some will survive. Others ... they will not.'

And I think, *If she's capable of this, what else has she done?*

I remember his voice trying to reach me across the ether. Then fading away.

'Where is he?' I demand. 'Where's Malik?'

'Dead,' Akuji says.

Vidhan makes a choking sound in his throat. I feel cold. Numb.

'No. You're lying,' I tell her.

'Am I?'

'I'd know if he was dead. I'd feel it.'

'Do not overplay your hand, Ana Moon. Sword or no sword, you are not born of any noble blood. You are nothing. A nobody. What have you done, what *one* thing, to earn such prominence?'

'Guess we'll have to wait and see,' I reply curtly.

'We have seen already, no?' She looks at Graziani. 'Rodolfo has pointed this out. How easily I routed you on that mountain in Tir.'

'But you saved me. Why not just kill me then?'

'Because, Ana Moon, you are no good to me dead. Not yet.'

'How could you do this?' I demand, feeling rage build inside me. '*Why?*'

'My name,' Akuji says, watching us, 'is Mara Graziani. You already know my brother, Rodolfo Graziani, the Marchese di Jöve.'

He smiles and tilts his head. 'A pleasure,' he says.

'But,' Vidhan says, 'Akuji . . . it's –'

'I told you,' she spits. 'My name is Mara. I am an agent of the Order. A spy. And a spy must be like water and take the shape of the vessel. Akuji Na was the name of the first Collective Pathfinder I killed. An Ares girl, Fallen on the wrong side, moderately skilled with a katana. I liked her name. Do you know what it means?' She pauses, smiles. 'It means *Dead and Awake.*'

'What is it you want?' I ask. 'You and *him.*'

'The Graziani,' she says, moving to Rodolfo's side, running her hand across his shoulder, 'come from an ancient aristocracy – a line of assassins. The Pathfinder gene has always been in our bloodline. And every Graziani promises undying loyalty to our great benefactor, Master Kei Shinigami, who – for centuries – has funded our underwater realm. Under the onslaught of the tides, our castles and lands are expensive to maintain. But, while the other worlds will fold and crumble, Jöve will not. We will endure. For this, we are not just indebted to the Order, we are not just loyal to the Order, we *are* the Order. It is in us – our blood.'

'You're insane,' I tell her.

She smiles. 'Our parents were killed for their allegiance. By that devil, Mother.'

My breathing is shallow. I feel a cramp in my stomach.

'So then . . . this is what?' I ask. 'Payback?'

She says nothing. Gazes coldly back at me.

'Vidhan and Malik,' I say. 'They're your family too. Don't you see that? How long did you travel with them? *Years?* You can't possibly –'

'Don't *you* see,' she snorts. 'It was an act. They mean nothing to me.' She says it forcefully, as if convincing herself more than me.

'I don't believe you,' I say. 'You can't think that. You *can't.*'

'Kuji!' Vidhan cries. 'Tell me this ain't real.'

'My name,' she says, over-enunciating, 'is Mara. Akuji is dead.'

'What do you want from us?' I say, trying to subdue the panic in my gut.

Mara paces round us and I turn, following her with my eyes, hand on my sword. Ready. Prepared. 'You have no idea how much I have endured,' she says. 'How long I have waited for this moment.'

'Why break cover now then?' I ask. 'What's changed?'

'Everything,' she says. 'We have found a way to the seventh and now we have so much more. Ra. The Wraith. *You*. A pawn in our long game against the Collective.'

'Well, if it's me you want then let Vidhan go.'

'Hell, no,' Vidhan says, wincing in pain. 'Not in this bloody lifetime.'

Mara smiles. 'My sole ambition, at first, was to get an insider's understanding of the Collective, find a way to strike at the heart – Mother. Then, like a bolt from the sky, you arrive. You, gifted with that blade at your hip and then the Wraith. These two things alone are worth more than you could ever imagine. But bringing you to Shinigami . . . *that* will be the final nail in the Collective's coffin.'

'So you're taking us to the pyramid? Shinigami's place in Venetia?' I say, thinking about Bea.

'When the tide falls,' Mara answers, nodding.

'No!' Vidhan yells. 'Not without Malik.'

Rodolfo laughs 'Come, come. *Certamente*, you can see you have no choice in the matter? Why not accept your fate? And our . . . *hospitality*.'

He, like his sister, is circling the space, tall and straight-backed, closing in on us in an ever-tightening coil.

'Like hell you're takin us!' Vidhan bawls and leaps across the space.

Four things happen at once. One on top of the other.

First, Mara arcs her body and spins in to attack Vidhan.

Second, Vidhan disappears.

Third, Mara's fighting sticks stab into the empty space where he was standing before.

Fourth, he reappears at her left shoulder.

Vidhan roars in anger and lashes out – a wild haymaker that Mara easily ducks, but Vidhan has hell in his eyes. He delivers a kick to Mara, right under the ribs, and she flies to the side. Vidhan flies after her, undeterred by the fact that he's unarmed and bleeding. It happens so fast, so unexpectedly, I'm rooted to the spot.

Then I swivel on my toes to face Mara's brother. I draw the sword.

Too late. Rodolfo's staff comes whipping through the air with a sound like a crack of thunder and slams into my shoulder. A white flash of pain and I roll backwards into a corner. I flip to my feet, growling like an animal.

What happens next unfolds in slow motion, dreamlike.

Mara's fighting sticks cut the air in a blur.

Vidhan smokes out of the way.

I run into Mara, but she sidesteps me with ease and I flounder and crash down. From the ground, I see Vidhan come at her again. He's sweating heavily now – pale and grey in the face – and he catches her in the hip with a side kick. But it's a feeble attempt. Rodolfo swings his staff round his body like he's Bruce Lee and slams it home across Vidhan's back, sending him careening across the space towards Mara. She watches him hungrily. Then she does a little pirouette move. Swinging her fighting sticks like a ballerina. Agile. Beautiful. Deadly.

She catches him across the cheek. Vidhan staggers back, reeling drunkenly. His arms hang limp. A cut opens on his cheek.

Mara looks at him, calm and calculating. She swings her fighting sticks.

I drag myself up on to my knees and scream. 'No! Please, *no*!'

She turns and gives me a blank look. 'It is not him we need,' she says. 'It is you.'

Vidhan comes to life in this moment of reprieve. He makes a desperate lunge at her. But Rodolfo steps forward. With callous skill, he wheels, spins his staff through the air and brings it down hard across Vidhan's temple.

Vidhan drops to his knees. He turns to me, stunned.

Blood pumps down the side of his face.

And the light in his eyes is snuffed out.

46

The metal grate is cold and bites into my cheek.

I don't mind. It could slice me to the bone for all I care. My fingertips trace a cut on my temple and come away sticky with blood. I deserve it. I choke back a sob. Vidhan Blue, the Professor, who made me feel like I belonged, like I mattered. Who dreamed of a beach on the far side of the Earth where the sand is yellow and reaches to the moon and back. Vidhan is gone. Dead.

'You cannot escape,' Mara says. I can hear the smirk in her voice. But I refuse to look at her. 'Where would you go?' she adds. 'It is futile.'

I don't answer. I feel numb.

'And do not presume you will be able to Fall out of this cell into the next world. No pathways in here. You are trapped.'

I say nothing.

'*Calma*,' Rodolfo says from the doorway. 'Enjoy the ride. You shall be there soon enough.'

I keep myself pressed to the floor. I don't answer. I listen to his footsteps leave the space, but I can still feel Mara here with me. She hasn't moved.

'You are upset with me?' she says. 'We went too far, killing him?'

I let myself become petrified, as hard as wood. I know how to do that.

'My brother gave him a worthy death,' Mara says. 'Something . . . noble.' Her voice catches at the word and I hear her sharp intake of breath, as if she's composing herself. When she speaks again, it's with a raised voice. 'But I have no need to explain myself to you. What my brother did was self-defence. It was . . . it was *necessary*,' she adds emphatically.

A tear. It falls warmly down my cheek to the floor. I let it.

Mara lingers in the doorway, waiting for a response that will never come. 'Judge me,' she says. 'Do what you must. It will change nothing.'

There is, in her voice, a hitch. A tinge of pity? Regret even?

Wake up, I think to myself. *It's your imagination.* Mara Graziani – to harbour such hate for so long, without once revealing her identity – must be incapable of pity. I look at her boots and I see the sword, Ra. The point stabbing into the metal grate next to Vidhan's head. She took it from me. I see the chain hanging from her hand. The Wraith snatched off my neck. And me, too stunned to do anything but let it happen.

Then a hissing sound. A thump. The door closes.

And I'm left alone. With Vidhan's body.

I roll on to my back and I bang the back of my head on the floor. I've let them all down. Bea. Frankie. The Old Man. Mother. Gabriel. AM-41. Malik. Myself. Everyone. But especially Vidhan.

My throat closes. I feel dizzy.

I lie still, listening to the ship's engine thump somewhere beneath me. The floor tilts suddenly and my stomach drops. It feels like we're rising.

What difference does it make?

I slam my head down again and again on the hard grate. All that power I'm supposed to have and I let it happen right in front of me.

Vidhan is dead. His blood on *my* hands.

And Malik . . .

No. Stop. What would Bea tell me?

Get up, Moon. Stand up. Do something.

I roll my head and stare at the body slumped on the floor. He looks smaller somehow – a shadow, not a person. He's fallen in an awkward way and his left arm sticks out weirdly and the thumb of his left hand seems to point at me.

What are you showing me, Vidhan?

And then I remember.

I lift myself up off the floor. I take a deep breath and I haul out Vidhan's bent handbook from where I stuffed it right inside my jeans, up against my skin.

The Book of Seven.
I flip to a very specific chapter.

FALLING

Moving through the fabric of one realm into another is known as a **FALL**. It is, at the core, a **QUANTUM LEAP** into another dimension and involves moving through space *and* time. Though rare, there are instances of people Falling between worlds and disappearing altogether, or reappearing with knowledge beyond the ordinary.

I skip forward a few pages, skimming the parts I know, and arrive at this:

PATHFINDERS are an ancient order of superhumans. What allows us to Fall with such control, and to deal so effectively with the Reapers and quotidian enemies that beset all Pathfinders, are four inborn **ABILITIES** that, in many instances, mirror the properties of quantum physics. Pathfinder abilities may include:

TELEPATHY
Pathfinders can communicate across distances, without speaking. They form words in their minds and throw them to the receiver; at the same time, they may also 'read' other Pathfinders' thoughts.

COMBAT

Pathfinders have a natural predisposition for weaponry and warfare, although they are not gifted equally. Where one might be peerlessly skilled with a sword, another may be a master of pistols. The weapon will always choose the Pathfinder. Never the reverse.

SUPERPOSITIONING

Light, refracted, will appear in multiple places at once. In this way, Pathfinders can also be in two places at the same time. If practised and honed, this ability will allow you to move, briefly, at the *speed* of light. A skill that, when deployed in combat, offers advantage, allowing the Pathfinder to swiftly evade enemies or to attack unseen by the naked eye.

TUNNELLING

In the same way light passes through an obstacle (glass, for instance), Pathfinders* can tunnel through barriers by envisioning themselves beyond the barrier. Thus an experienced Pathfinder can pass through solid walls by willpower alone.

* Masters only. See APPENDIX for details

47

'It's the same with divorce,' I tell Bea, walking home from the horror film (which lived up to our expectations – just enough jump scares to keep us interested. It was about a loner with multiple personalities, one of which was a monster).

'What's the same with divorce?'

'You get divided,' I say. 'You go to the courts and they ask you a load of stupid questions and that's that. One week here, one week there. On and on. And it feels physical, you know? Like you're split down the middle. Into two people.'

'Moon, get over yourself.'

'But that's how it feels. Two sets of clothes. Two sets of rules. Two families.'

'And, just so I'm clear, that's bad?'

'I'm tired of being split, Bea.'

Bea stops walking and looks at me. I look back at her.

'The world hits you,' she says. 'Hard. It turns upside down and back to front. And that sucks. And it feels like the end. But maybe it's only the beginning . The start of something new Not better. Just . . . different. You know?'

'Yeah. Sort of.'

'I mean, maybe we can consciously change things. Take something bad and think it better in our heads. I suppose what I'm trying to say is this, Moon: don't let yourself be defined, or limited, by one thing. You're so much more than that.'

'I am?'

'Yeah,' Bea says, grinning. 'You're Ana bloody Moon.'

48

I stand at my cell door, feeling galvanized. I place my palms against the door, cool under my skin. I can feel the engine's thrum right through me.

I am made of atoms. The door is made of atoms. We're the same. No different. This side of the door. That side.

I close my eyes. I imagine Mother in the room, watching me, sitting cross-legged, lids half closed, exhaling a plume of blue smoke. I think about Vidhan. I think about the text in the Handbook's appendix:

Flex your muscles and shake them loose. Start with your toes and work your way up your body, all the way to your head. Relax every muscle. Every sinew. Breathe in deeply and exhale. Don't hold any tension. Relax.

I follow the commands. I breathe. I roll my neck. I relax. I let everything go.

Focus your mind on your breathing. Think about nothing else. Let yourself sink into relaxation. Feel the approach of sleep, but don't lose consciousness. Rest at the edge. Hold yourself between wakefulness and slumber.

I empty my mind. I let myself sink. I find I can do it easily, without trouble, as though I've known this skill all my life.

Visualize your body. Your torso, your arms, your legs. Flex your muscles. Not physically but with the mind.

I move my body, clench and unclench my fists, all with my mind. And I begin to vibrate.

You are ready. Do not pause. Do not hesitate. Go.

In a state of complete calm, without hesitation, I slide my arm through the door. Right through. There's resistance at first, then nothing, up to the shoulder. Now it feels cool. There's a breeze on the other side. I snatch my arm back.

I breathe. I listen to my thumping heart. I calm myself again. I don't think about Vidhan's body. It's not him. Not really. I focus on the atoms racing round my body like stars and the atoms in the door. I concentrate on merging them. That's all. Then I go.

I step through.

*

Here I am. Beyond. I look back at the door in amazement, and, when I put my hand against its impossible firmness, I'm hit by a stunning realization: *I walked through a metal door, as if it was air. It's not solid after all, it's a facade – atoms swirling, vibrating, bound by nothing but gravity.*

Crab-like and silent, I creep through the empty ship. The engine noise is now a comfortable murmur and the interior is plush and roomy, nothing like the metal cell I left behind. I walk along a tunnelled corridor towards a bright light and I feel as if I'm walking into oblivion, towards the light at the end of death.

Maybe this *is* a death. Death of the old self, birth of the new.

Then out you come and take your first breath and the world you knew vanishes and here you are – in a new one.

The corridor climbs upward on a gradual slope towards the end.

A door.

I open it and step on to the ship's bridge.

At the controls sit three figures. Akuji – no, Mara – is belted into her seat, staring out of the window. No sign of Rodolfo, her brother. Two others. Pilots maybe? Bodyguards? Reapers in their human form? They wear helmets with opaque black visors and I can see nothing of their faces. All three wear headsets. None of them turn when I enter the room.

The sky beyond them is bright through a slanted, all-around windscreen. And I see them – faded and paper-thin – the two floating moons. Clearly, the ship has lifted out of the water and I lean forward and look below. The sea has fallen away, drained by the shifting tides of Jöve. Beneath us, the ground is bizarre terrain. Apart from what you'd expect at the bottom of the sea – craters and deep ravines and purple rivers of kelp laid flat – huge skyscraper crystals tower up into the sky. And between them, rising from the strange surface, a multitude of tubular-shaped buildings with darkly curved windows, like something out of a sci-fi film.

I drag my eyes away from the view and scan the cabin. And that's when – for once – things go my way.

The sword. I see Ra laid out in a storage compartment low in the wall. I pad silently over to it, crouch and lift the blade. And, when I stand and remove the sword from its scabbard, it makes a beautiful, unmistakable sound.

Shiiing!

Mara turns. A look of shock and dismay crosses her face, almost instantly giving way to white-hot anger.

The two men swivel round and see me. They're up and out of their seats in a blur, reaching for the guns on their belts. I swing the sword and lunge at them. There's no soul-searching. No hesitation. I don't think about it.

Two clinical blows and they both go down.

Then I turn my attention to Mara. She's managed to struggle out of her harness belt and I see her go for her fighting sticks, an arm's length away, stowed under a bulkhead. Too late. I intercept her and point Ra at her throat.

'Ah-ah-aah,' I utter, adrenalin pumping through my veins. 'I don't think so.'

'Take it easy,' she says.

'Don't worry,' I reply. 'I'll give you a noble death.'

The ship makes a whining noise and, without warning, we begin to pitch. The floor tilts violently and I lose my footing. I drop to my knees and slide across the space, then leap up just in time to see Mara retrieve her sticks.

The craft begins screaming towards the ground, engines roaring. Mara circles the bridge like a cat, as silent as falling dust. On her chest I see the Wraith.

'The mechanics,' she says. 'In your cell door. They must have failed.'

I shake my head and smile. 'You're scared,' I tell her, 'and you should be.'

She springs forward, jack-in-the-box fast, and her sticks whip through the air in a blur of flashing strikes. I fall into a defensive position. My hands vibrate with every blow she lands. I get a nick on my cheek. A crack to my ribs.

I leap backwards and she flies at me, catching me flat-footed. I feint left and her sticks whip in that direction, following me.

I spring right, out of the way. Too late. An edge snags me. I feel the burn. A cut to my arm, slicing my mustard hoodie open. Not deep but I feel the blood flow.

She comes at me again, eyes on fire.

She swings and I dive right and leap through the air.

She misses.

The ship lurches. It's diving hard now. The floor is at a thirty-degree angle.

'Do that again!' I shout at her, panting hard. 'Come on!'

She paces. The tip of one of her fighting sticks drags on the floor, but not from fatigue, rather to lure me into an attack. A ploy. I steady myself. I hold the sword in both hands, tip to the roof, waiting.

'You should know,' she says, 'I have never lost a fight.'

'There's always a first,' I say, and we fly at each other.

Our weapons clang and ricochet and we exchange blows, then leap away and pace. She twirls her sticks, like a drummer in full flow. I keep my sword steady, controlled. Again we engage. We pull away. We pace.

I feel strong, like a newly oiled machine.

No longer afraid. No longer a Noob.

Entangle. Detangle. The Wraith jumps on her neck.

Now we back up into the corridor, leading into the hold space.

I walk backwards. She follows me.

She strikes, her sticks lightning fast. They cut the air. I evade the onslaught and then turn and run down the sloping corridor to regroup, get some space. She hurtles after me. I break out of the corridor, back into the hold and wait for her, breathing hard. She follows, leaning against the pitch of the ship.

Between us lies a body. My heart clenches. My hands cramp. Vidhan.

Mara's eyes flick to it and back to me. A shadow of something in her expression. Pain?

'His death,' she says. 'It was unfortunate.'

'*Unfortunate?*' I spit back at her.

'What could I do?' Mara says. 'His loyalty to the Collective, and Malik, was ironclad. He would never join us. But *you*.' Her voice hitches. 'Come with me, Ana, beyond the Gateway. I promise you, we can live a life beyond imagining.'

I step sideways, watching her, sweat rolling down my back. 'I don't think you understand. There *is* no you and me.'

'We're the same,' she says. 'We're no different.'

I stab at her and she springs back.

'We're *nothing* alike,' I tell her. 'You're a monster.'

'Am I?' she says. 'Why? What makes me the monster and not you?'

'You betrayed us. Me. Malik. All of us. You, and your brother, you killed Vidhan. He was kind. He loved you. And you killed him. He didn't deserve that. But I'll tell you what he does deserve – vengeance.'

Mara looks at me, deadpan. 'You see?' she says. 'We *are* the same.'

Then she does something I don't expect. She lowers her weapons.

It's as if she's decided to give in. Either that or she's resting. And, because neither of these two scenarios seem possible, my senses are put on high alert.

Suddenly Mara reaches out and, with the back of her fist, slams a red button on the wall. The outside door – the one that snatched us from the water – heaves open. A gust of wind sucks me towards it.

Mara attacks. Thrust. Cut. Parry. A lethal choreography. And, all the while, the ship plummets to its inevitable demise.

Ra becomes an extension of me. It's as if I was born with the sword in my hand. When I move, the sword moves. When the sword moves, I move.

We dance back and forth. Attacking. Defending. Counter-attacking.

But Mara's movements are becoming tight. I see the fatigue in her eyes. Wielding two weapons is exacting a toll.

You're tired, I tell her in my head.

She stumbles. Rests on a fighting stick, tip to the ground. I've caught her a few blows, not many, and not with much effect, given that her suit appears impregnable – but the hits have left a reminder on her skin, I can tell. She's not unbreakable. Her swagger is leaching away. She swings weakly. Rests again, breathing hard.

'So,' she says. 'You've learned . . . to fight.'

'No,' I say. 'I've always known.'

I spin and kick her in the chest and she staggers backwards. She reaches the open door and teeters back, staring at me.

'Tell me where Malik is!' I shout over the tumult of a shrieking engine and the tortured wind. 'I know he's not dead. Tell me, and I'll let you live.'

She glares at me and says nothing.

I bring Ra down powerfully and strike a fighting stick out of her hand. It flies into the ether. I move the sword to within a few centimetres of her neck. 'Tell me!'

'My brother!' she yells. 'He's gone to sell him!'

'He's *what*?'

'Venetian skin traders. Pathfinders fetch a hefty price in the river camps of Paris Nouveau. They bet on them. In the fight arenas!'

The wind screams, the engine thunders.

I look at her in fury, battling an urge to sink the blade into her jugular.

'I'll take you!' she screams. 'I know people there.'

I calm my breathing and contain the anger spiking in me. I try to read her thoughts and get nothing, no sign of any internal conflict or misdirection. If she *is* lying, it's a perfect lie.

'I should kill you!' I shout.

'You could. But then Malik dies!'

Fighting the compulsion to kick her over the edge, I hold out my left hand. She looks at me. She looks at the sword in my right hand. Then she slaps hold of my left wrist and I draw her swiftly back.

A mistake. In a bright blur, she snatches something from behind her back – Vidhan's short-blade – and slashes at me.

But I'm not here. I'm a shadow. A glimmer. Somehow, just by thinking myself out of the way, I've ghosted to the side. As elusive as light. A blur.

One split second in front of her, the next out of reach. The move catches us *both* by surprise.

Mara's pale eyes flash wide. 'Superposition,' she murmurs.

I don't bother answering. Malik said I'd improve – get faster. He was right.

I grab Mara's shoulder and, using her own momentum, I swing her round in a 180-degree arc, ripping the Wraith off her neck. Then I heave her away from the edge as hard as I can. When I release her, I whip down with the flat side of the sword's blade, smashing her over the head. Mara makes a yipping sound and goes down. Then the ship jolts to the side and she slides the wrong way.

She's gone – sucked out of the door.

I watch her drop into a bank of fog in dismay. She disappears.

With a sick jolt in my gut, I realize I'm next. I'm on a ship with no pilot and we're going down. Fast. I stabilize myself, stuff the Wraith into my back pocket, drive Ra home into its scabbard and fasten the ties to my belt. I step back further from the edge, scanning the sky for a pathway. Waiting.

Here. A shimmering? No time to be certain. I run. And, when I hit the edge . . .

I leap.

The sixth is a realm divided. Blighted below; ugly to the bone. Exalted above; or so believed.

Shrouded in cloud. Air thick and heavy. Forest as far as the eye can see. Cities grow intertwined with trees. Normals here eke out a brute existence. Pathfinders are treated as gods, and monsters. Tread carefully in this world of shadows. The Order – under the elder master, Kei Shinigami – reigns in **VENETIA**.

VENETIA

49

It repeats. The nausea, the puking and the crackling in my head. I'm in a vortex of pain. My bones ache. They feel rubbery. Like the Handbook says, it's as if my body has been force-fed through a meat mincer, bit by bit. I fight wave after wave of pain, disorientated and confused. The air is thick. It's hard to breathe.

I made it through the pathway. *Just.*

And I think, *If I made it through, maybe she did too.* *Akuji.*

No. Mara Graziani. I don't see her, though. I don't see anyone.

I drag myself through dense woodland. White clouds hang low over the canopy above. I push thoughts of Vidhan from my head. An urgent, primal shout rings out and I freeze, sword at the ready. I force myself to stay frozen for a count of ten.

They arrive. Swinging from branch to branch, high in the trees, a troop of monkey-like creatures with long, brightly coloured tails. They whoop and chatter and hurl down rotten fruit – and God knows what else – from above.

Venetia. Realm six. My fifth world away from Sol.

If *The Book of Seven* is anything to go by, not a great place for a Collective Pathfinder to find herself. But here I am. Alone. No one to watch my back. With nothing but a sword and a vial of Reaper blood. Yet what can I do but go on?

Malik needs me. Bea needs me.

And I will find them both.

I head south, following a beaten path through the woods I can only hope leads to Paris Nouveau.

I see the horseman trailing me from miles off through the dense trees. A lean and long figure.

He – I can see it's a man as he draws near through the dark wood – takes his time. Disappearing, reappearing, until he's close enough for me to see his speckled grey is a flea-bitten mare, sixteen hands and flecked with sweat. She clips alongside me, about three metres away, between the trees. The rider – in a waistcoat and a high-collared jacket – is armed. But I know he's not a Pathfinder. Surprisingly, I *feel* it. His weapon, jammed in his belt, is an ancient-looking pistol, front-loaded, like something from the nineteenth century. His hands rest on the pommel of his saddle and he leans across and spits a jet of saliva through his teeth. He wears a bowler hat, sloped over his eyes. Young, tanned, prominent Adam's apple. He's assessing me.

I stop. I turn round and I face him, feeling no fear. I'm too far gone for that.

He brings the grey mare to a halt and she shakes her dappled head and whinnies. My gaze settles on the canteen tied to his saddlebag.

'Could use a drink,' I say. My voice is hoarse, almost unrecognizable.

He reaches back, unclips the canteen and throws it across to me. I pull the stopper greedily and I lean back and take a long gulp, making sure the poncho falls aside, revealing enough of the sword to let him know it's there. I thank him, replace the stopper and hurl the canteen back. He clips it back in place, watching me.

'Where are you headed?' he asks.

'South.'

'Paris Nouveau?'

'That's right.'

'My name is Claude Duval,' he says. 'Highwayman, bounty hunter and, for those with a big enough purse, gun for hire.'

'I'm Ana Moon.'

'Pathfinder?'

'Maybe. Maybe not.'

'No. You are. I can tell. But you're not of the Order. I can tell that too.' He nods at Ra. 'Any good with the sword?'

'Draw the pistol and find out.'

He smiles. 'You're a stranger in a strange land,' he says.

Just then a red fruit zings past his hat and, effortlessly, he moves his head to avoid getting hit and snatches it out

315

of the air. He turns the fruit over in his hand. It looks like some sort of pulpy red melon. My stomach growls. He flings it hard at a tree trunk and it splatters like blood.

'Poisonous,' he says. 'Once them Gizzards sink in their fangs.'

'Gizzards?'

He raises a finger to the canopy. '*Gizzards.*'

Right. Those monkey-things. Good to know.

He points into the trees. 'Paris Nouveau is that way.' I squint in this new direction, a difference of degrees, which means I would have been miles off track.

'How far?'

He shrugs. 'Too far to walk.'

'How much for the horse?'

He smiles and tips his hat. Knocks leafy debris from the rim. 'Not for sale.'

'I might take it anyway.'

He laughs. '*Ah bon?* Is that a fact? Welcome to try.'

'So what is this? A mugging? You're offering your particular services to anyone you think is weak?'

'Think of it as a road tax,' he says, nodding. 'But you're not weak.'

'No. I'm not.'

'One more day, no food, no water? You will be.'

'And you reckon you'll wait. Rob me when I'm too broken to stop you?'

'Something like that.'

'I'm gonna need that horse,' I say. 'And you as a guide.'

He smiles down at me.

I realize, as I say the words, that this is not me. This new Ana Moon is almost unrecognizable from the girl who left Sol. How many days ago? I've lost count. The days and worlds are bleeding into each other.

Who am I? What have I become?

The grey mare stamps and Claude Duval makes a clicking sound between his teeth to settle its nerves. 'What is it you want in the capital?' he says.

'I'm searching for someone.'

'Not a safe place for a Pathfinder.'

'So I heard. But I'm going regardless. I'm looking for one of my kind. His name's Malik Habib. He might've been travelling with a psychopath assassin called Rodolfo Graziani. Those names mean anything to you?'

He shakes his head. 'This Malik,' he says, 'is he your man?'

'Look, are you gonna help me or not?'

'*Ça dépend*. What's in it for me?'

'Not dying, for starters.' I draw the sword, slowly, and turn it so he sees the sun glint off the blade.

'Some weapon,' he says.

'Help me or don't,' I say. 'Your choice.'

He makes his choice. He reaches for his ancient pistol. A premeditated move, announced with a flick of his eyes, and, before he can draw breath – let alone shift his weapon – *I've* moved. I'm at his side now and the cutting edge of my blade lies against the artery of his thigh.

He looks at me in blank shock. I've got myself a ride.

50

We travel a day and a night, sharing the horse, riding through northern France – in Venetia. The woods are dense and crowd the path. The Gizzards follow us for a while, chattering, hurling fruit, then fall back. The forest leaps with sounds. Featherless birds flash lizard-like through the velvet green, and hairy, frenzied bugs scatter into the roots under the grey mare's trampling hooves. The only people we see are either solitary opportunists or shady groups travelling in packs. We avoid them all, swinging wide arcs around them, staying downwind, hidden in the trees.

It rains. Spitting cold, ice-needle thin. Duval is surly and says little in the downpour. We pass the night in silence, huddled round a smoking fire under his tarpaulin. I tie him with his own rope to a tree before falling asleep.

The night is dark. The sky starless.

On day two the rain stops. We arrive at the banks of a sluggish, mud-coloured river carrying an assortment of steamboats. We watch them from the treeline. Then we move on, flanking the banks of the River Seine. We come to a lone hill and ride to the top. I drop from the horse, holding the reins, and step forward, sword in hand, taking care to keep Duval in my peripheral vision.

When I see where he's led me, and what lies before us, I lower my hand a fraction and let the tip of the sword rest on the ground.

'That dung pile there?' Duval says behind me. 'That is Paris Nouveau.'

There is the Eiffel Tower, intertwined with trees, one-third its normal height and in the process of being built. There, the cathedral of Notre-Dame, on the Île de la Cité. And, all about the cathedral, in the rubble of old edifices, thousands of lean-to tents and rough-made buildings with chimney stacks sending black smoke pumping into the air. Everywhere the trees muscle through the buildings, as if the forest is trying to reclaim the city. But it isn't the city that holds my attention. It's the gargantuan pyramid hovering in the sky over the Seine. The surface gleams in the dim sunlight, as if the entire structure is made from golden solar panels. It looks like the Great Pyramid of Giza, but *floating* in the air. And, from the pyramid, they soar.

Reapers.

I watch them circle. One of them dives towards a bird, a dove maybe, white against a bruised and stormy-looking sky. The Reaper snatches the bird out of the air, devours it mid-flight, and then wheels back high, rejoining its pod over the Basilica of the Sacred Heart of Paris – Sacré-Coeur, Montmartre.

I turn and look at Duval. 'Can you see them?'

'I see them.'

My hand falls instinctively to the Wraith on my neck and I watch the Reapers drift in the sky. None come to investigate. The Wraith is working, it seems.

Whirring turbines chop the air. A chugging sound.

'What's that noise?' I ask.

'Anti-gravitation engines.' He points at the pyramid. 'For that god up there.' He says this half in awe and half with what seems like distaste.

'You think Shinigami's a god?' I say.

The highwayman spits and throws open his arms. 'I do not care one way or the other. But the river camps here are full of worshippers. They crawl out from all corners of the world.'

'Why?'

'To be led to the seventh. Why else?'

'But not you.'

'Not me. They are, how you say, tilting at windmills.'

'You don't think it exists?'

'I did not say that. I know there are worlds beyond this one. I have seen enough Pathfinders come and go. But me, I have a simple credo.'

'What's that?'

'The grass is not greener.' He lifts his hat, flicks it clean with the back of his fingers and replaces it. 'Look, are we finished here? You and me?'

My hand falls on the sword. 'Not yet. Tell me about the fight arenas and the skin traders.'

Duval sucks his teeth. 'Skin traders are merchants. They look for prizefighters. The best of these are like you, Pathfinders. They sell them here at market and the camp masters who buy them force them to fight in the arenas.'

'Down there in the river camps?'

He nods and draws out from his pocket a lump of what looks like brown sugar for the horse.

'You're afraid,' I tell him, watching the grey mare snaffle it from his hand.

'Just not interested in dying.' Duval tips his chin. 'Cremations,' he says. 'Look.'

I see a horse-drawn cart turn into what looks like a burial ground with long, lime-covered pits. We watch a team of workmen in long black coats undertake the grim task of unloading dead bodies wrapped in white cloth from the cart. They heave the corpses, one after the other, into the pits. Then I see them pass a lit torch through their hands and they set the bodies ablaze.

WHUMPH!

Up in flames they go. Columns of dark smoke rise.

'The fighters that lose,' Claude says, 'burn together.'

The bodies are engulfed by smoke and fire.

The highwayman watches me. 'I have done what you wanted. I have led you here. We had an accord. The pistol, *s'il vous plaît.*'

'Not yet.'

'What more do you want? *Merde!*'

'For one thing, your *veste.*'

'My *jacket?*'

I use the sword tip to lift his lapel, revealing his grimed skin and the taut tendons of his neck. 'Your jacket,' I repeat.

He grumbles and shrugs it off and throws it on the ground. I flick off the poncho, lift the jacket with my sword and, watching him, shrug my arms into it. It smells of mould and smoke and it's heavy.

'How do I look?'

'Like you're wearing my jacket.'

I smile.

'My pistol,' he says.

'Where do they take them?' I ask. 'The Pathfinders?'

The highwayman curses and mumbles something under his breath. 'Mostly to the main arena,' he says. 'Notre-Dame.'

'The *cathedral* is a fight pit?'

'The biggest.'

I look out over the sprawling city of Paris Nouveau and I know two things with absolute certainty: Malik is here and he's alive. I feel it in my bones. An invisible thread connects us, pulling taut. I'm tempted to send my thoughts out to him, to tell him I'm here, but I get the feeling it'll attract unwanted attention.

And there's something else I know. She's here too, in that pyramid in the sky. Bea.

'How do I get in?'

'To the fights? You pay.'

'How much?'

'Ten francs.'

'How much do you have on you right now?'

'*Me?*' He gives me a nonplussed look.

'C'mon. We both know you've filched from everyone who's crossed your path.' I step up to him and dig the sword's tip into his thigh.

'*D'accord,*' he says. '*Calmez-vous.*' He rummages through his pockets and produces a handful of gold coins. Counts them out. Twenty-four francs.

I take just the ten I need and flick him up my poncho. 'Fair trade,' I tell him. 'Your life and a poncho, for a coat and a horse ride.'

Duval spits.

I point up at the pyramid in the sky. 'And how do I get inside *that* thing?'

'Bad idea,' he says, shaking his head.

'*How?*' I repeat.

He shrugs. 'Rubbish ships.' He indicates what looks like a landing zone, a few streets away from the cremation pits, where the trees have been sawn down and removed. And next to the landing zone is a hulking pile of rubbish, flocks of wheeling seagulls and bent figures crawling over giant mountains of waste. 'The Order's ships carry rubbish from the pyramid to the dump, twice a day. My cousin, Jean-Marc, he's the dump manager.'

'The family success story,' I tell him.

Duval grins, leans across and spits again.

I give him the pistol and let go of the reins. 'Leave,' I tell him. 'Don't look back. I'll find my own path from here.' I say it confidently and I mean it, but I'm not certain where the confidence ends and the bluster begins. I'm barely holding it together.

But I won't let anyone see that.

Not now. Not yet.

51

A flash of lightning. Thunder. Rain.

I'm on my own again and even with the sword I feel vulnerable. I pick my way through the sodden campsites of the Île de la Cité – alone. I pull the lapels of the rank-smelling jacket to my cheeks. Taking that was a good idea. It's waterproof, and hides the sword more than the poncho did, allowing me to blend in. I crossed the Pont Neuf from the Right Bank and now I'm walking up Quai de l'Horloge, a stone street teeming with people, heads bowed in the deluge. It feels like I've stepped back in time. Horse-drawn carriages trample up the cobbled streets and throngs of people, blurred in the grey rain, retreat to their tents and lean-tos and derelict buildings.

Lightning flashes and Notre-Dame is lit up. The black spire, still standing in this world. The gargoyles. The famous flying buttresses. A masterpiece of Gothic architecture. All in the shadow of the pyramid. It's hard not to be awestruck. But I'm no tourist and this is no holiday.

I turn right off the river into the rue d'Arcole, densely tree-lined, their roots thrusting up through the stones. The rain is coming down so hard now it's difficult to see more than a few paces. I pass a tavern spitting drunks out and into the street. A brawl ensues. Bottles swing. Punches fly. A man comes staggering towards me and I reach for the sword, but, before I need it, a woman rears up behind him and smashes a bottle over his head. They fall to the ground, grappling.

I move on.

Now I stand in an open courtyard facing Notre-Dame. A masterpiece of Gothic architecture. It's hard not to be awestruck. But I'm no tourist and this is no holiday.

Two guards, dressed in riot gear – helmets with black, opaque visors and carrying batons and pistols in their belts – stand at the entrance and oversee the passage of a long line of people into the building's dim interior. I can see scanning metal detectors just inside the huge doors. No getting in that way with a sword. Horse-drawn carriages and then metal detectors. Carts and flying ships. Venetia is an unholy mix of old and new. A reminder, I suppose, of the way Shinigami has cross-contaminated worlds with tech from other realms.

I see a huddle of Hare Krishna types walking through the crowd. They wear loose-fitting robes, beaded necklaces and their heads are shaved. One of them swings a heavy incense ball, sending up puffs of blue smoke. I can't catch everything they're shouting in their language – a version of French – but it's along the lines of, 'Repent! For it is by the hand of Shinigami that we ascend to the seventh.'

I watch them snake towards me and I think about legging it, but I don't.

'Will you give yourself to the living god, sister?' the one with the incense ball says to me in thick French, full of zeal, swinging the chain as he speaks.

'Don't come any closer,' I warn him in English. Duval had said the city is full of migrants, so I figure I won't be the only one who doesn't speak the lingo.

'A foreigner,' he says. He's reed-thin, wet through and weasel-faced. I say nothing. He watches me and says, 'Will you give yourself to the living –'

'No,' I say, cutting him off.

He pauses. Eyes me up and down. 'You come for *le spectacle, n'est-ce pas*?'

'Maybe.'

'You are in luck. It is a good day. They have captured a new Pathfinder. He fights soon, in there.' My heart jumps. *A new Pathfinder. Malik?*

'*Cherchez-vous des billets?*' he asks. 'Tickets? They are twenty francs.'

'*Twenty*? I only have *ten*.'

He narrows his eyes and says, 'Pathfinders are not cheap.'

'I need another way in,' I say, lowering my voice, pointing at the guards and the metal detectors. 'Is there a way past the guards?'

'*Sans billets?*' he says, raising his eyebrows. 'Without tickets?'

'That's right.'

'*C'est pas possible.* There is no other way.'

I see a few members of the crowd turn to me, and one of the guards looks up, and I'm wracking my brains, trying to come up with a plan, when I remember. I almost start laughing.

'Never mind,' I tell Weasel-face and I move off.

'Wait!' he says, and makes to grab my arm, but I ghost away.

I shoulder through the crowd and arrive at the south-facing side of the building. I pass a gate and walk down a stone path through a wild garden until the crowds begin to thin. When I'm certain no one is looking, I scramble over an iron fence and drop on to the other side. Moving at a half-jog, I reach the building and put my hand against the structure. I feel its vibrations – the crowds inside chanting.

The wall is ancient and, I'm certain, at least half a metre thick.

Atoms. That's all we are. Every living thing. Every solid object. Dancing neurons.

I take a step back. I breathe. I empty my mind. I don't think about anything but my breathing. I let myself sink into relaxation.

And I walk through the wall.

Long ago, with the Old Man and Frankie, I stood in queue and we walked through the towering front doors of Notre-Dame and stared up at the first Rose Window. I recall being quickly bored and begging to leave. I was seven. But I can still remember the echoing stillness of the cathedral. Rows and rows of pews and a suffocating fragrance of incense, candlewax and polish. None of that is here now.

The first thing I notice is an enormous sand-filled pit, surrounded by a high mesh-wire fence, where rows of pews once stood. Next, tiered seats rising to the stained-glass windows and holding a heaving, volatile crowd. The last thing I notice is the smell. A stink of body odour mixed in with blood.

I've emerged under one of the seating stands with a clear view through legs to the pit and the two fighters squaring off. One of them is a monster of a man, stripped to the waist and built like a circus strongman – thick-necked, barrel-chested, arms and shoulders like legs of ham. His eyes are black and soulless. Dead.

A Reaper. No question. Shifted into its human form.

The other fighter wears a hood that hides his face in shadow, but I can see the twin gleams of his dark eyes. And I know, in a heartbeat, it's Malik.

He cocks his head to the side, as if listening to a faraway sound. He knows I'm here.

'Can you feel it *building* inside?' a voice booms in English – clearly for the benefit of all the foreigners packed into the place – and a cheer goes up.

I search for the source and find him. A tall, maudlin-looking man addresses the gathering from a jutting wooden platform, using a loudspeaker to amplify his voice. He wears an austere black suit. His face is daubed in ceremonial white paint with black rings under his eyes.

'The *rage*!' he shouts. 'Embrace it. Breathe it in. Taste it. Ask yourself. Who am I? What am I capable of? Will I remain down here, mired in muck and blood? Or is my place in the seventh, with the living god? Salvation is at hand today. Redemption. You win, you rise. But how far will you go for immortality, for perfection? Will you bleed for it? Will you *kill* for it?'

Another wild cheer.

My heart thuds in my chest. My hand drops to the hilt of my sword.

'Are we *ready*?' the man in the black suit shouts.

The crowd goes wild in response. They begin to chant. 'Fight! Fight! Fight! Fight!' They stamp down on the wooden stands until the whole place seems to throb and vibrate. And now, through it all, I feel Malik's voice in my head.

You came after me.

He's looking right at me. He peels his hood back. He looks fearless.

That's more or less what happens when you follow someone, I think back to him, hoping all the noise and chaos will drown any sign of telepathy.

Vidhan? he thinks to me. I shake my head and send him nothing in response. What is there to say? And I can tell, by his reaction, that Malik understands.

Akuji?

She betrayed us, Malik.

'We have a prize fight for you today!' the man in the suit cries. 'Captured in the Northern Sea – a bona fide Pathfinder!'

A raucous cheer and some ringing boos.

'He will face none other than the ten times undefeated champion of the Île de la Cité – Le Monstre!'

The crowd goes mental again, stamping, cheering.

Ana, Malik thinks to me – calm, unworried – when the noise lessens. His eyes are dark and fierce. *Get my pistol. It's in the armoury below ground.*

'LET THE FIIIIIIIIIIIIIIIGHT BEGIN!' the man in the suit roars.

52

Malik's opponent – a head taller, at least thirty kilograms heavier, made almost entirely of thick slabs of muscle – rushes him. At the last second, Malik blurs out of the way. The strongman throws out a meaty forearm and Malik ducks under it and he's away and out of reach.

In the same second, something makes me turn and look up into the crowd, up to the platform. And here I see someone who makes my stomach churn. He's standing next to two guards and he's pointing at me with his long staff.

Rodolfo Graziani. Vidhan's murderer.

I run. I bolt round the stands until I find what I'm looking for: a steep ramp leading into the bowels of the place. I race down, moving so fast the guard at the entrance, distracted by the fight behind me, doesn't see me. I reach a maze of corridor tunnels dimly lit by kerosene lamps, and find a fork in the path.

I pause, breathing hard. Then a feeling pulls me to the right and I veer off in that direction.

A few turns later, the sound of the crowd and the fight above fading, I arrive at a dead end, and here is a caged-off, padlocked area filled with multiple shelves of weapons and a sign on the wall reading MANÈGE MILITAIRE.

That's when I smell it – a rotten stink. I freeze.

A Reaper guards the cage. Wings reach to the tunnel roof and walls. Its black eyes swivel and its nostrils flare, taking in the air. But the Wraith round my neck renders me invisible to the creature.

I think about the Reaper that took Bea on the Tube. The fear in my gut. The way it cradled Bea in its wings; the ferocious way it looked at me.

I cut it down. One thrust aimed at the heart. The Reaper chokes and slumps to the ground, bleeding plum-coloured blood. I step over it to the gate . . . and I smoke right through it.

The room is stockpiled with an array of weapons. Guns, swords, knives. An arsenal. But I'm guided by a feeling in my gut to Malik's matt-black pistol. I find it on a middle shelf, tagged with his name. I seize it, rip off the tag and shove it down the front of my jeans. Then I grab a clip of ammo next to the gun and, within minutes, I'm sprinting back up the tunnels, listening to the crowd grow more boisterous.

I hurry up the ramp and I'm out and into the periphery of the pit. A wall of noise greets me. Screaming and yelling. The drumming of a thousand feet.

In the arena, Malik's opponent has him in a headlock. They have battled their way right up to the fence in front

333

of me and Malik's face is pinched like a waffle in the mesh wire.

He sees me and his eyes light up, despite the meaty forearm across his throat.

Now! he shouts into my head.

With a burst of energy, Malik worms out of the headlock. He runs up the side of the mesh wire and, using his opponent's heavily muscled arm as leverage, somersaults over his back. He's free. At the same time, I swing the sword and split open the wire fence. I throw Malik his pistol. He catches it deftly, turns and fires a bullet into the demon's head. *Blam!*

The fight's over.

Out of the corner of my eye, I see a pair of guards descend on us, wings sprawling, changing from humans into Reapers as they come.

Escape. That's all that matters now.

We run.

I'm fairly certain Malik can't walk through walls, so I lead us straight to the front gates. We weave through the crowd, a mob hot on our tail, and barge our way forward until we meet a throng of guards blocking the gate entry.

Spearheaded by Rodolfo Graziani.

Malik fires his pistol. The sound leaves a tinny whine in my ears. He misses Graziani, hits a guard. We cut our way through the melee and charge out of the gates – Malik firing and reloading, and me slashing left and right with the sword – and burst on to the street. Behind us, the mass of guards follows fast.

Outside, it's still pelting down with grey rain. I feel a thrill at emerging from the claustrophobia of the cathedral fight pit. We've done it. We've escaped.

And then my heart sinks. We come to a skidding standstill.

Here, barring our path, stands Mara Graziani.

In her right hand, she holds the reins of a horse. A muscular, russet-coloured stallion, stamping its forelegs, eyes alight, coat slick and gleaming in the wet. Then, before we can do anything, Mara draws Vidhan's short-blade from her belt.

She throws it.

I watch mesmerized, unable to move, and I know that I'm done for. It's coming for me, my heart. But, in bewilderment, I watch it slice through the space between Malik and me.

And, when I turn, it's just in time to see the blade sink to the hilt into the chest of a guard – a guard millimetres from shredding us with a sword. He goes down with a strangled cry.

'Go!' Mara Graziani shouts, holding out the reins to me. 'Do not make me regret this any more than I already am.'

For a split second, I'm not sure how to react. And then I understand. I know what this is. Redemption.

I'd seen it in her eyes, heard it in her voice. The pain and the guilt. Vidhan was her friend. Her clan. No other allegiance could ever wipe out the things they had endured together. In the end, Vidhan and Mara were family.

Something she realized too late.

The horse stamps and rears. The stark whites of his eyes stand out as bright as the white star on his chest. I leap at his mane and haul myself on to his back. He rears again and flashes his hooves and I hang on and watch Mara sprint past Malik and plough headlong into the fray of guards following us. Malik backpedals to me. I bring the horse to him and throw out my arm. He runs, catches hold of my hand, leaps up and slots in place behind me. He winds his arms round my waist, and we go, hooves clattering over the cobblestones. At the last moment, before we veer down a side road, I turn the horse and we look back. A crowd, led by Rodolfo, surrounds Mara. I see the bright flash of her fighting sticks. I swear she looks at us then. Just a glance. And then I see a blade punched into her.

Mara drops to the ground. She's gone.

I grit my teeth and pull the horse round. 'Are you holding on?' I shout.

Malik yells something back, snatched by the wind.

We ride.

53

I don't read the road signs or panic about which direction to go next. I know the way. It's in me. The horse is a muscular thoroughbred and smooth-gaited and he too seems to know our destination: the rubbish dumps outside the city and the ships that rise from there to the pyramid above. I'm up out of the stirrups and leaning forward and Malik grips my waist and my hips and I feel wild. On our left, we're flanked by a swollen, swift-flowing Seine. We bolt down the road, swerving wide-eyed cart drivers and pedestrians.

'Whoa! Slow down!' Malik shouts from behind me. No chance.

We fly on at full tilt, white-knuckled, hair thrown back by the wind. I use my body weight and my knees and jabbing heels to keep the horse quick and on course. A glance over my shoulder confirms no one is following.

But for how long?

I think about *her*. Akuji. Mara.

Her parents were killed by the Collective. By *Mother*. It doesn't matter how. It doesn't matter what they did to deserve their fate. What matters is how it forged the ones left behind. I think about what it must take, having one goal in mind and keeping it secret – holding it close – for so long. Vengeance. Spending years deep undercover, not speaking, plotting your revenge, waiting for the right moment. And then, when it comes, being unable to follow it through to the end. *Why?*

Perhaps the people she spent her days with changed her, made her something else.

We race up a rutted road, worn by years of traffic. Ahead, I see a line of twisted trees and, beyond that, a mountain of steaming waste and, descending from the sky, a fat-bottomed airship with a name etched in black on the underside.

SHINIGAMI

I steer the horse in that direction. I can see the cremation pits now and we blast past them and up a hill, through the gates of the dump. On either side of us tower huge walls of rubbish and the stink claws at the back of my throat.

We arrive at the dump station – an L-shaped, tin-roofed warehouse backing on to the landing zone. I pull the horse to a stop in the rain and swing out of the saddle. I'm down and looking up at Malik. My legs are shaking from the ride and I can see Malik's feeling it too. He eases down off the horse, looking pale.

Then his eyes flick up and I see him go for his gun.

I swivel. Two armed men are standing in the rain. One of them has a shotgun levelled at us. He looks about forty and as hard as nails. Unshaven, wearing a wide-brimmed hat from which rainwater sluices. The other carries a front-loading pistol. He wears a bowler hat, just so . . . and a poncho.

'You owe me ten francs and a jacket,' he says.

'Highwayman!'

He nods. 'This here is my cousin, Jean-Marc.'

'Right,' I say. 'The dump manager.'

Jean-Marc says nothing.

'You know these guys?' Malik says out of the side of his mouth.

'Better tell your Pathfinder friend to drop his gun,' Claude Duval says.

I glance at Malik. His pistol is levelled at them both and he has that gunfighter look in his eye. I turn back to Duval. 'I think it's the other way round.'

Amazingly, Duval responds by pocketing his weapon. Jean-Marc watches him, side-on, and he too lowers his gun.

'Smart move,' Malik says.

'You are in the clan of Akuji,' Duval says. 'Not so?'

I'm at a loss as how to respond. Malik doesn't speak either.

'She told us to get things ready,' Duval says. 'And for her we do what we must. There is not much time. Follow us. Now or never.'

They turn and walk briskly towards the building. Malik and I don't move.

Duval turns and shrugs. 'You want to get on the next ship? You have two minutes.'

Beyond the warehouse, we find a battered-looking hulk of a ship in the landing zone. A pair of workers in blue overalls and face masks operate a waste-removal machine. Hydraulic lever arms haul a giant skip from the roof, swinging it over the front of the ship, where it upends and drops rank effluent on to a slope of rubbish. The workers see us approach, but don't look bothered. Duval stands next to us in the pounding rain. He points to the side of the ship – a door left open.

'In there,' he says. 'They know you are going with them.' He waves at one of the workmen. 'That's Jean-Pierre. My other cousin.'

'What did she do?' I ask him. 'To make you help us like this?'

'Mara?' Duval looks up at the sky and blinks. Then he looks back at us.

'My cousin's daughter,' he says. 'She disappeared one day. From this property. Vanished into thin air. It was the Pathfinder, Akuji Na, who brought her back from the other world. If it was not for her . . . Well, the Duvals are in her debt.'

'No black and white in the multiverse,' Malik says under his breath.

But something doesn't add up. 'You said she asked you to get things ready for us,' I say. 'When was that?'

Duval glances at his cousin. 'After I left you, I came here, to see my family. She was here when I arrived. She said she had seen us. You and me.'

I think about the journey here with the highwayman, two of us on the flea-bitten grey mare, ghosting through the forest, avoiding anybody and everybody. One of the figures in the trees must have been her. Following. Watching. Deciding.

'She looked different,' Claude says.

'Different?' I ask.

'Older,' he says. 'But also . . . broken.'

I don't want to hear more. And I don't want him to know what we saw outside Notre-Dame. He doesn't need to. I shrug off the jacket and hand it across. 'The ten francs are still in the pocket,' I tell him. 'Keep the poncho.'

'*Merci*,' he says, taking the jacket back from me. 'Now go,' he says. 'Or don't. The waste ships run on time.'

54

The ship's interior is cold steel and devoid of any comfort. We find six unpadded metal bucket seats with harnesses attached to the wall and I sit down and strap myself in. The sound of the machine being operated is so loud it renders everything else mute. The ship shudders right through my bones. Then the noise cuts out.

Malik slumps down in a seat opposite me and stares at the harness. He pulls out his pistol, double-checks the chambers. Finally, he attaches himself.

'Vidhan,' he says, looking up at me. 'He's dead, isn't he?'

I nod. I can't answer.

'And it was her,' he says. '*Mara.*'

I shake my head. 'She knifed him after the Fall, but it was Rodolfo. *He* killed Vidhan. Malik, she was a spy working for Shinigami.'

He shakes his head and I can see tears welling in his eyes. He looks away and wipes his eyes with the heel of his palm. Then he takes a deep breath.

'I just . . . I can't understand. How could she?'

'Mother killed her parents. That's what she said.'

Malik drops his head into his hands and blows out his cheeks. He drags his fingers up and down through his hair until it seems like he's about to draw blood. Then he slams his fist into the wall of the ship.

I say nothing. I sit there, watching him. Feeling powerless.

'How many more?' Malik says, shaking his head and staring out at the ceaseless rain. He's asking himself, but I answer regardless.

'Just one,' I say.

Malik looks up at me. His hair is wild. His eyes are wet and darker somehow. More beautiful. 'You've changed,' he says quietly.

'In a good way or a bad way?' I whisper back.

He forces himself to smile. 'That was some riding back there.'

'Trophies, remember? The lessons paid off.' And, before he can protest, I lean across the space and snap open his harness.

'The hell you doing?' he says.

'The Wraith,' I tell him, dragging out the vial from the chain on my neck. 'It can only be me from here, Malik. We both know that.'

I can't believe I'm saying those words. Especially when going alone feels like such an obviously bad idea. In the films, whenever the good guys separate, Bea and I scream at them to stay together. They never listen. Then one of them ends up dead.

'No,' Malik says, shaking his head, trying to attach himself again.

But I reach across and grab hold of his wrist. 'I can do this, Malik. I can.'

We sit here – saying nothing, looking at each other – in a flying ship on the outskirts of a city in a parallel universe, worlds away from home.

Malik pulls me towards him, takes my face in his hands and kisses me. His lips are warm and taste of rain and salt and tears. Heat radiates off his body. I keep my eyes open and stare into the darkness of his irises and my stomach flips and the walls throb and my heart jackhammers. Then he pulls back.

Sudden. Unexpected. Over.

Did I imagine it? Dream it?

Hell, no.

I pull him back by the lapels of his jacket and kiss him hard.

Malik growls, low in his throat. He kisses the hollow of my temple. My closed eyelids. My cheeks. My mouth. He feels good under my hands. There's an ache in my gut. I've Fallen, floated through the fabric between six worlds and come out the other side. But nothing – not the weightlessness, nor the Fall – feels like *this*.

His tongue in my mouth. Mine in his.

Atoms mingling, dancing. Exploding.

This is it. Right here. This is what it means to let the continents go – to let the rest of the worlds (all seven of them) drop away into insignificance. I'm as close to death as I'll ever be, but I couldn't possibly feel more alive.

'Should've done this before,' Malik murmurs, hot against my skin, taking the words right out of my mouth.

The workmen enter the ship, killing the moment.

Malik and I separate.

The workmen, without speaking, strap themselves into their seats. One of them mumbles something into a wall intercom. There's a loud hissing noise. The ship's engine grinds. And Malik stands. I feel an immediate wrench in my stomach. Malik steps backwards, out of the door, watching me. My eyes don't leave his.

'Malik!'

Go, he says into my head. *And don't come back for me. Stay away, Ana.*

I don't get a chance to answer.

With a jolt, we lurch up into the air and then we bank steeply and gravity throws my weight against the harness. The sound of the wind screeching outside is fierce. The door is still open, like an army helicopter, and rain flies in and drenches us. We scorch up above mountains of waste and the ship turns hard left again and throws us back into our seats. Now the door closes and we knife into the sky, up to the golden pyramid. Up to Bea. And to the ends of the Earth.

And all I hear is Malik's voice in my head.

Go. Stay away.

I know why. He thinks anyone who gets close to him dies.

But I won't listen. Malik's right, I've changed.

55

I'm standing in a long corridor, some two and a half metres high and sloped downwards at about thirty degrees. Brightly lit, starkly white. I'm not sure what sort of material the tunnel is made of, some sort of glass maybe, smooth and hard. The light source is within the walls. It's been at least five minutes and I've seen no one yet. On docking, the workmen ushered me out of the landing bay, looking skittish, then opened a PERSONNEL ONLY door and pointed through it. I stepped inside and they shut the door behind me. I walked on. Alone.

Now I come to a fork. One corridor veers left and the other right. There are no signs.

I'm close. I know Bea's been through this tunnel. I don't know how I know it. It's a feeling, a sense of her. But I can feel something else too, merged with her presence. Something dark and immense. Pulling me. A malevolent force.

I choose a path on instinct. And I move. The sound inside the corridor is a low, almost organic humming sound, and I move the length of it, sword in hand, feeling dizzy, disorientated. My feet are almost off the ground. I'm as light as air.

His lips on my temple, my cheeks, my mouth.

His breath a whisper on my skin.

The graze of his stubble.

His blood-caged heart a hand's-length away.

I shake my head to focus.

I climb upward, for a long time, until I come to a door. I try it.

Unlocked.

I step through and enter a vast room with liquorice-black marble floors and sloping floor-to-ceiling windows that look out over the sprawling megacity of Paris Nouveau. The room is quiet and, worryingly, empty. I expected a sprawl of Reapers, hundreds of them, waiting. The men in suits in their visors. Not this emptiness. It sends a shiver up my spine.

And that's when I notice it.

The object in the centre of the room. Not an object. Something else.

Raised above three steps is a huge, spherical blackness suspended a metre or two above the polished marble. At the edges it shimmers brightly, emitting little solar flares of light. A crackling noise, like static, comes from it and the air around it vibrates. The darkness inside the sphere is a dense, profound blackness. A yawning mouth waiting to feed. I stand in front of it, mesmerized. Then I reach out to touch it and feel an immediate current pulling me to the hole, sucking me in. The hairs on my arm stand up. A chill runs down my spine. A feeling of impending doom.

I look up. The stone ceiling, high above, converges at a point right above the centre of the room. Around the edges stand an assortment of relics and busts and various artefacts. On the walls hang extraordinary paintings. I recognize them from art class. Here's the swirling madness of Van Gogh's *Starry Night*. Here is *The Garden of Earthly Delights* by Hieronymus Bosch. Three extraordinary panels, ranging from heaven to hell, and a weird panorama of paradise lost between them. And here is Goya's *Saturn Devouring His Son*. A grisly, macabre painting. It shocked me the first time I saw it. Saturn emerges from the darkness and, with wide mouth and bulging eyes, he goes about consuming the corpse of his own son.

'Impressive, is it not?' a cold voice says behind me. A hint of sibilance.

I swing round. Here stands the god and the devil. And he's like nothing I imagined.

For starters, *he* is a *she*.

'Some call it monstrous,' she says. 'But I see only beauty.' I assume she's talking about the painting, but then I'm not sure. She might just as easily mean the dark pulsing mass suspended in the air. Or even herself.

She wears a long robe, like the kind Gabriel and the masters wore at the Council Meeting in Ares. Her hair is silver-grey and shorn to the skull, like a Buddhist monk. Her eyes are sharp and as green as the sea. She's small. Of indeterminate age. A Japanese woman you might pass on the street and not give a second thought to. Yet, despite her unimposing physical size, she has a presence. She takes up

348

space in the room. She feels potent somehow, a figure of terrible beauty and power. Undoubtedly, this woman is Master Kei Shinigami.

She stands at the entrance. Two guards flank her and, from behind, half a dozen more – like black-clad storm troopers – file into the room, their reflections throwing sprawling wings on the polished floor.

And there, in his ermine-collared coat and his suit of patterned black armour, stands her assassin, Rodolfo Graziani.

'Welcome,' Shinigami says, 'to my humble abode.' Her voice is cold. 'We've been running circles round each other. Me hunting you; you hunting me. The inevitability of this moment almost gives me chills.'

I stand with my arms pinned to my sides and stare at her.

'Where is she?' is all I manage to say.

Shinigami raises her eyebrows. 'A terse greeting but understandable. Your friend is, after all, the reason we have the pleasure of your company.'

'She's here. I know she's here.'

Shinigami smiles. The smile does not extend to her eyes. 'Ana Moon. The one and only. How we are honoured today, Rodolfo.'

The assassin stares at me with cold hate, then bows his head in deference. 'We are honoured,' he mumbles.

'Forgive his raw manners,' Shinigami says. 'He's bitter today. His sister, once loyal, fell to the wrong side. As you know.'

'People make mistakes,' I say. 'It happens. She made a mistake. And then she made amends.'

'Yes,' Shinigami says. 'And paid with her life.'

Graziani makes a sound in his throat. I clench my fist round the sword's handle.

Shinigami watches me with untroubled eyes. 'Look at you, all that fire in your belly. You have me to thank for that, Ana Moon.'

'*You* made a mistake too,' I say through gritted teeth. 'Your Reaper came for me but it took Bea. How smart is that?'

Shinigami clasps her hands behind her back and paces the room. Her robe shifts as she walks and I see the sheathed weapon on her back, a black sword – a katana. She pauses at the angled windows and looks out. The rain has stopped and the sun is rising. A huge disc in the sky, diffused golden by the tint in the glass.

Outside, the Reapers fly.

'Useful creatures,' she says. 'Delightfully compliant.' She turns and smiles at me. 'Yes, they failed to bring you to me. But look. Here you stand.'

I'm not sure how to respond. So I don't.

'Has it not occurred to you,' she says, 'that everything, up until this moment, has been . . . inevitable?' She shakes her head. 'A *mistake*? There are no mistakes in the multiverse. Merely different paths to the preordained.'

There it is, I think. *Her weakness. Pride.*

'Ana Moon,' Shinigami says. 'You don't yet know who you are, do you?'

I open my mouth to answer, but no words come. I'm not sure how much she knows about the prophecy. Have her spies told her everything?

'Most people,' Shinigami says, 'are slaves to their moods and their desires. They drift through life without resistance, pawns in a game of chess. Even Pathfinders Fall like this, unconsciously. It's the reason so many of them become lost. But masters. Oh, we rise above. We move the pawns. We *create* the world we want.'

She circles in towards me and I step backwards. The pulsing darkness is right next to me now.

'Tell me,' Shinigami says. 'You carry Ra, mightiest of all Pathfinder weapons. You've achieved so much, so soon. Through my Reapers and spies, I have seen it all, every step of your journey here. So what are you? Master or pawn?'

I look from her to the sword in my hand and say nothing.

'You know what I abhor?' she says. 'Weakness.'

Then she does something extraordinary.

She draws her sword as fast as smoke and she flies at Graziani.

She brings the black blade down with a snapping sound.

And she decapitates him.

In horror, rooted to the spot, I watch his head roll, smearing a path of blood across the floor. Shinigami calmly resheathes her blade and looks at me.

'Weakness in the bloodline,' she says, kicking the head aside. I stare at her in shock.

351

'Weakness is a pathogen,' Shinigami says. 'It must be destroyed. The multiverse is sick, overpopulated with the faint-hearted and the feeble. So I will do what I *must*. I will annihilate what is left of the multiverse and build a new order out of the ashes of the old.'

'You're off your meds,' I tell her, squaring my shoulders.

She smiles and says nothing. Her eyes are implacable. I look at Graziani's headless body. I look at the black sphere at the centre of the room. Its shimmering, pulsing edge of fire.

'The Seventh Gate,' Shinigami says. 'Here, over Paris Nouveau, undetected for millennia. Until *I* found it and built my fortress round it. Perfection lies beyond this gate. Power to build this new order. I'm certain of it. But finding the key – the one in Mother's prophecy that will open the gate to *and from* the other side – has proved infinitely more onerous than finding the portal itself. Every Pathfinder, every Normal I've sent through has not returned.' She steeples her fingers like Dr Augur. 'Now this could mean,' she says, 'that, once there, they are so enthralled that they never desire to come back.'

'What have you done with Bea?' I ask, breathless. 'Is she –'

'On the other side, yes,' Shinigami interrupts. 'Like all the others. And, like all the others, there she remains. Not one returned. Even on pain of torture. Would *you* not return if I held a loved one at knifepoint?' She looks at me strangely and a thrill of panic shoots through my body. 'I admit,' she continues, smiling, 'I was at a loss.' She says all this as if reciting a poem. Lost in the cadence of her reasoning. 'Until I heard about you. This Moon girl from Sol with powerful abilities.' She lets the 's' linger. 'So I snatched you from your world and brought you here and sent you through the gate. And I waited. And waited. And finally I realized my mistake. We had caught the wrong girl. But at least we knew who the *right* girl was. Since then, my Reapers have been tracking you down, hunting you, driving you towards this moment.'

'What is it you want?' I snarl.

'Isn't it obvious? I want *you* to step through the gate, Ana Moon. I want you to walk into Kronos and return. With or without your friend.'

'And what then?' I ask, staring into the darkness. 'You'll let us go?'

Shinigami throws up her hands. 'Once you return, and the pathway flows so I may enter and return myself, yes. *Then* I will release you.' She looks at me. 'You and your *friends*.'

The extended 's' sound, delivered by the sibilance in her voice, alerts me. Friends. Not friend. The plural matters.

Behind her, I see why.

Pushed into the room, bound and gagged, a knife at his jugular – Malik. He's bruised. His nose is bleeding. It looks like he's taken a beating. He blinks at me and sags in the grip of his captor, one of the Reaper-guards.

I try not to let Shinigami see the emotion in me. I allow no panic, no surprise on my face. I look back at her.

353

'Fine,' I say as calmly as I can. 'We have a deal.'

Three things I know, with absolute certainty, as I say this. First, she's telling the truth – Bea *is* in the seventh. I know it in my gut. Second, she's lying – she won't release us. Why would she? Third, *I'm* lying – there *is* no deal. But there's also no choice. I walk to the gate, hair swirling, electricity in my skin.

I look at Malik. And I step into the dark.

The seventh. Pathfinder masters overwhelmingly agree that whatever wonders lie in **KRONOS** will be tempered with forces of equal and opposite power. As above, so below; as below, so above. It is a belief long held that the seventh takes you to the darkest corners of your mind. Into the shadow.

The elder master, Mother, has written that the seventh will be whatever the mind craves. A dream. A nightmare. It will reflect what's inside. If your spirit is light, it will be a paradise. If you have darkness in you, you will see only darkness and it will be hellish, from first moment to last – an inescapable prison.

KRONOS

56

Black. In every direction – behind me, ahead of me, to either side – nothing but an absolute infinity of black. I look down and I see the ground is black and, above me, the sky is black. There's no sound. I spin round, trying to see the vast room inside the pyramid, where I stepped into the hole. Nothing. It's gone. Replaced by the profound dark. The soundlessness. I'm not puking and I don't feel my teeth ache. I don't *feel* anything. When I walk, there's no squeak of my trainers on the ground. I hear nothing. Not my breath nor the beat of my heart. Black.

That's all.

I walk on through a world dipped in oil. Numb. Alone.

Then I feel it. A current at my feet.

I see now I'm walking through dark water pooling at my hip. I look up and, as I watch, the sky moves through many shades from midnight black to brilliant cobalt blue. And now the water I'm wading through is clear and turquoise and the ground beneath my feet is sand. Shadows pass at my thigh and I get a tingling sensation up my spine. I'm not alone in the water; there's movement. A turtle finning away.

I follow.

Now, rising from the blue, a beach shimmers in the heat ahead. And strung between two palm trees, lying in a hammock, I see an old woman. In an instant, I find myself right in front of the hammock and the woman swings out easily and looks at me. She's wearing a white kaftan robe and sandals. Eyes hooded, half closed.

So, she says, straight into my head. *It's you.*

'Mother! You're *here*?'

Perhaps, she says. *Or perhaps you're imagining me.* She looks at the foam-flecked sea. *Now that I think about it, perhaps I'm the one dreaming you.*

Mother walks to the water's edge and I follow her. She sits down, elbows on her knees, and stares out over the blue. I sit next to her and dig my hands into the wet sand. Waves pound against the restless horizon.

'This beach,' I say. 'The waves . . . they remind me of something.' And then I remember. 'It's Vidhan's beach. He surfed here when he was a kid.'

Mother nods. *It's possible*, she says. *A promise you make to someone. That could mean something here. Or not.*

She stands abruptly. *The seventh*, she says in my head, *is everything you ever wanted. Love. Hate. Truth. And truth, when you find it, can be dangerous.*

I look up at the faint outline of a moon in the sky – a ghost – there despite the brightness of the day, sharing the sky with the sun.

Seawater, bright with sunlight, whispers up the beach and the moon sucks it back. I watch the flow, mesmerized. I'm transfixed by a cloudy phosphorescence in the water. The air is warm and I feel salt on my skin. When I turn to look at Mother, she's gone. I look up and down the white-gold beach and out to sea, to a set of swells rising and breaking far away. When I squint against the sun, I think I see the outline of a surfer paddling hard, dropping down the face of a giant wave. But it could be a trick of the light. I step into the water, guided by instinct.

Up to my thighs.

My hips.

My chest.

A wave breaks, crashes down close to the shore, and I'm thrown off my feet. I'm flipped upside down, spinning, a sea of foam and panic in my chest.

I let go. Let myself become limp. The current carries me.

I feel it pulling. And pulling.

And I allow it.

I'm in the deep sea, on my back with my arms outflung, beneath a vaulted metallic-black sky drilled with a billion stars. The world tilts and the stars are below me now and I fall out of the water into them and float through a wilderness of night, the air cool on my skin. I'm treading water through the stars. The Earth turns. The sun rises. A solar flare arcs across the dark. A bright burst of light. Then whiteness.

*

The next thing I know, I'm standing in front of a terraced house, in daylight, blinking. The street, a cul-de-sac, is empty. I'm alone. Not a single person, not a car, nor a cat or dog in sight. The whole area is deserted. The stillness is immense. I remember the dream I had about walking through an abandoned city. And Bea's interpretation – virginity. She was wrong. I know the meaning of the dream. It was a premonition. A warning. A dream about death. I look at the house and the hairs stand up on my arms. I feel a prickle at the base of my neck. I know this street, this house. I've been here before. Cedar Lane. London. Bea's house.

Each step to the gate takes an effort of will, as if I'm walking through still wet cement. I stand at the gate, open it and walk through to the whitewashed front door. An ordinary four-panelled wood door. I lift the brass lion-head knocker.

But, before I let it fall, the door swings open.

'Moon!'

57

I stare at her with a clobbering heart, butterflies in my stomach, a tingle in my scalp. Here's the face I know. Sharp-eyed and bright, the careless wedge of hair. The face I've dreamed of seeing for so long, the face that's drawn me across seven worlds. She's wearing the same outfit she wore on the Tube that day she was taken. A lime-green jumpsuit no one else could ever get away with wearing.

'Bea –'

'Moon,' she says. 'Where have you been?'

'But –'

'C'mon,' she says, laughing, holding the door ajar. 'We're having tea.'

Tea?

She steps aside and I walk past her in a daze, sword banging against my thigh.

The hall is in shadow. People laughing somewhere within.

I glance back at the road and it's gone, replaced by a field of golden wheat rising and falling in a quiet wind. The sky above a perfect blue. Bea shuts the door and we glide through the hall into the sitting room, and the voices there.

I feel nervous. Excited. Inexplicably frightened.

Beams of sunlight slant into the room through windows thrown open, and a thousand motes of dust float in the light, whirling through the air like stars.

Here, sunk in armchairs round a coffee table, four adults.

Mrs G. Bea's mum. She wears a summer dress, hooped gold earrings and a necklace of jangling stones. She looks up as we enter and smiles.

Next to her – wearing a suit with a white shirt, collar undone – is a small dark-haired man. I recognize him immediately.

Avi Gold. Bea's dad.

'Ana,' he says, standing. 'Trouble on the Tube? Should've taken a taxi.'

'Mr G.?'

'Come,' he says. 'Join us.'

'But . . . you're . . . I mean, this is –'

'Ana, love. Sit here. Next to your father and me.'

The voice snaps my head round. I'd almost forgotten the other two people in the room. And, when I turn to look at them, my throat closes and the room spins.

Frankie. She taps the cushion on the settee next to her. On the other side of the cushion, holding Frankie's hand, the Old Man. My mouth opens and closes and I walk towards them, joy bursting in my chest. Frankie and the Old Man. *Together.*

Not *just* together. *Hand in hand.*

I know this can't be real, but I float over to the settee anyway. And then, mid-stride, I stop. The sword. Not one of them has said anything about the blade tied to my hip. That is *not* normal. Not. At. All.

I look at Bea and I snatch her wrist.

'Hey!'

'Bea, I need to talk to you,' I whisper.

'No!' she says firmly, shaking her head.

'Bea, this is important.'

'NO!' she says again, her voice ratcheting up.

I glance at the others in the room – our parents. They look confused. Their eyes shift from Bea to me. Seeing them here, like this, after so long, makes my lungs fill up with air. I feel like bursting. Like hurling myself across the room at them, hugging them both. But something tells me to wait. I turn my back on the room and face Bea. I hold her shoulders and spin her towards me. She tries to turn away but I don't allow it. 'This isn't them, Bea. This isn't real.'

'Ana,' she says, squirming. 'What do you mean, *real*?'

She pulls away and I haul her back and turn her face to mine. I can't even blame her. She's been trapped here for how long – weeks? Months?

'Look at me, Bea. All this . . . it's an illusion. It's not real. I know it seems beautiful. I mean, of course it does.

Your dad. I can't imagine what it must feel like, seeing him again. And my parents, under one roof. It's incredible. But it's not *real*.'

'And that matters?' she says.

'Yeah. It matters.'

'Why? What's wrong with living here? Can't you see, Moon? My dad, he's alive here. He's *alive*. And your parents, look at them, they're *together*. All that pain. That hurt. It's gone.'

I grab her elbow and yank her arm.

'It's not real, Bea. These people . . . they're not what you think. They may look like them, they may even behave like them, but they are *not* them. It isn't real.'

'So what? What do I care what's real or not?'

I pull her backwards with me through the open doorway, down the passage to the hall. She resists but I'm stronger.

'I need to show you something,' I say. 'Just . . . trust me, OK?'

'Show me *what*?' she says, struggling against me.

We get to the front door and I turn awkwardly, still holding her arm, and I fling open the door. We're hit by bright sunlight. 'This,' I say.

As far as the eye can see, in every direction around the house, is a sea of golden wheat. No roads. No houses. No cars. *Wheat*. That's all. Like something out of a cereal ad. Blue, cloudless skies and golden wheat drifting in the breeze. I let Bea go and we stand at the door, staring out at Kronos. I think about the soaring skyscrapers of Lūna and the falling red ash and the devastation of Ares. I think about Gabe dropping from the sky. Tir and AM-41, a poncho-wearing cyborg. I think about freight-surfing and kissing Malik and underwater cities and pyramids in the sky. And Reapers.

I turn and look at my best friend.

'Bea . . . listen to me. I've travelled so far to find you. And –'

'So far?' she says, cutting me off. 'I've only been here. At the parentals' house. That's a fifteen-minute cycle from yours, Moon.'

'Bea –'

'Moon,' she says, dragging the hair out of her eyes. 'I'm home. I don't care about all this.' She waves her arm, indicating the fields stretching into the distance. 'I don't.'

I look out over the fields and the impossible blue sky, wracking my brain.

'How long have you been here?' I ask.

'Here?' she says, glancing down the corridor. 'I mean . . . I don't know. Like, a day? It feels like a day. But then . . . OK, maybe longer. I can't really remember.'

'Doesn't that bother you?' I ask.

'I'm *home*,' she repeats emphatically.

'Right. But you don't remember how long you've been here, and I bet you don't remember how you got here, do you?' I ask.

'I do. I was . . . with you, right? We were walking home from school through the woods . . . and then . . . and then I was here. That's all.'

'You don't remember the Circle Line? What happened?'

'Nothing happened,' she says, shaking her head. 'I came right here.'

I feel a spurt of panic in my gut. I think about Malik waiting – bruised and bloodied – a knife at his throat. 'Do you remember the fight at least?' I ask Bea.

'With Erika Jürgen? Course. How could I forget that?'

My heart skips. *Now we're getting somewhere.*

'Yeah, that was crazy,' Bea continues. 'The way you pulled her off me! I've never seen you like that. You were something, Moon. If it wasn't for you –'

'Wait. No. That isn't how it happened. *You're* the one who pulled her off *me*.'

'You crazy? Moon, it was *you*.'

Now I'm the one with a warping, bending memory. My head spins.

'But –'

'You really let her have it, Moon. It was impressive, gotta say.' She looks down the corridor again, takes a step away from the door.

My heart beats hard. I shut my eyes and I'm on the path again. In the woods. With Bea. And, like a bulldozer, Erika Jürgen comes.

Next thing I know she's got me – no, that's wrong – it didn't happen that way. She's got *Bea* pinned up against a tree. It happens fast. Her hand is at Bea's throat and then I'm the one pulling Erika off Bea and I'm hitting her and hitting her and, at the edges of my vision, everything bends. The light turns silvery. It shimmers.

368

I remember now. It was me. *I* was the one doing the beating. *Me.*

The multiverse tips.

And then I think about Mother.

A promise you make to someone. That could mean something here.

'Bea,' I say. 'D'you remember what you said to me that day? You said you'd do whatever it takes, go to the ends of the Earth for me.'

Bea looks at me. She says nothing. But she stops moving away from the door.

'You said, if you were mad and lost, I'd pull you back from the brink. Bea, you *said* that. You said it's who I am. Well, I'm here now. I'm pulling you back.'

She shakes her head. Looks down the passage. A man's voice floats to us.

The Old Man? No. Bea's dad.

I grab hold of Bea's arm, willing her to come with me, begging her with my eyes. This isn't her world; it's not where she belongs. Bea's eyes are swimming with tears. She looks confused, lost, smaller than she was before.

'Don't make me leave, Moon. Please,' she says, her voice cracking. 'You don't understand. He's been gone for so long. It hurts.'

'I know it hurts. I know.'

'It never stops hurting. It never goes away. It hurts so bad.'

'Bea, I know. I know it does.'

She's crying now. Tears flow down her cheeks.

I yank her to me, pull her close and we hug.

'You have to come with me,' I whisper against her skin. 'You *have* to.'

'Why?' she says, sniffing, wiping her eyes. 'Give me one reason.'

I pull the wedge of hair away from her face. I take her hands in mine. I look her in the eye. 'Because,' I tell her, 'back in the real world, she's waiting for you, Bea. Your mum – your *real* mother – she's waiting for you to come home.'

And that's when I feel a shift in the atmosphere.

We're not alone.

Frankie and the Old Man are standing side by side in the corridor with us.

'You need to come back,' Frankie commands. Her voice is weirdly harsh. 'Your father and I, we're waiting for you, Ana. Come back to us.'

I feel a warmth pulling me down the corridor to them. Something needful. Now it's *me* taking a step away from the door.

Bea stiffens next to me. She's stopped crying.

The Old Man holds out his hands to me. There's something not right in the way he looks at me. Something in the eyes. 'Come,' he says sharply. 'We'll go back to Bristol. Just the three of us. You, me and Frankie.'

I take another step. Something's wrong here. But it feels so good, so warm with them. *We'll go to Bristol. Things will go back to the way they were.*

Bea grabs my arm. 'Moon! Snap out of it.'

'But, Bea, they're –'

'Not your parents. Look at them. Just look!'

I look at them. And I see.

Their eyes are crazed. And black, like oil. They're taller than they should be. Necks bent. Heads tipped against the ceiling. Their arms look like spiders' legs.

'Bea?' I say.

'Moon?'

'Run!'

58

We make it into the wheat, driving our shoulders through, just as they explode out of the door – loping – on all fours, like animals. I feel a spike of fear. But, in the field, I think the odds are even. We press on, getting whipped and cut. Behind us, they come, two burrowing creatures. A sharp wind knifes through the wheat and the light shifts. I hear my name called over and again. 'Ana! Come back to us, Ana!'

I stop running and, panting hard, I turn to look behind.

'Ana, no!' Bea shouts. She grabs my arm and pulls. Just in time.

A figure crashes through the plants and flies past us, right where I'd been standing. That wakes me up. I haul out my sword.

'Ana?' Bea says.

'Shh,' I say. We're back to back, waiting. The wind howls.

One of the figures explodes out of the wheat and, without seeing it properly, I pivot and slash the sword left to right. There's an awful screech and the wheat rustles and something tunnels away from us. Then silence. We stand there, panting.

A moon eclipses the sun. The wheat field darkens. It folds round us like water. In the blink of an eye, we're suddenly in a black sea. I hold on to Ra for dear life as giant swells heave and dip around us. We swim drunkenly through blood-hot water. In another blink, the sea becomes as black as oil and drops away and we find our feet in sand. We're alone, on land again. Darkness all around.

We walk through a silent darkness, wordlessly, hand in hand.

Now we see a pinprick of light.

It grows into a large, bright hole. Bea looks at me, wide-eyed, following my lead. We keep walking and the hole keeps widening, until we see the room beyond.

Then we step through.

It takes a moment for my eyes to adjust to the brightness. The pyramid. The commanding view of Paris Nouveau. The extraordinary works of art. The Reaper-guards. Malik. Still bloodied, gagged and bound, but wide-awake now. Eyes fierce. And everyone still in the same position they were in when I stepped into the gate. Including the elder master, Kei Shinigami.

She comes hungering towards us, rapt and light on her feet. 'It worked!' she cries. 'I *knew* you were the key. And now the seventh is mine.'

I glance at Bea. She doesn't look shocked or scared. But that's Bea.

'I remember you,' Bea says to Shinigami. 'And this place.' She looks round the room, staring. 'Bloody hell,' she says. 'So much money. You'd think you could have hired a better interior designer. It's a little tacky but –'

She must see Malik then, because she stops speaking abruptly.

'Hey!' Bea shouts. 'Hey, Moon! It's *him*. Dreamboat.'

'I know,' I say.

An image springs into my head: Gabe looking at me intently.

Ana. We want you to kill Shinigami.

'How long was I gone?' I ask Shinigami, trying to buy time, to conjure up a plan. I don't have one. Get Bea – bring her back. *That* was the plan. It stopped there.

'How *long*?' Shinigami says in a tone suggesting she's affronted by my question. 'A second, a blink. What does it matter? Kronos is all that matters now.'

'And it's exactly how everyone said it would be,' I tell her, looking at the Seventh Gate, which is surprisingly silvery-blue now, not black. And not as forbidding. It vibrates and shimmers, like any other pathway between worlds.

'I knew it would be,' Shinigami says, her voice febrile. The expression on her face moves through a multitude of emotions: hunger then greed, then pride and triumph. She unsheathes her obsidian-black sword.

'Fate,' Shinigami says, 'drives everything. You cannot change the past, or alter the things that have made you what you are. Destiny is immutable. It was always mine to find the seventh and create perfection, as it was yours to open the path to true power for me. And now, since you are surplus to requirements, your destiny is death.'

Shinigami's sword sings through the air. She leaps at me so fast she becomes vaporous, like smoke.

I leap to the side and parry her black blade.

Ra vibrates in my hands and my arms shake, right up to the shoulders.

We circle each other. In my peripheral vision, I see Bea restrained by a pair of guards and Malik wrestling his own. A stink rises now and I see some of the guards transform into their Reaper form, pink-skinned and vile.

Shinigami strikes. I defend and dance back. She comes after me, forcing me further backwards, until we're moving through the space like prizefighters, her advancing relentlessly, me stumbling back. Our swords cut the air.

Shinigami moves with terrifying speed, faster than Vidhan and more skilled than Akuji. Quick and lithe, like a viper. When she attacks, it feels as if ten swords are slicing through the air at me. And, no matter how fast I move, or how quickly I defend and counter-attack, she's always a step ahead, coming at me, eyes alight.

It's not long before I'm streaming with sweat. My muscles begin to seize up and spasm. I find myself standing in front of the Seventh Gate now. Feeling the dark pull of it, my feet almost lifting off the ground.

I know I'm no match for Shinigami. In terms of raw sword-fighting talent, she has me easily beaten. She's blazing-quick. It's almost a thrill being this close to someone of such incomparable skill and coiled energy.

Almost. Mostly, it's terrifying. Compact and efficient and light on her feet, her strikes are so easy, they're almost lazy. Her footwork is a blur, impossible to read. I keep searching for a chink in her defences. I cancel out the others in the room. Narrow my focus to Shinigami and our two blades whipping through the air like lightsabres.

She cuts me across the shoulder. Not deep, a surface wound, but it burns and I can't stop the yelp that escapes my lips.

'You're shaking,' she says.

She's right. I am. My whole body is shuddering. I spin through darkness and despair. I lunge at her and miss. Swing again and stumble past her.

She's a machine. An automaton. She keeps on coming.

She cuts me again. A deeper slash this time, across the stomach. I gasp and swerve out of the way of her next strike. I see the triumph in her expression. She knows we're close to the end now. We move round the room and I see a gap and thrust, but she slips out of the way like mercury and Ra stabs into the pale face of Goya's *Saturn*. Shinigami laughs.

I pull the blade free, sweating. A surge of panic tears through me.

I curse my mistakes, the poor timing, the clumsy manoeuvres. Everything I've learned, everything Akuji – no, *Mara* taught me disappears.

I'm a Noob again. A beginner. Nothing in comparison to Shinigami.

How long until the end now?

How much time before I feel the steel of her blade cutting through my throat?

Will it hurt, I wonder?

Will I even see death when it comes?

I jerk my body out of the way of another brutal strike and stagger back.

I recall the tent in Lūna and Mother hitting me time and again, so long ago. Coming after me and hitting me and hitting me. I think about fighting Mara, high above the desert plains, and the relentless, unforgiving way she came at me.

And that's when I remember.

You get stuck in your mistakes. It is why you lost. Put them behind you. Let go. Find a way to win, from inside.

I let go. I float. I feel the Seventh Gate pulsing. Pulling.

And I think about a line from *The Book of Seven*.

If you have darkness in you, you will see only darkness and it will be hellish, from first moment to last – an inescapable prison.

Everything else the book has said has been true. Maybe I need to trust it one more time.

'You were right about one thing,' I tell Shinigami, breathing hard. 'I can't change the past, but the future, *my* future, that's up to me. And yours is the seventh.'

Shinigami smiles coldly. Her black sword whips through the air . . .

I ghost out of the way. I move so fast, it feels like I'm stepping outside my body, and the room around me, and everyone in it, becomes frozen in time. In the final second, I can tell she knows it's over. She must see something in the darkness of the gate that terrifies her, because the expression on Shinigami's face morphs from triumph to horror. Her sword hovers in mid-air, arcing towards my neck. In slow motion, almost in freeze-frame, I step round her and deliver a brutal kick to the side of her knee. I hear the bone pop.

Time accelerates.

Shinigami roars in pain and falls forward . . . into the silvery-blue.

And disappears.

At that precise moment, every Reaper in the room disintegrates. They shriek and fall, shattering into pieces, which then float away like shreds of ash.

I stare into the gate for a long time afterwards, half expecting Shinigami to explode back out, sword flashing. But no one emerges. The silvery air is placid and calm, like a skin of water hiding a body dropping unseen into a bottomless dark. The Reapers are gone. Shinigami is gone. And now I know she will not return. The certainty of this becomes something that simply is that way. Like the sun rising and falling. The good and the bad. Heaven and hell. *This* is the Seventh. All that's left is me. And Malik.

And Bea.

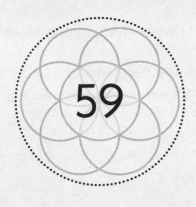

59

The three of us find our way back to the landing bay and stand on the bridge, door open to the sky and the searing wind. Malik, Bea and me. The sun is high overhead and the sky metallic-blue. Malik takes my hand. Electricity flies between us, like sparks jumping the two terminals of a battery.

'Look,' Bea says, peering over the edge. 'I don't mean to interrupt this little moment here, but if I could just ask one bloody important question.'

'Fire away,' Malik says.

'What the *hell* are we doing?'

'We're Falling,' Malik says. 'What else?'

'See now, here's the thing,' Bea says. 'When you say Falling, I hear *dying*.'

Malik looks at Bea and clutches her hand. 'Trust me,' he says.

Bea frowns at me and I can see she's freaked out, even if she's playing it cool.

'It's OK,' I tell her. 'You'll be fine. Everything'll be fine. I promise.'

'Wait,' Bea says. 'Just wait –'

We don't. We run and, together, we leap.

Then we lift.

We float.

And we Fall.

The Welsh of **SOL** have a beautiful word, among many — *hiraeth*. It means 'a longing for home'. It's an idea all Pathfinders carry with them. The Pathfinder way is hard, beset on all sides. Returning home, to your birth world, is not just a yearning; it's a necessity.

SOL

60

'Want me to wait here?' Malik says.

I shake my head. My hands are trembling. I can't catch my breath. I step up to the door, insides churning.

A burgundy-red door. *The* burgundy-red door. Red not black. I look at the number above the lintel. 7 Underwood Lane. The 7 offset, tilted to the left. Malik stands next to me, weaponless. We removed my sword and his gun and stored them at the Haven. I figure I'll find a more appropriate hiding placc later, when things have settled. If they settle.

'Two hours,' I say. My chest is tight. 'You're sure that's all it's been?'

'Like I said,' Malik says, 'time is different in each world.'

'But it took so long to get back,' I say, stalling. 'Kronos to Venetia, then Jöve, Tir, Ares and Lūna. And all the way from Paris to –'

'They'll be expecting you, Ana. Like I said.'

'And what do I say about you?' I ask, looking at him, heart thumping.

He shrugs. 'Tell them I'm a friend.'

A *friend*.

We said goodbye to Bea at the whitewashed front door of her terraced home on the real Cedar Lane. Actual cars on the road. And trees. And people. No wheat.

'So I suppose this is it,' Bea said, looking at her house, and then at me.

'I suppose so,' I said.

'He won't be there,' she said.

'No,' I answered quietly. 'He won't. But *she* will. Your mum.'

Bea nodded and inhaled deeply. Breathed out. 'Will it hurt?' she said, looking at Malik.

He shook his head. 'You won't feel a thing.'

'And I'll forget everything?'

'Yup.'

'You're sure? *Every*thing?' she asked again. 'All that weird Falling and getting sick business and . . . everything else I saw there.'

'Everything,' Malik repeated.

'Why can't you just let me remember?'

'It doesn't work that way. You're a Normal,' he said.

'First time you've been called *that*,' I said, laughing.

Bea gave me the finger.

Malik positioned himself in front of her, placed his hands on her shoulders, straight-armed, and stared into her eyes. Then – without a word uttered, without a sound – he wiped her memory. I knew it must have worked, because, when Malik turned her round and pushed her gently towards her home, she didn't look back.

We stood unobserved – *unremembered* – on the far side of the street and watched Bea lift the brass knocker and let it fall.

A few seconds passed. Then the door opened and out spilled a warm light.

Bea stepped inside. The door closed.

'So let's see,' I say now to Malik. 'I go out for a couple of hours and come back with a new friend. A friend who looks like *you*? Yeah, right. Forget it.'

'What's wrong with the way I look?'

'Absolutely one hundred per cent nothing. Which is exactly my point. You look like you've been Instagram-filtered.'

'Which filter?' Malik says, grinning.

'The hot one. And . . . oh *bloody hell*.'

'What?'

'The book!'

'What book?'

'I was supposed to be getting a book for school.'

'Look,' he says. 'If you're not gonna knock, I will.'

'All right. All right. Just . . . gimme some space here.'

He steps back. I take a deep breath and square my shoulders.

It's hot. The sky is a limpid blue.

I knock.

61

The door is thrown open and what greets me is this: hair –
shaved on the top and sides and, at the back, drawn up
into a ponytail of beaded dreadlocks. Ears – pierced and
run through with twisted ash-black bones. Goatee, grey
and clipped. No moustache. A silk kimono bunched in
his fist. Moroccan Frenchman and frequent nudist, Gad
Moudnib. Aka the Hippie.

'Ana!' he says. '*Ça va?*'

'Gad!' I fall into the front room and give him a bear hug
and I slap him on the chest. 'You won't believe how good
it is to see you.'

Gad narrows his eyes. 'You have been in my secret stash
again?' He looks at Malik suspiciously. 'And this? Who
are you?'

'This is a friend,' I say. 'Gad, Malik. Malik, Gad.'

'*Enchanté,*' Gad says.

Malik shakes his hand. Without his pistol, he looks
uncomfortable and awkward. 'Good to meet you, sir.'

Gad raises his eyebrows. '*Sir?*' He turns to me, flashing a smile. 'I like him.'

'Hey, Gad?' I say.

'*Oui?*'

'Do me a favour – don't ever buy a suit, OK? Stick with the kimonos.' He frowns and gives me a confused look.

'And never cut the dreads,' I add. 'You're perfect the way you are.'

He throws open his hands. '*Mais évidemment, ma chérie.*'

We find the Old Man in his ceramics studio off the terrace. A terrace that's open to the sky. No conservatory. The studio is steeped in dry heat from the kiln and a hot stone smell assails us at the door. The Old Man – at his kick wheel, wearing a canvas smock and sandals – has his hands cupped round a lump of clay. He taps a foot pedal and the wheel spins. He digs his thumbs into the clay and draws it up between his fingers, pushing and moulding. The clay changes shape as we watch. Miraculously, a fine-neck pot emerges. The Old Man looks up with red cheeks, only now aware of us standing here. He blows air up over his nose from his bottom lip to swish the hair out of his eyes and he frowns. 'Hello? Who's this then?'

My heart leaps. It's *him*. The Old Man. The way he was. Un-blind.

'I'd shake your hand,' the Old Man says, brushing his forehead with the back of his hand. His palm is grey with wet clay.

'That's OK,' Malik says.

'This is, uh . . . this is Malik,' I blurt.

The Old Man looks from Malik to me and my heart pumps in my chest. I feel like pinching myself. I'm home. I'm *home*.

'Ana,' the Old Man says. 'Are you OK?'

I open my mouth to speak, but I can't find the words. What do I tell him about the places I've been and the things I've seen? I know the answer. Nothing. I can't. Not ever. Not one thing. He'd have me shipped off to an asylum. And that gets me thinking about Vidhan. It hits me like a punch to the gut. He's gone.

'Ana?'

'Uh-huh?'

'You're staring.'

'Am I?'

'Are you sure you're OK?'

'Yeah. Course I'm OK.'

'You look frazzled.'

'I'm not *frazzled*.' I glance at Malik, feeling *exactly* that – frazzled. Dizzy and wide-eyed, dazed by all this sudden family intimacy.

'And?' the Old Man says. 'Did you find what you were looking for?'

Find what I was looking for? How does he –

'You said you needed a book . . . *Equus*, right?'

Right. The book!

I haul out a folded sepia handbook from my back pocket. Wave it in the air. 'All sorted,' I say, quickly shoving *The Book of Seven* back in place.

'Looks beaten up,' the Old Man says doubtfully, glancing at Malik.

'It's second-hand,' I say.

'And Malik is . . .?'

'A schoolfriend,' Malik interrupts. 'We met each other at the bookshop I was looking for research material . . . for my art class.' I flash him a look.

'Oh?' the Old Man says, his interest piqued.

I'll say this for Malik. He knows how to read people.

I step in regardless. 'Dad, listen . . . I forgot my phone at Frankie's. Is it OK if I go over and get it and come back in time for dinner? I won't be long.'

The Old Man shakes his head. 'First the book, now the phone?' He smiles at Malik. 'Some people might say you were distracted.'

'Back in thirty?' I say, flustered.

'Don't be late.' he says. 'Gad's making his signature dish.'

'Couscous with merguez?' I ask, amazed at how easily I'm slipping into normal after so long. Real things. Backchat. Evening meals.

'Malik?' the Old Man says. 'Care to join us?'

Malik looks at me. 'No . . . I mean . . . I'd love to but I really should be –'

'Nonsense,' the Old Man says. 'Of course you're joining us. It's done.' He looks at me and he winks and I beg him with my eyes not to say anything else.

'Ana!' he says, calling me back as we turn to go.

'*What?*'

'Do you know what you did?'

'Uh . . . *no*?'

'You called me Dad.'

'No. I don't think I did that.'

'You did. You *did* do that.'

'I'm pretty sure I didn't.'

'*Dad!*' he says. He smiles and he mouths something like, *My God, he's lovely.*

That's it, I'm outta here. I grab Malik by the arm and shove him out of the door.

We arrive at Frankie's just as her black Range Rover Sport is pulling serenely into the driveway. She emerges silkily from the front seat, still wearing her dark suit. The door thunks closed and she strides up to us, steely-eyed, jangling her keys.

I feel like rushing up to her and kissing her. But I don't. I stand next to Malik and wait.

She sees him and gives me a questioning look. 'Frances,' she says, holding out her hand to Malik, taking the initiative. Classic Frankie Solana.

'Malik,' he says and they shake. 'A schoolfriend.'

'*You're* a schoolfriend?' Frankie says.

'He's a year above me,' I cut in.

'How old are you, Malik?' Frankie says, raising her sculpted eyebrows.

I squirm again. 'Frankie!' Between her and the Old Man, Malik will be scared off in no time.

'What? It's not OK for me to ask?'

'No. Listen, it's OK,' Malik says. 'I'm used to it. I look older than I am, I know. But I'm eighteen.' He's lying again – he's easily nineteen.

Frankie looks at me and pockets her keys. I'd slipped on a new jumper at the Old Man's house, and I washed my face and my hands and made myself presentable, so Frankie wouldn't freak out. I can tell she isn't totally comfortable with Malik being here, but she can also see that I'm happy.

'How'd it go?' I ask her.

'The meeting?' She looks surprised. 'Didn't know you cared.'

I shrug and say nothing.

She gives me a guarded smile. 'A success, I think. We'll have to see. And you?' She glances at Malik. 'How was the . . . uh . . .'

'The appointment?' I ask, thankful that Frankie's tactful and smart enough not to talk about shrinks in front of a good-looking boy. 'It was fine.'

'Good,' she says. 'I'm pleased. But . . . what are you doing here, Ana? You're meant to be at your father's.'

'I know,' I say. And then I lurch forward and give her a hug. Nothing crazy, just a quick embrace. A sniff of that Frankie aroma. Coffee, leather and chocolate.

Now she looks genuinely shocked. 'Ana –' she says.

'I just . . . I wanted to see you,' I blurt. 'Plus, I left my phone in my room.'

Frankie laughs and looks at Malik. 'And there's the real reason. Come on inside, Malik.'

She leads the way up the drive and I follow, heart in my throat.

I close my bedroom door behind me, and Malik and I look at each other. My breath quickens and then we're kissing and his hands are in my hair and his dark eyes are locked on to mine and I'm lost in them and the room is spinning, spinning.

'Are you really here?' I ask him when we break apart. 'Am I dreaming?'

'I'm here,' he says. 'You're not dreaming.'

'That's a relief.'

He grins. My stomach flips. 'Promise me something, Malik.'

'Sure. Anything.'

'Promise me you'll never wipe my memory. Like you wiped Bea's.'

'What are you talking about? Why?'

'Just promise.'

'OK. I promise. Why?'

'Because, Malik Habib, I don't ever again want to live in a world where I'm not one hundred per cent certain that you exist.'

He kisses me.

'I'm sorry,' he says as we draw apart again.

'Sorry? About what?'

'About what I said, in Venetia. About staying away from me.' His voice falters. 'I was wrong. It's just . . . Issi, then Gabe and Vidhan. It breaks my heart.'

A wave of sadness rolls over me. 'And mine,' I say. 'But *Bea's* alive. And we're the reason. Gabe and you and me. And Vidhan.'

Malik nods and I fall into his arms. 'If it ever gets too sad,' he whispers, 'we can always go and look for Vidhan's double. Just . . . to see him again.'

And it dawns on me. Out there, in a world apart, a different Vidhan Blue is still breathing. Not the same but *alive*. It's a realization that doesn't bury the pain, but it sears off a layer of hurt, like burnt skin – just the idea of him. Another Vidhan.

We say nothing for a long time.

We don't speak about Akuji – or Mara – and we don't speak about Shinigami.

Is she dead? She's in hell, that's all I know for sure. And the Order? In ruins. Collective Pathfinders, not long after we left Venetia, overran the pyramid fortress and blew it out of the sky. Now the Seventh Gate is guarded. And the multiverse is free.

'What's all that about your phone?' Malik murmurs, breaking my reverie. 'You didn't leave it here. It's been in your pocket the whole time.'

'I wanted to see her, that's all.'

'Your mum?'

'Yeah. Mum.'

My phone buzzes and I snatch it out of my pocket. It works. It bloody works! Wi-Fi. Internet. 4G. We're back in the real world now.

Moon!

Bea!

U home?

Yeah. I'm home.

Parental has caved in to pressure.

What do u mean?

She's repealed her decision. We can hang out again.

    Officially.

She's all heart.

Lol. I've missed you, Moon. Feels like f**kin forever.

Tell me about it.

Heard about Erika? She's out of hospital.

Really?

Yeah. So don't feel bad.

I don't. She deserved what she got, Bea. All of it.

Jeez! Who are *you*?

I start typing and then stop. Malik is at the window, looking out. Beyond him, the trees are black against a darkening sky.

I feel it then – a pull – an ache, deep in my gut, dragging me to look at the road outside and the wide sky beyond. The hairs stand up on the back of my neck and somehow I recognize this feeling. It's a signal. Someone, somewhere out there in the vast multiverse, has Fallen. And I will find them. Because that's what I do now.

I live between two sets of parents and seven worlds.

Life is not a straight road. It's a path through the woods.

And who am I?

I'm Ana Moon. Pathfinder.

Acknowledgements

I wrote *The Between* thinking of my two children, Adam and Brune, and my niece, Amelia. Like so many modern families, they move almost endlessly between homes. I wanted a story that could invoke this mood of transience. Something with echoes of *Alice's Adventures in Wonderland*. A feeling of always being elsewhere.

Thank you, as ever, my fearless agent, Stephanie Thwaites. None of these words would have found their way near a printed page without you.

Thank you, my brilliant editors, Ben Horslen and Beverly Horowitz, for never losing faith despite deadlines falling into parallel worlds. And thank you, Alexandra Hightower and Stephanie Barrett, who blithely turn hot messes into prose.

Thank you, my family. Mom and Dad for indulging so many story conversations. Mostly, thank you, Delphine, Adam and Brune, without whom this book would have been finished far sooner. And for being such beautiful muses.

I'm grateful to you all.

About the Author

David Hofmeyr was born in South Africa and lives in London and Paris. In 2013 he graduated from Bath Spa University with an MA in Writing for Young People. His first book, *Stone Rider*, was published in 2015 and was shortlisted for the Branford Boase Award for first-time novelists. He divides his time between writing and working as a strategist for Ogilvy & Mather. *The Between* is David's second novel.

STONE
RIDER

DAVID HOFMEYR

Available in paperback, eBook and audio

ONLY

Adam Stone wants freedom and peace.
He wants a chance to escape Blackwater,
the dust-bowl desert town he grew up in.
Most of all, he wants the beautiful Sadie Blood.

THE

Alongside Sadie and the dangerous outsider, Kane,
Adam will ride the Blackwater Trail in a brutal race
that will test them all, body and soul.

STRONGEST

The prize? A one-way ticket to Sky-Base
and unimaginable luxury.

WILL

And for a chance at this new life
Adam will risk everything . . .

SURVIVE

For loads more about the things you love, make sure you follow Penguin Platform.

PLATFORM

🐦 @penguinplatform

▶ YouTube youtube.com/penguinplatform

📷 @penguinplatform

tumblr. penguin-platform.tumblr.com

SHARE, CREATE, DISCOVER AND DEBATE.